Corpse In The Chard

Published in the UK in 2023 by The Cotswold Writer Press

Copyright © Anna A Armstrong 2023

Paperback ISBN: 978-1-7394217-0-0
eBook ISBN: 978-1-7394217-1-7

Cover design and typeset by SpiffingCovers

Corpse In The Chard

ANNA A ARMSTRONG

For Richard,
Thanks for all the fun.

I am not what happened to me.

I am what I choose to become.

Carl Jung

Chapter 1

'Granny!'

Amelia, at nineteen, had mastered the art of vocal horror. Red-haired and petite, she was currently a Goth with cascades of curls that tumbled down her shoulders to her black laced corset. She crossed her arms and tapped her Doc Marten-clad toe with such vigour that it made her stiff tutu rustle.

Dee sighed; she could guess what her granddaughter's next comment would be.

'Mummy isn't going to like this!'

Yes! There it is! A statement both true and full of foreboding.

Dee swallowed. 'No, dear.' She raised her eyebrows and looked hopefully at Amelia. 'Perhaps it could just be our little secret.'

'Granny! How can you keep a corpse in your lettuce patch a secret?'

'Chard, dear.'

'What?'

'He's lying in my patch of chard.' Dee gestured across the immaculate rows of vegetables, all neatly kept and punctuated by willow wigwams for the peas and beans. 'The lettuce is over there – it's not ready yet.'

Amelia rolled her eyes and said, 'The point isn't the type of veg, it's that you have a dead body in your garden. It's not the sort of thing you can ignore.'

Dee nodded. 'Well, obviously we'll need to tell the police. I just thought, perhaps we don't need to tell your mother. After all, it is only a small corpse!'

'*Granny!* The size of the corpse is not really the issue, any more than whether it's in amongst the chard or the lettuce!'

Amelia's green eyes flashed and her curls quivered with fury.

'I suppose not,' Dee murmured sadly as she surveyed the scene. 'Such a shame, the chard was nearly ready to pick and I do so like it fresh. Now it's all squashed.'

Together they regarded the flattened early leafy veg; compressed by a corpse, it was already wilting in the morning sunshine.

Their meditations on the perils of combining spring salad with stiffs were rudely interrupted by an appalled cry of, 'Mother! How could you?'

The voice that rang out across the peaceful garden silenced the previously-singing birds. Amelia had been right – Mummy, otherwise known as Zara FitzMorris, did not like it. Indeed, all five-foot-three of her was trembling with rage, from her well-coiffed Titian top to her designer heels. She flung out a beautifully manicured hand and pointed an accusing finger at the body.

'What *do* you think you're doing? And after all the trouble you caused last time!'

Dee flushed. Unable to meet her daughter's glare, she glanced uncomfortably at her own ballet flats and shifted her weight from one foot to another. 'It's not as if I go looking for dead bodies, darling.' She shrugged her narrow shoulders. 'They just sort of find me.' A thought suddenly struck her and she risked a peek at her furious daughter. 'Anyway, how did you get to hear about it? We haven't even phoned the police yet.'

'Your neighbour, Mrs May, rang me to say she thought that I ought to know that you're at it again.'

'Well, really!' muttered Dee, scowling at Mrs May's side of the fence.

With her elfin chestnut hair, slight figure and simple top and trousers, Dee resembled a redheaded Audrey Hepburn in an unaccustomed rage. As she glowered at the border between her little haven and that of the enemy, Mrs May, she spotted the woman herself.

Mrs Elizabeth May's wizened face, topped by her tight grey perm, peered back at her through the fence.

Dee raised her voice to be certain that it would carry and declared, 'You would have thought she'd have better things to do than to snoop on her neighbours! For a start, she could at least put a bit of effort into that concrete yard she calls a garden. A garden should have some points of interest – unlike some people's.'

With sudden remorse, she realised that she was being less than gracious.

Dee FitzMorris, get a grip of yourself! I really shouldn't let a dead body make me forget my manners! There must be something I can say about Mrs May that is polite and charitable while at the same time having at least a hint of the truth about it.

She was still struggling with how to combine all three elements when Zara spoke, pinching her lips together and pointing an accusing finger at the corpse.

'Mother, generally when people talk about making their garden interesting, they are referring to a water feature – or even a whimsical gnome – *not* a cadaver.'

With more haste than thought, Dee blurted out, 'I meant all the effort I put into planting my tubs and obelisks. Even my vegetable patch is a joy to behold – just look at the way I've interplanted nasturtiums and marigolds with carrots and lettuce. My garden is a positive masterpiece and that's even before we get on to my flowerbeds and fruit trees. Have you noticed the apple trees are just coming into bloom?'

As you can tell, Dee has a passion for her garden which always looked beautiful but was perhaps at its finest now in late spring when the bright aquilegia rose above the hardy geraniums, and fragrant honeysuckle scented the air. Her garden was vast – long and thin, it was a medieval strip from the days when a cottager had to grow their own food. Somehow over the centuries, it had remained intact.

Zara was not to be swayed by apple blossom and returned to the facts. 'With a dead body in it.'

Dee nodded, hesitated and murmured, 'Yes.' She looked at the human remains dubiously. Reluctantly she admitted, 'It does rather detract from the general ambience.'

Amelia had been staring intently at the deceased, narrowing her green eyes and with her head tilted to one side as she concentrated. 'Granny, Mummy ... there's just one thing that's bothering me ...'

Zara gave an exaggerated sigh and exclaimed, 'Honestly Amelia! You're getting to be as bad as your grandmother. Here we are standing in your grandmother's back garden – not enjoying tea and scones like any normal family, but contemplating a corpse! And you are saying that there's just one thing bothering you!'

Dee was acutely aware that Mrs May's steely eyes were upon them and that she was listening to every word. She preferred not to wash her dirty linen in public and a dearly departed in the chard most definitely came in the category of dirty linen.

She whispered, 'Lower your voice, Zara. We don't want the neighbours listening in to our private discussion.' Turning to her granddaughter she added, 'So Amelia, dear, what is worrying you?'

'Why is he dressed as a clown?'

The three of them gazed down at the man's elongated shoes with their bulbous toes neatly lying in an elegant ballet fifth position and at his vivid oversized yellow checked suit. His gloved hands were crossed at his stomach while his white face paint was smooth and clear. Happy eyes were drawn over his rigid lids and a jolly smile was painted around his mouth.

'I suppose he really is dead?' asked Amelia.

Dee didn't look up, but just nodded and murmured, 'Yes dear, he is definitely dead. That smell is formaldehyde – he's been embalmed. At least he looks peaceful.'

Zara glanced from her mother, small and serene, to her daughter who was not much taller than her grandmother and equally intrigued by events. She declared, 'You two are incorrigible, calmly chatting over a clown corpse. I'm going inside to call the police and to put the kettle on.'

Zara swished up the garden path with an elegant swirl of her emerald wrap dress and a gentle tinkle of multiple gold bangles.

Chapter 2

Detective Chief Inspector Nicholas Corman was not having a good day: firstly; the Flying Scotsman model train he'd ordered had not arrived in the morning post. It was a new version that actually puffed smoke as it went along. Its non-appearance meant that he would not be spending his evening as he had happily anticipated. He'd imagined a few pleasant hours setting it up and watching it chug around the elaborate track in his spare room.

Secondly; his Sergeant Josh Park's sloppy eating habits had struck again. Nicholas liked his life and possessions to be like his mind – clean and orderly. Now, thanks to Josh, he had toffee popcorn all over his immaculate trousers and valeted car.

Josh was sitting beside him in the passenger seat of his – now less than pristine – car. He directed a withering glance at the offender but the boy's finely defined Korean features remained totally undisturbed.

Why does he insist on snacking in my car? Surely he realises it's both unsanitary and unprofessional? Nicholas pulled his stomach muscles in. *And how does he retain his washboard abs whilst constantly stuffing his face with sweets?*

As if the first two irritants were not bad enough, now the third annoyance of the day: here they were driving along winding country lanes on their way to what, Nicholas suspected, had to be a hoax call about a dead clown.

The address of the alleged incident was innocuous enough; Little Warthing was one of the many picturesque villages nestling in the gentle Cotswold Hills. It was quintessentially English, a village made of attractive sandstone set on a hill. The houses were a quaint mismatch of homes built over many centuries; medieval cottages huddled next to grander Georgian residences with a few Tudor dwellings squeezed in the gaps. The magnificent church, erected as far back as 1175, took centre stage at the bottom of the hill, and history simply oozed from every corner. It was easy to imagine crusading knights and their more humble neighbours going about their daily lives in this village, worrying about their bills and laughing over babies and toddlers in much the same way the present-day residents did. It was a village more famous for its cream teas and hollyhocks than dead clowns.

Nicholas turned off the high street and down a side road, his mind still not at peace.

What were my parents thinking of? 'Move out of London,' they said. 'Find somewhere pretty. You need a fresh start after the divorce.' Not once did they mention the prospect of fruit loops reporting clown corpses ...

Nicholas and Josh found the house easily enough; Honeysuckle Cottage was the archetypal adorable cottage to be found on many a postcard in the Cotswolds. It was medieval in origin, a delightful honey colour with small windows, a wobbly slate roof and a sturdy oak front door. It was far more attractive than the ugly grey bungalow to its left. Nicholas glanced at that pebble-dashed monstrosity and sighed over the madness of the planning boards in the seventies.

He refocussed on Honeysuckle Cottage and noted that the front door seemed perfectly respectable, with no hint of it harbouring anyone intent on wasting police time with bogus calls about dead bodies, let alone clown corpses.

They knocked and were greeted by a teenage Goth. She was small, but smiling. Her black, studded corset, short tutu and biker boots were certainly striking, as were her flaming red hair and black lipstick.

'Mum, the police are here,' she called nonchalantly over her shoulder.

The girl surveyed Nicholas with cool interest, then her eyes alighted on Josh Parks standing behind him and there was a pause.

Both Josh and Nicholas were used to the effect Josh's looks

tended to have on any lady under the age of a hundred. His physical appearance might have been the result of genetics, but the twinkle in his eye he had developed himself over the last twenty-one years.

The Goth smiled, 'Oh hello, I'm Amelia.' She reached behind Nicholas and held out her black nail-varnished hand for Josh to shake. She turned the shake into a grasp and dragged the young man into the house. '*Do* let me show you our body!'

Nicholas, left on the doorstep, was less than impressed. *I can't understand why women find him so attractive! The boy can't even comb his hair properly!* He followed Amelia and Josh into the cottage and was struck by its inviting scents of lavender, beeswax and baking.

The hall opened into a sunny kitchen filled with plants. A large white Persian cat shot him a disdainful green-eyed look and walked across his path. By the kitchen table stood one of those frightening women of a certain age, all lip gloss and attitude. Such females were especially disturbing to Nicholas as he had been burnt before; somewhere – probably shopping on Oxford Street – there was an ex-Mrs Corman.

'Ah, Inspector. How kind of you to come. I'm Zara FitzMorris.' As she spoke she was unashamedly assessing him.

He failed to notice that she had much the same appreciative glint in her eye that her daughter had had when she'd regarded Josh, but Nicholas Corman was a modest man, unaware that his chiselled jaw, thick dark hair and greying temples were distinguished. As yet he was ignorant of Zara's penchant for the shiny shoes and immaculate tailoring that marked out an 'English Gentleman'.

She even sounds like my ex-wife. And what is it with 'How kind of you to come'? Does she think this is a dinner party?

'Are you the householder?' he said abruptly.

'No! That would be my mother.'

'Then it's her that I need to speak to.'

Nicholas spoke curtly but Zara remained unruffled.

'I'm here, Inspector. Just making the tea!' called a cheery older woman holding a kettle.

Not a dinner party – just a little tea party!

The older lady was as slim and as small in height as both her daughter and granddaughter. She even had traces of their distinctive red hair, but what struck Nicholas most was the warmth of her smile, which he ignored as she introduced herself.

'I'm Dee FitzMorris. Do have a cup of camomile; I grow the flowers myself. So soothing when there are dead bodies about.'

Nicholas took no notice of the glass teapot with yellow floating flowers but queried the surname.

'FitzMorris?'

'Yes,' put in Zara, pouring out a cup of tea. 'It's rather good as a surname, isn't it? So much nicer than being called something like,' she paused and contemplated the ceiling then smiled with satisfaction at selecting an alternative name, 'say something like, 'Grub'. I really couldn't see myself going through life as Mrs Grub. But as luck would have it my husband was a very distant cousin from centuries back, so I kept FitzMorris.' Her grin became mischievous. 'And Mother changes husbands so often, she felt it cut down on the paperwork just to stick to FitzMorris.'

Nicholas Corman felt he was losing control of the situation. 'About this body ... do you know the deceased?'

Dee put down her tea cup and looked at him thoughtfully. 'No. Well, that is ... it's so hard to tell with the paint on his face. I do feel there is something vaguely familiar about him.'

Her eyes shifted from his face to his clothes and all thoughts of dead bodies – known or unknown – were forgotten as she exclaimed, 'Oh Inspector, do let me get that popcorn mark off your trousers—'

'It's quite all right. So you—?'

'Honestly, it won't take a moment. I used to run a boutique, a bridal boutique it was, so there's not a stain that I can't deal with!'

Nicholas felt he should be more in command of this interview. 'When did you find the body?'

'About one hour ago. It would have been sooner; normally I'm straight out in my garden with my morning coffee, but today it was after my Taekwondo drill. It's so important to keep flexible, don't you think, Inspector? And martial arts are so good for flexibility and balance.'

Dee was regarding him expectantly and Nicholas blinked back at her, momentarily lost in a vision of this tiny granny engaged in unarmed combat.

At the mention of Korea's own martial art, Josh perked up. 'Wicked! Which club do you belong to?'

Nicholas attempted to keep focused. 'Can we stick to the matter in hand?'

Apparently, this was a forlorn hope as Zara now interrupted, 'Mother, he hasn't got time for martial arts; he's far too busy with his model trains.'

Nicholas took a second wide-eyed look at Zara; under her cool gaze, he had a sensation of being on display rather like a cod at a fishmonger's.

She smiled and explained, 'You're so neat and meticulous that your preferred hobby has to be model-making. There is a hint of old Hollywood glamour about your dress choice so I should think you have a passion for something classic ... The Flying Scotsman?'

He suspected he was gawking fish-like with surprise written all over his face.

Zara was still smiling. 'My mother has a knack for clothes and what they say about people, whereas I sell homes so I'm rather good at assessing what makes people tick.'

'It's unnerving isn't it?' stated the small Goth standing by the French windows.

He transferred his look from grandmother and mother to the granddaughter.

'Their scrutiny makes you feel out of control, doesn't it?' Amelia scanned his orderly combed hair, pressed suit and polished shoes. 'And you need to be in control.'

'And you are?' he asked, immediately feeling both out of control and foolish as he recalled that she had already said her name at the front door.

'Amelia FitzMorris.'

'Occupation?'

'Student. I'm studying psychology. I'm not sure if I'm going to specialise in family…' She paused and her eyes stared directly into his in a way that returned him to the unpleasant sensation of being a gawping fish on a fishmonger's iced display – then, in a chilling tone that held more than a hint of a threat she added, 'or criminal.'

Zara took pity on him and suggested, 'Amelia dear, why don't you take that nice young sergeant out and show him Granny's clown corpse?'

Happily, Amelia obliged, seizing Josh's arm and hauling him through the French windows and into the garden beyond.

Relieved, Nicholas decided to concentrate on the grandmother. 'So Mrs FitzMorris—'

'It's Ms, but call me Dee; so much easier.'

'Dee, when exactly did you find the body?'

'Like I said it was about an hour ago, straight after my—'

'Taekwondo,' Nicholas supplied and was rewarded with another smile.

'Of course, had it been yesterday, it would have been quite different but then yesterday was a bit unusual.'

'Unusual?'

She nodded. 'I needed to be in the woods at dawn.'

'You needed to be in the woods at dawn?' Baffled, Nicholas raised his eyebrows together.

She smiled and nodded again.

'Why?' he felt compelled to ask, although he knew they were straying from the corpse.

'I'm a citizen scientist and we're researching woodland songbirds, so I needed to be there for the dawn chorus.'

'Citizen scientist?'

'Wonderful organisation; scientists who need data for their research call on us, be it hedgehog counting or plastic bottle collecting.'

'So after that, you—'

She finished for him, 'Did my Taekwondo forms. So important to stay flexible.'

'Quite. So then you went into the garden and ... it must have been quite a shock.'

'Yes! But rather interesting at the same time.'

Nicholas' mouth fell open and he blinked several times as he tried to collect his thoughts. 'Interesting? In what way was it interesting? Was it because he was a clown?'

'Yes, Inspector.'

'How could you tell he was a clown?'

She gave him a compassionate look tinged with pity, which made him squirm. 'The bright suit and stage makeup were a bit of a giveaway. Did you know there are lots of different types of clowns and you can tell a lot about a clown from his makeup?'

'His makeup?'

She smiled and nodded as if she was encouraging a small child while she affirmed, 'Yes there are lots of different ways for a clown to make up his face.'

Nicholas cleared his throat. 'You know a lot about clowns. A special interest of yours?'

Dee shrugged. 'Not really, but there has been a rather good series about them on Netflix.'

Josh and Amelia returned.

'Hey Gov,' announced Josh.

Chief Inspector Nicholas Corman winced. *Does the boy have to call me that? It must be the result of a childhood spent watching police dramas.*

Josh continued, 'You should check out the clown – wicked makeup.'

I must have a serious word with him about being professional and suitable use of language.

'Yea! Totally wicked! Did you see that programme on Netflix?' Amelia asked.

'Yeah! Wicked!'

'Yeah.'

It took all of Nicholas' self-control not to roll his eyes. Mustering every atom of professionalism he had, he resumed, 'Dee, your neighbour said that you were at it again – that implies you're in the habit of finding dead bodies?'

Dee sat up very erect and fixed him with disdainful green eyes. 'Inspector, have you ever had a relationship break up?'

He felt himself go hot. *How can this woman know about my messy divorce and heartbreak? Are there no secrets from these women?*

She regarded him for a few moments in silence and then said, 'I'll take that as a yes. Then you know that it is the height of rudeness to mention an old relationship when you've embarked on a new one!'

'What …?' he stammered, but got no further as the forensics team arrived.

Driving away, he was still dazed. Eventually, he commented, 'Remarkable.'

Josh opened a bag of Toffee Crunch and noisily shoved a handful into his mouth, sending a shower of crumbs over both the car and the Inspector. 'Yeah, it's not often you get three generations of redheads.'

'I was meaning three generations of ladies with such acute observational skills. Still, one comfort is that this will be easy to solve – after all, there aren't many clowns around.'

He drove out of the village and totally missed Blossom Bim Bam bicycling along. She was wearing a pink sparkly skirt and had a cute dot of red paint on the tip of her pert little nose. In her bicycle basket was her sparkly wand and blowing in the wind behind her was a bunch of brightly-coloured balloons. On top of her mass of blonde curls sat a straw hat with an enormous daisy on it. Nor did Nicholas notice Ken Pilbersek, who went by the stage name of Joseph Popov; he was standing sadly at the bus stop, his car having failed to start that morning. He had a grumpy white face with a shiny red nose; his own sparse hair was covered by a bright orange wig and a cap that matched his brightly checked suit. Wistfully he watched Blossom Bim Bam cycle past.

Chapter 3

The reality of what had happened did not strike Dee until later. Somehow over the twenty-four hours preceding her discovery of the corpse, all her bravado and curiosity seeped out of her.

When night came, sleep eluded her, regardless of numerous cups of camomile tea. In vain she tried to lull herself to sleep with a Lavinia Lovelace historical romance.

I wonder if I should try one of Lavinia Lovelace's Goth romances. Amelia loves them. Or perhaps even one of her racy romances set in exotic locations that Zara's got?

But, for once, no amount of romance could calm her troubled mind.

The next day when she looked at herself in her bathroom mirror, her reflection was not encouraging. Her normally full-bodied pixie bob hung limply and her skin looked dry and dull, with fine lines splaying out from around her eyes and mouth.

She didn't have the energy for her morning exercise regime and her shower with lemon gel failed to invigorate her. She pulled on a forgiving jersey dress in navy with a tiny brown motif and a pair of tan ballet flats – it was an undemanding outfit which required no thought. Out of habit, she popped on some bangles she'd picked up in Marrakesh. Her mind was still in a whirl as she tried to process what had happened.

Taking my statement and fingerprints and things took forever, though I suppose everyone at the police station was very kind really and it was sweet of Josh to pop out and get me some camomile tea.

She shuddered at the recollection of the unpleasant instant coffee she'd first been offered. She sighed and walked downstairs. The kitchen was bright with morning sunshine flooding through the French windows. Cat purred and wound herself around her ankles asking to go outside; obligingly she opened the door and watched as she padded over the lawn. The grass sparkled, there'd been a shower giving Dee's world a freshness which on any other day would have lifted her heart.

On this particular morning, she gazed out at her beautiful garden unable to appreciate the leaves in all their new green spring glory or all the promise of the sprouting lupins and other traditional cottage garden plants. All Dee could think about was the desecration of her little haven by forensic officers in white overalls.

She couldn't face having her morning coffee outside this morning, however much the sun was shining and the birds were singing. She acknowledged that she'd have to venture out to refresh the bird feeder nestling among the fragrant apple blossom but otherwise, she decided not to go into her garden. She sat morosely at her kitchen table nursing her coffee until bleak thoughts threatened to overwhelm her.

This will never do! Get a grip, Dee FitzMorris! I must get out of the house and do something.

She rather regretted having refused Zara and Amelia's request to spend the night. *It would be nice to have had some company; still, I have lots of friends in the village and if I pop out to run some errands I'm bound to run into all sorts of folk.*

Cheered by the thought she put her mug in the sink and reached for her wicker basket. She had some freshly made watercress soup in the fridge so all she required to go with it for a delicious lunch was some crusty bread and a bit of cheese, both of which Sophie's deli would supply.

And then I may as well treat myself to some freesias – they always smell so heavenly and it will be a good opportunity to meet the new lady who has taken over the florists. While I'm there, I might look for some inspiration for the two pots by my front door – the dwarf tulips are looking a little tired. And thinking of inspiration, I'll pop into Robert's interiors shop – the sitting room could do with a refresh and he always has so many beautiful things.

Feeling hopeful she armed herself with a touch of tinted lip balm and headed out of the door.

Her newfound positivity was quickly quashed; she was barely out of the door when a couple of teenage boys openly stared and pointed at her. She felt hurt. *I can't remember their names but I'm sure I helped both of them with their reading when they were at the village school. I seem to remember that the spotty one couldn't get the hang of his 'ph's and 'th's.* Dee had been volunteering at the village school for so long that there was barely anyone under the age of thirty in Little Warthing that she hadn't read with.

There was no sign of movement from the Flying Pheasant, her local pub. This was a shame as she was on good terms with the Rossillina family who ran it.

I could do with a hug from Gina this morning, thought Dee but then she reflected, *although, with Gina's ample bosom and warm-hearted enthusiasm, there's always the risk of suffocation with any hug.*

Gina's friendliness made her perfect for being in charge of the front of house while her husband, Francesco, was in command of the kitchen.

Funny to think I helped both of their children to get the hang of reading, first Alex and then her brother Marcello, and now Alex has just finished her accountancy exams. Dee was extremely fond of Alex with her glorious dark curls, black eyes and her fiery personality, *Of course, Alex needed a strong character; it's not easy being a teenager in a wheelchair but she's always taken life full on and enjoyed herself – especially her tennis.*

Happy thoughts of the Rossillina family had soothed away the unpleasantness of the pointing adolescents, but worse was to come. In order to reach the shops on the steep-hilled high street she had to walk past Mrs May's unattractive bungalow and then Peter Wilson's home. Retired Police Chief Peter Wilson's cottage might be more appealing than Mrs May's bungalow but his personality was just as dreary.

To Dee's dismay, there he sat on his stripy canvas deckchair outside his front door. As was his habit, he had the radio on full blast.

I wonder why Mrs May puts up with that noise, day in, day out. The racket is bad enough at my home and at least I have one house space as a buffer. It isn't even Classic FM, which would be bad enough but the constant drone of the Ashes, on long wave. Still, I suppose it's better than when he listens to Meatloaf's 'Bat Out of Hell'.

She ignored his hard stare and continued musing.

He's definitely one of life's eccentrics. He wears his blazer and orange and yellow MCC tie but has a ponytail. I should think he must have had an interesting childhood. I must get Amelia to profile him for one of her psychology projects ...

She smiled at the thought.

Buoyed up, she gave him a cheery 'Good morning' which he responded to with a silent glare that made her feel strangely guilty.

It must be some gift he picked up from years of interrogating criminals, but I don't know why I feel so bad. I haven't done anything wrong.

As if in confirmation of her innocence there was a brief fine mist of a shower coming out of the blue sky and a sudden glimpse of a rainbow; heartened, Dee walked on.

She was soon at the high street – or what passed for a high street in a village. Trailing down the hill the shops gave the impression of toppling, as though they only clung on to their footing by determination. The village council had vigorously insisted that all shop fronts and pub signs were in keeping with the village's ethos; it gave the impression of being the stage set for a Dickens' drama. Dee rather liked all the painted shop signs and the way the shopkeepers took pride in artfully displaying their wares in their windows. The sweet shop was a wonderful example with twisted candy canes, brown and beige humbugs and bright pink bonbons, all displayed in beautiful glass jars.

She turned uphill, negotiating her way past a little knot of tourists who were blocking most of the pavement as they admired the quaint architecture. Late spring and early summer heralded the start of the tourist season. Dee felt honoured to live somewhere that people as far away as China and America wanted to travel to. She was far more patient with their endless photo-taking than many of her neighbours.

She reached the deli. The smart dark-blue sign above the window stated *Sophie and Son* and an awning in the same colour protected the delectable food displayed in the window from the sun's rays. Inside it was cool. Dee inhaled the myriad inviting smells; the mouthwatering scent of the fresh crusty bread in the nearby baskets vied for attention against the vivid green herbs – all picked that morning – the sharp, refreshing mint contrasting with the delicate thyme. Vibrant yellow lemons added a splash of colour while a variety of red tomatoes cried out to be made into a salad with some of the pungent basil. Dee had to avert her eyes from a bunch of glossy dark-green chard with its distinctive red stem.

Best of all, there was Sophie herself behind the counter. Tall and slim, she wore a trim blue apron with the same logo as the shop front. Her blonde hair was pulled back into a ponytail and, in her crisp white shirt and jeans, she definitely did not look old enough to have an adult son.

Sophie had come over from Boston to study English Literature at the prestigious Oxford University and somehow never left. Dee always thought of her son, David, as being a youthful and admirable Atticus Finch from To Kill a Mockingbird. *But am I just falling into cultural stereotyping? And wasn't Atticus Finch in the Deep South rather than Boston?*

Sophie saw Dee over the heads of two customers whom she was advising on which of the many local cheeses they should try and gave her a warm smile. Dee felt so overwhelmed with gratitude, she had to blink back her tears. Despite her mouth being dry she managed to return a slow smile. She selected a small round granary loaf and popped it into the brown paper bag provided. The two customers had made their cheese choice; they were large ladies, both with too much makeup on and thick ankles displayed beneath their floral skirts. Dee thought they looked vaguely familiar and gave them a smile which froze on her face when the larger of the two women nudged her neighbour and in a loud whisper announced, 'That's her!'

'Who?' asked her companion, gawping at Dee.

'The clown killer!'

'You never! Let's get out of here before she takes a bread knife to us!'

They hurried out of the shop but not before both Dee and Sophie heard one of them mutter, 'Can't think why the police let a dangerous woman like that roam the streets.'

Dee thought her legs were about to buckle under her; there was a pain in her chest and she felt dizzy. The next thing she knew Sophie had her by the arm, supporting her.

'Oh Dee, I'm so sorry.' Sophie's accent still held a hint of her Boston birth but Dee was only aware that her blue eyes were full of compassion. She had to battle not to start crying.

'That's quite alright,' lied Dee. 'Actually, I just popped in for some cheese.'

'Alright, if you're sure you are okay.'

Dee nodded and Sophie went reluctantly back to the counter.

'I'll have some of Geoffrey's Goat please,' Dee said, annoyed that her voice sounded so shaky. She tried to instil some levity by adding, 'You know he claims it always tastes so good because he keeps his goats happy by singing Puccini to them.'

Sophie gave a polite grin but she was still eyeing Dee with concern. Dee thought Sophie was about to say something but they were interrupted by the arrival of the formidable Vivian Plover and her downtrodden husband, Christopher.

In honour of spring, Vivian had ditched her tweed skirt for an equally rigid Liberty print. As ever, her sensible shoes and firm lipstick were in evidence. Her hair was dyed and permed in a way that was reminiscent of Maggie Thatcher at the height of her powers. Actually, Vivian resembled Maggie in many ways, only she was a lot less cuddly.

Her smile of greeting didn't reach her eyes as she acknowledged both Dee and Sophie. Woodenly she explained, 'We came in for some cheese as the Lord Lieutenant and his wife are dining with us tonight, but I can see you are busy so we'll come back later.'

Before Sophie could say a word she had turned on her heels

and marched out. Her husband, Christopher, who, despite the weather, was clad in his thick winter tweed jacket and heavy cords, gave them both an apologetic smile but hastened to follow his wife when her shrill, 'Don't dawdle, Christopher!' rang out.

'Oh Dee ...' murmured Sophie, her voice trailing off as she was lost for words.

'I'm sure it will all blow over – storm in a teacup and all that. Now I really must get on, I want to call in at the florists and Robert's.'

Dee hurried away, painfully aware that if she spent any more time in Sophie's kind presence she would totally break down.

With her basket containing cheese and bread and her head firmly down Dee walked briskly up the hill. She firmly avoided making eye contact with anyone on the high street and only succeeded in not colliding with anyone by watching out for their feet on the pavement. By looking down she did manage to avoid any hurtful looks from passersby, but it also meant that she missed out on enjoying the idyllic scene of picturesque honey-coloured homes nestling next to the shops with their small neat front gardens and welcoming tubs and pots all sprouting fresh growth. Climbing roses were budding hopefully on many walls and hollyhocks were starting their steady ascent skyward. The earlier shower had given the air a delightful freshness which mingled with the smell of freshly cut grass. The birds chirping in amongst the translucent leaves and the bees buzzing in flowers all proclaimed that summer was on its way. At that moment, though, Dee cared little for such matters; she just wanted to reach the florists.

She had walked at such a pace that she was a little out of breath. She paused outside the florist shop both to catch her breath and to admire the scene before her.

My! What an improvement!

The previous village florist had gone in for rather more bright helium balloons proclaiming 'Congratulations!' than flowers. The closest they had got to flora were dismal pot plants wrapped in acres of plastic with garish ribbons stapled on. Now everything had changed; the shop front itself was a discreet blue-grey designed to show off the flowers' beauty. On either side of the door were shelves of fashionable terracotta pots with healthy green ivy, bright cyclamen, fragrant white jasmine and all manner of other plants. Inside, Dee could glimpse buckets full of voluptuous peonies and elegant long-stemmed lilies.

She pushed the door open and was greeted by a heady scent and an attractive young lady.

'Hello,' beamed the woman, as she looked up from the bouquet of roses she was assembling. She had a wonderful smile, warm brown skin and tight black curls peeking out from under a bright red twist of a headband. Debussy played in the background and Dee just knew they were going to be friends.

'Hello, you've made everything look quite beautiful. I came in for some freesias but now I'm here I feel quite spoilt for choice.'

The lady's smile deepened. 'Well, the freesias are there.' She indicated a sweet-smelling bucket overflowing with yellow and white flowers.

Dee selected a bunch of them and went over to have them wrapped and to pay for them. By way of conversation, she enquired, 'How are you settling into the village?'

'Wonderful; everyone has been so friendly. As you can imagine, I've had to work flat-out to get this place in order but hopefully things will settle down now and I can get to know a few people. By the way, I'm Sam.'

Dee put the freesias in her basket and smiled back. 'Delighted to meet you, Sam. I'm Dee FitzMorris.'

She had hardly got her name out when she saw Sam's friendly face change to a picture of terror. Her smile froze, her eyes opened wide and her dark skin paled.

Word spreads quickly in a village, thought Dee as she hurried out of the shop.

She was feeling so despondent that had Robert's interiors not been on her route home she would have abandoned her original plan of calling in.

But as I'm walking past the door anyway, I may as well pop in and pick Robert's brain for some ideas about my sitting room.

Besides which, it will be a delight to see him and, who knows, if he isn't too busy, he might make us a cup of tea and we can have a little chat.

Dee was very fond of both Robert and his husband, Paul. Although she was friends with both of them she was, without a doubt, closer to Robert. He always had time for a catch-up and was rather easier company than Paul.

Of course, it could be that Paul is rather military, both by career and nature, added to which Robert's interior business is in the village so I see him around whereas Paul works in Cheltenham.

As it turned out it would have been better had she just walked past Robert's interiors shop.

He always made sure that the exterior of his shop was as appealing as the goods inside. Dee admired the two bay trees under-planted with lavender in their lead pots on either side of the entrance. The shop's windows had been given a suitably seasonal refresh and displayed contemporary floral fabric draped over a cream chaise longue. There was a wacky twisted standing lamp nearby which contrasted rather well with the antique gramophone record player, complete with its enormous horn, which stood on a small side table.

The bell tinkled as she pushed the door open. There was a delightful soft scent of potpourri which she knew he made himself from roses and lavender from his garden. To her disappointment, instead of being warmly greeted by Robert, she was met by his assistant. The girl was thin, blonde and decidedly unwelcoming.

Barely bothering to acknowledge Dee, she simply snapped, 'Robert's not here – he has gone to have a site meeting with a client.'

Defeated, Dee walked quietly out of the shop, thinking, *I shouldn't have come to the village today; I should have stayed at home.* She thought of her little cottage and the sanctuary it provided and hastened away to the safety of Honeysuckle Cottage.

Her home was almost in sight but her ordeal was still not over and there was more unpleasantness to come.

Nearly there! Still no sign of life from the Flying Pheasant but thank goodness I don't have to face Peter Wilson again – he seems to have taken both his large bulk and his noisy radio inside.

She was just at a level with his empty deckchair when she spotted Ken Pilbersek rushing along the pavement towards her, wearing his clown costume and makeup. *I suppose I should think of him as Joseph Popov rather than Ken Pilbersek.*

He pushed past her without a word, but Dee thought he glowered at her. She sighed. *Well, that's hardly surprising. After all, he may earn his living as an actuary but he is a professional grumpy old man. I won't take that look he gave me personally, he glares at everyone. I doubt if his middle-aged face still has the muscle ability to smile; decades of looking daggers at all and sundry has probably hardened his expression into a permanent pout. It's quite extraordinary that he chose to be a mime artist clown in his spare time.*

As if one clown was not enough for an outing, Dee spotted a pretty lady clown bicycling down the road. She had a large sunflower on her straw hat and her basket was overflowing with colourful balloons and bunting.

And here comes Julia Fryderberg – now with her sunny disposition she was born to be Blossom Bim Bam! I can easily imagine her entertaining children at a party.

Dee gave Blossom a warm smile and a wave while thinking, *It's odd that generally, clowns are few and far between and yet, Little Warthing has two in residence – and now a third turns up in my vegetable patch!*

Whereas Dee had half-anticipated a rebuff from Ken, she could not deny it was a hammer blow when Blossom just cycled straight on and ignored her. *She's cycling faster than normal and she does look extra-flustered, so perhaps she's running late for a party and didn't notice me.* As much as Dee tried to be rational, in her heart she suspected that news of the clown corpse in one's chard did not make for village popularity.

The humiliating snub was noticed by someone else other than Dee.

Mrs May coolly observed Dee. She was wearing her habitual nylon attire, one of those shapeless dresses that double as an overall and were so popular in the seventies. As usual, her thin lips were tight, but Dee noticed they had a satisfied twist to them. She was standing on her front step, a mop in hand which was bathed in the acrid smell of bleach that was so strong it penetrated the neighbourhood and obliterated any scent of spring. It was a solemn daily duty of hers to vigorously clean her front step but today Dee thought she was more intent on gloating than cleaning.

With more dignity than she felt, Dee managed to say, 'Good morning, Mrs May.'

She had hoped to be able to sweep past with no more being said. Her welcoming front garden beckoned her; full of beautiful flowers, overflowing with life but Mrs May had other ideas. Brandishing her mop, she barred Dee's way. Not for the first time Dee wondered who permed her hair. *They should be reported and struck off the Hairdressers' Guild.*

Mrs May's eyes were cold, an icy grey that suited her complexion. 'You don't seem to be popular, do you?' she sneered, then gave a short laugh. 'Must be a bit of a shock for you. After all, you've always been Little Miss Popular, haven't you? Even back at school, everyone fell for your Pollyanna persona.' Mrs May savoured the moment, watching Dee closely while slowly shaking her head in mock sympathy. 'Well, not any more! People have finally wised up to you!' She spoke with glee, then, realising that Dee was not going to grace her with a reply, she continued, 'Make no mistake about it; evil will be punished.'

As if on cue, the vicar arrived – or what passed for a vicar in their little village. Dee was a bit vague as to where his parish was; the village chapel was converted into a trendy coffee shop years ago and the magnificent parish church was at present without a member of the clergy. The last one had retired shortly after the harvest supper and the pumpkin-carving competition, and they had struggled all winter relying on retired clergy for the odd service. In some cases, the services had been very odd indeed.

Dee understood that clerical hope was at hand as apparently a keen young female vicar had been appointed, but she hadn't started yet and for now, all Dee had by way of spiritual counsel was the chap in front of her in a dog collar. She knew nothing about him other than he had started popping up around the village last autumn at about the same time the previous vicar left and that Zara had briefly been quite keen on him, as had several other local ladies.

He spoke with charm and concern. 'Ah, Ms FitzMorris.'

'Call me Dee,' she said automatically.

It appeared that Mrs May despised the vicar even more than she disliked Dee. At the sight of him, her tart expression curdled. Cantankerous to the last, she stomped back inside.

The vicar, undismayed, sent the slammed front door a benign smile and murmured, 'Bless her; she is evidently a troubled soul.' He then turned his bright Hollywood smile on Dee. His blue eyes were mesmerising.

Talk about film star good looks! It's easy to see why this chap is a great favourite with all the local ladies! I can see why even Zara was smitten for a while. Then, as she looked more intently at him, another thought struck her. *Actually, upon reflection, he isn't so much good-looking as fascinating. It's unfortunate that he's so long-limbed as it makes his hands seem disconnected from his body when he moves them, and his Jehovah's Witness suit does nothing for him, but you can easily overlook all that when he is directing those eyes at you.*

There was a flash of light as he lifted his right hand and the sun glinted off an exceptionally expensive watch. *I wonder if that was a gift from a grateful parishioner. After all, clergy aren't paid a fortune.* While she observed him she was struggling to recall his name then suddenly it came to her: *Justin Harper. How could I forget! We had weeks of Zara saying 'Justin says ...' or 'Justin is so clever, he ...' Ridiculous of her to have a schoolgirl crush at her age!*

He was still exuding warmth and general ecclesiastical love towards Dee.

She continued to look at him. *I wonder why Zara suddenly went off him in such a major way. Personally, I don't trust anyone who smiles like that all the time! I find them disingenuous. His teeth are unnaturally straight and white – I wonder whether he just wants to show off the expensive dental treatment he has had.* She thought of Mrs May accusing her of being a Pollyanna and decided to give him the benefit of the doubt. *Disingenuous or not, today I need some company.*

'Would you like to come into my house for a cup of tea?' she heard herself ask, aware that the invitation stemmed from her feeling rather low after the morning's rebuffs rather than a wish to get to know this vicar better.

Dee was surprised with the ease with which they found themselves transported from the pavement to the kitchen table with a pot of camomile tea in front of them. Justin Harper, otherwise known as Vicar, had perfected the art of looking at one with concerned interest. His body language conveyed that he had all the time in the world to listen to her.

'How are you doing?' he asked.

'It all seems a bit surreal.'

He was quick to reflect back. 'So the situation doesn't feel real? What does it feel like?'

Cat, who had been prowling noiselessly around the table, started to purr, rubbing her feline body seductively against the vicar's legs. Dee hoped he wasn't allergic to cat hairs.

Vicar Justin was just allowing Dee the space to consider what it did feel like, when Zara walked in.

'Hello? Mother?' She caught sight of Justin Harper, dog collar and all, ensconced at the kitchen table and she momentarily froze.

'Ah, Zara,' he smiled and flashed those impeccable teeth at her.

'Call me Ms FitzMorris. And I'll call you Mr Harper.'

Oh dear, thought Dee.

She knew all too well that, for her daughter, good-looking men fell into two categories: either they were good-looking men she found interesting – like Chief Inspector Nicholas Corman – or they were good-looking men she disliked – like Vicar Justin Harper. In either case, she made no attempt to hide her feelings.

'I was just talking with your mother about the sad demise of Andrew Bernier.'

Dee put down her cup with a clatter. 'Andrew Bernier? He lived on the next road over. He was forever walking his boxer past on his way to the woods. Never had a poop bag to hand, used to make a terrible mess of the pavement. He wasn't a clown.'

'No, I think he was something to do with taxes. An accountant of some sort,' confirmed Vicar Justin.

Zara placed her hands on her hips and gave him the full benefit of all her assertiveness training. 'More to the point, how do you know who the corpse was? The police haven't released that information.'

Vicar Justin's smile did not falter. If anything, it took on an even more kindly edge as he gently addressed them both. 'Someone in my position has their sources.' He rose. 'I'm sure you two have a lot to discuss, so I'll leave you in peace.'

Dee saw him to the door.

He pressed her hand warmly into his. 'Do call if there is anything I can do for you.'

She had already gone back inside so she missed him brushing against the fragrant rose bush by her gate and being delighted when a jewel-like red ladybird flew onto his hand. He carefully held it up to the sunshine and watched as it ran through and over his palm; a perfect little piece of God's creation.

His smile deepened as he carefully curled his hand into a fist and obliterated the bug. With great precision, he meticulously wiped the yellow gunk off his hand using a pristine white handkerchief, before continuing down the road humming.

He could squash anyone who came against him as easily and happily as he had that ladybird. Life was certainly good. Now he was the one with power; a far cry from his dismal childhood in that care home.

Chapter 4

The Flying Pheasant was an attractive pub; wooden panelling and quirky oil paintings of comic pheasants lined the wall rather than a flat-screen TV. If you wanted to catch the latest sporting event you were better off at one of the rowdier pubs on the high street. People came to the Flying Pheasant for the crackling fire and the excellent food. The atmosphere was calm, the only disturbance being when the resident black Labrador bumped into the chess set. It was a classic country pub but with a contemporary twist provided not only by the artwork but also by numerous touches like seasonal flowers in scattered jam jars.

It was early morning so there were no customers but the daily preparations were underway ready for the lunchtime rush.

Francesco strode from his kitchen into the front of the pub; he had his notebook in hand and Italian temper on show. His nostrils flared as he declared, 'Would you believe the market-garden bloke just made his delivery and there's no sodding basil!'

His wife, Gina, didn't respond, she was fiddling with her wedding ring and gazing at the door where Mrs Jenkins was clattering about, laden with her mop and bucket and other cleaning paraphernalia.

Cheerfully their cleaning lady called over her shoulder, 'Hi there, Francesco, can't stop, I'm due at the Plovers' and you know what a fuss that cow Vivian makes if I'm late. I feel sorry for that husband of hers – she's always on about the mess Christopher makes of her precious kitchen floor but to my mind, the poor man is bound to, what with him being so keen on his garden and with that sweet spaniel of his always by his side. Still, like I say, can't stop! Cheerio!' With that, she slammed the door and left.

'Gina, didn't you hear what I said? No sodding basil! I'm

going to have to change today's menu. Thank God he brought some great asparagus.'

His wife still didn't say anything. He took a step closer to her; she was a bit taller than him, voluptuous and normally vivacious. She looked pale beneath her Mediterranean complexion.

'Gina!' he insisted, starting to get worried. 'What was that woman gossiping about this time? I know she's good at her job but really …'

Gina turned to face him, her black eyes stared vacantly. 'The police know it was Andrew Bernier.'

Francesco shrugged. 'So?'

There was an edge to Gina's voice as she snapped back, 'He shouldn't have been left there in Dee's garden! Poor Dee!'

Scowling, he placed his hands on his hips and let out a loud breath before saying, 'Like I told you, her garden is the obvious place to get rid of a body. It's in the centre of the village but with a discreet back entrance. And everyone knows she never locks her gate.'

Gina wrinkled her forehead. 'But what about Dee?'

'Like I told you – she's tough, she'll get over it!'

'And Alex? Do we tell Alex?'

'No!' His voice was sharp. 'She'll find out through work and it's best she doesn't associate us with his death. Just remember our daughter's life will be far better now he's gone.'

Robert and Paul's home was outstandingly beautiful both inside and out but that was only to be expected with Robert's heightened sense of style. The kitchen was a showcase for his taste and attention to detail. Bespoke, not only did it look perfectly in keeping with the house's ancient history but it functioned to perfection, right down to the way each drawer slid in and out with ease. Paul was sitting in the bay window overlooking the back garden. The small round table was laid for breakfast. He already had his coffee and was just waiting for Robert to get back from Sophie's deli with fresh croissants. Brunch was a rare treat when pressures of work permitted.

When Robert walked in, his blond hair was slightly ruffled and along with a fragrant bag of croissants, he had a worried air. 'I just bumped into Mrs Jenkins,' he said.

Paul's dazzling blue eyes flashed and he clenched his teeth, making his sharp jawline taut. Throwing back his Grecian nose he declared, 'Don't tell me that the first late morning I've had in months is going to be ruined by that woman banging around and gossiping at the top of her voice about everyone in the village?'

Robert shook his head and came to sit down. 'She comes here this afternoon after she's been to the Plovers'.' He put a golden crescent croissant on each plate. They were plump and inviting and Paul seized his with relish. 'The police know that the corpse in Dee's garden was Andrew Bernier.'

'Who?' asked Paul absently, not looking up from putting Fortnum and Mason's Burlington Breakfast marmalade onto his pastry.

He was surprised by the note of irritation in Robert's voice when he replied, 'I told you about him!'

'Oh yes, that accountant chappy you had some bother about with your mum's inheritance.'

Robert looked at his devastatingly good-looking husband as he sat relishing his croissant and decided it was probably better if he didn't know any more details of his war with clown corpse and accountant, Andrew Bernier.

The big insurance company where Alex Rossillina worked as an accountant was in the nearby market town. Alex was not the only inhabitant of Little Warthing who made the brief commute to their impressive office each day. Ken Pilbersek, aka Joseph Popov, was a senior actuary at the firm and Julia Fryderberg, aka Blossom Bim Bam, was his junior.

On this particular morning, the building was alive with the latest news. Ken heard it from Julia. He'd been walking past her cubicle and noted she was absent from it. *Late again! Why can she never be on time?* He gazed at her collection of pink glittery pens that were scattered over her desk among various important spreadsheet printouts. Actually, there was so much debris on the surface he was amazed she could find her work at all.

He sighed and shook his head sadly. *Should I have another word with her about her office cubicle? It's hardly the right professional image! What have balloons in the shape of a sausage dog got to do with statistics? And I'm bound to get complaints about that vase of pink roses setting off people's hay fever.*

He sighed again, his grey, sullen features looking even more morose. His attention was diverted by a flurry of activity at the door. He looked up and there she was, her blonde curls attractively tousled and exuding agitation. She was struggling to get her pink mac off and as she shrugged her arms free he couldn't help, momentarily, being caught off-guard.

Get a hold of yourself, man! This is hardly the conduct of a senior actuary, let alone an honourable clown! Despite himself, he could not help looking at Julia again and once more feeling a frisson of excitement; there beneath her flamboyant outer shell was a neat starched grey suit. *What is it about her that's so ...*

'Oh Mr Popov, have you heard the news?' Her blue eyes were wide and her words came out in little breathy gasps.

Ken looked around the office to make sure no one had heard and then in a stern whisper, said, 'Miss Fryderberg, may I remind you that in the office I am Mr Pilbersek and never Joseph Popov?'

'Oh yes! Sorry!' she murmured, dropping her bag on the floor by mistake. The contents, including a string of pink silk trick hankies, a large faux flower with a water pump attached and a Tupperware box containing a cupcake, all pooled at Ken's shiny-shoed toes.

They both bobbed down to retrieve the items. As Ken handed her the cupcake their heads were so close he could smell her mint-fresh breath and see the trace of pink gloss on her pert lips. He swallowed.

'The police know the body is Andrew Bernier's! What are we going to do?' Her voice was shrill and her eyes overly bright.

Calmly Ken helped her to her feet and with his jaw set firm he declared, 'You, Miss Fryderberg, are going to have those figures I asked for on my desk by lunchtime.'

'But the police? They're bound to come.'

'I will deal with them,' announced Ken, throwing his shoulders back and holding in his ever-expanding stomach.

He was rewarded by a look of pure admiration from Julia.

It was lunchtime and the FitzMorris family was getting lunch ready. The windows were all open so the outdoor scent of flowers and fresh-cut grass mingled with the fragrance of mint, rosemary and lavender from the pots on Dee's window sills. Nestling in amongst the herbs were terracotta pots of abundant nasturtiums with bright buds in red and orange.

Amelia was placing Dee's delicate flowered plates on the freshly beeswaxed table. Her movements showed all the finesse and care of a ballet dancer, each movement imbibed with grace, which seemed odd as she wore a black leather-studded choker and a heavy pair of Doc Marten boots. The plates themselves were a mismatched assortment of antique porcelains collected by Dee from flea markets and family.

She tossed back her mane of red curls and announced, 'Well Granny, there is nothing for it! We will have to work out who killed the clown.'

Zara spun around to glare at her daughter, cheese platter in hand and green eyes blazing. Her expression was a contrast to her demure green wrap dress and low heels. 'I had been hoping for a quiet, civilised lunch – a bit of serenity in amongst all this ... this chaos.' She slammed the platter of fruit, cheese and biscuits down on the table. 'Let me tell you, Amelia FitzMorris, I will not have you leading your grandmother astray, and for goodness sake sit up straight. If you must be a Goth, at least you can be an elegant one!'

Dee looked from Zara to Amelia and said, 'Pass me the Brie, dear. I think Amelia may be right. I really can't go on like this. The village feels so ...' She crunched on a bit of crisp celery while she sought the right word. Eventually, she swallowed and said, 'Hostile.'

'Finding a corpse won't exactly make anyone popular,' agreed Amelia.

'That's what Mrs May said. Here, have some Black Bomber – it goes rather well with your lipstick.' Dee nodded, passing her granddaughter the cheese.

'She's a wizened old stick! What does she do that she has so much time to peek through her curtains?' asked Amelia cutting through the black wax coat and taking a generous creamy chunk.

'She's retired now but she used to be a librarian.' Dee took a grape and shuddered at a memory. 'She was a real stickler for rules. Poor little Henry Worth needed six weeks of counselling after she caught him eating a packet of Monster Munch behind the graphic novels. And I can't begin to describe what happened when I didn't return Lavinia Lovelace's *The Duke and His Blushing Bride* on time.' Dee tried to obliterate the unpleasant reminiscence with another grape then moved on to a fresh thought. 'Strangely enough, I was at school with her. I'd totally forgotten her until she mentioned it. I seem to recall there was something odd about her family setup. She definitely had a crush on your father, Zara.'

'She hasn't lived next door for very long, has she?' enquired Amelia, as she helped herself to a wedge of Camembert.

'No, dear … about eighteen months. She moved in when we were doing the glorious trip.'

'Three months of backpacking around Asia,' beamed Amelia, her little Goth face alight with happiness at the memory.

'That's right, dear. I think it was a bit of a shock for her when I got back and she discovered I was her new neighbour.'

'So she didn't hail you as her ideal neighbour?'

'Hardly, dear. She was unable to speak for a few moments then she stomped off, muttering something about me ruining her dream retirement and slamming the door behind her. It was all a bit awkward especially as I was left on the doorstep with the plate of chocolate brownies I'd baked for her as a welcoming gift.'

Zara cut off these happy recollections. 'Amelia – don't hog all the Camembert, and the pair of you can stop this ridiculous notion of becoming sleuths. We have a perfectly good police force and if you ask me, that nice Chief Inspector Nicholas Corman seems like a very capable chap.' A wistful note crept into her voice, her eyes fluttered downward and she exhaled a slow sigh.

Dee caught Amelia's eye and winked. 'I'd agree with you, dear, but I'm not sure I can wait for the long arm of the law to do its bit. Besides all my chard is ruined; it seems so personal. After all, why choose my chard and not someone else's?'

Amelia broke off munching on an apple. 'Honestly, Mummy, Granny's life is going to be rubbish if the killer isn't caught.'

Dee nodded vigorously. 'I was even snubbed at yoga! Not much *namaste* about that lot! Amelia is right – we have to do something and being on the ground, as it were, makes it so much easier. Let's start with the clown angle; that seems a pretty original touch.'

'In police dramas, Granny, they always start with the motive. Why would someone want to kill Andrew Bernier?'

Dee pushed her chair back and gazed up at the ceiling. 'You didn't see the size of his boxer dog's messes on the pavement! Why, only the day before he died, I ...' She trailed off as it suddenly occurred to her that it was probably best not to mention what had transpired between her and Andrew Bernier less than twenty-four hours before he had turned up dead in her back garden.

The fewer people who knew, the better.

Amelia prompted her. 'Only the day before he died, you ...?'

'Um? Oh nothing, dear. Back to the clowns. This village is rather over-endowed with clowns.'

'Well, I suppose two is more than most villages have, but it's not masses. They couldn't be more different. You'd better tackle the grumpy old man, Granny – he wouldn't talk to me.'

'Yes, dear. I'll make sure I *casually* bump into Ken Pilbersek.'

'And I'll corner Julia Fry— what's her name again?'

'Fryderberg, dear, or Blossom Bim Bam. She answers to both.'

Zara had been silently fuming. She regarded her mother and her daughter in horrified indignation. 'Mother! Amelia! I will not stand for the two of you behaving like Miss Marple. Although in your case, Amelia, it's hard to imagine Miss Marple as a Goth.'

'Zara, dear, you just concentrate on selling a few houses and don't worry about us,' said Dee placidly reaching for the celery.

'How can I not worry about you? It might be dangerous!' Zara was struggling to maintain her stern expression, waving an expressive hand in the air which made her gold bangle glint. With a rush of enthusiasm, she added, 'Besides which, you're doing it all wrong.'

'Wrong? How, dear?'

'You're not casting your net wide enough.'

'Who else do you suggest we interview?'

'I don't suggest you interview anyone! But personally, I think the vicar did it.'

'The vicar?' chorused both Dee and Amelia.

Dee spluttered over her celery. 'You mean Justin Harper? What possible reason could you have for saying that? He's a fine upstanding member of society. Besides which, Cat adores him.'

'Cat has always hated me,' commented Zara, throwing the feline a narrow green-eyed glare. Cat swished her tail and ignored her.

'Yes, dear. Now what is it you were saying about the vicar?'

Zara smiled at her mother. 'It's always the vicar who did it; you just have to see a dog collar on TV and you just know he's the guilty party.'

'I think that's a little unfair, dear.'

'Wasn't one of your husbands a vicar, Granny?'

'Yes, Amelia. Number three. Lovely chap. We were very happy together but then he died.'

'How, Granny?'

'Elephant. But back to Zara's vicar—'

'He's not my vicar! And besides, he's not even a proper vicar.'

'But he wears a dog collar!' protested Dee.

Zara held out her hand, gesturing towards Amelia. 'Well I don't know for certain, but it's all a bit fishy. He definitely isn't C of E – there are no tiresome bishops' meetings and precious little preparation of sermons or stepping in to do services. Anyone can wear a clerical collar. It may be illegal but one can still do it. Your granddaughter is dressed as a Goth. Do you really think that's her true identity?'

'Hello! I'm sitting right here.' Amelia looked more resigned than angry. 'Has it ever occurred to you that your refusal to accept me as I am is probably why I'm searching?'

Dee was full of concern. 'For what, dear? I'm always losing my reading glasses so I know how frustrating it can be to lose things.'

'My identity.'

Zara was baffled. 'So your true self is head-to-toe black?' She regarded her daughter – apart from her red hair and green eyes there was not a hint of colour – and gave an involuntary shudder.

Amelia thought for a moment. 'No. You're probably right. I'm thinking about a change.'

'Thank heavens for that!' declared her mother.

'I'm considering getting a tattoo.'

Before Zara could react, Dee helpfully butted in with, 'I've got a tattoo.'

Amelia and Zara stared at her whilst she placidly sipped her camomile tea.

Dee carried on with enthusiasm, smiling warmly at her granddaughter. 'It could be rather fun. We could be tattoo buddies.'

'Gross!' Amelia declared, wrinkling up her nose in disgust.

'Not at all, dear! It's a very sweet little red ladybird. I do adore ladybirds. And what's more, it's in a very interesting place. It's—'

'Mother! That's quite enough of that.'

Dee checked her watch. 'I have to go anyway. There's a citizen scientist project in the park at two-thirty. Funnily enough, we're counting ladybirds! So, just to recap, you, Zara, are planning on stomping around disapproving of your mother and daughter, whilst you, Amelia, are going to chat with Blossom. Meanwhile, I'm going to take on probably the grumpiest clown in the country. By the way, Amelia, whilst you're searching for your identity it might be useful if you look into clowns and their sense of identity, too. Gosh, this is going to be fun!'

'Right!' declared Amelia, with a swish of saffron curls and the clop of Doc Martens. 'I'm off to question an actuary who likes to act a clown about a murder while pretending I'm just making polite conversation.'

'Have fun dear!' commented Dee while filling the washing-up bowl with hot, soapy water.

'Are you in for supper?' called Zara but she was too late as her daughter had already shut the front door.

Chapter 5

The day could not make up its mind if it wanted to be sunny or full of showers. At the moment it was opting for sun and the birds were making the most of it and singing with gusto. Dee had redone her pots by the front door and had played it safe with lavender, but Amelia didn't notice as she was determined on her mission.

As luck would have it, she walked straight out of Dee's home and into Julia Frydersberg – aka Blossom Bim Bam.

Blossom was cycling past when her tyre caught on a pothole and spilled the contents of her bicycle basket over the pavement.

'Do let me help you with that!' declared Amelia brightly as she stepped into the road.

'Oh dear, yes! Oh, not my balloon dachshund! Oh, do you think that bunting will ever recover? Quick, catch the fake flowers before they roll under the hedge!'

Blossom spoke in a breathy scattered way that perfectly matched her riotous curls and flouncy pink dress. Her trademark straw hat, with a daisy on it, was the first thing Amelia restored to her and she hastily crammed it back onto her head.

Eventually, order was restored, or what passed for order in Blossom's rather chaotic world. Amelia handed her the various articles and she shoved them haphazardly back into her basket. Once she got everything ensconced to her satisfaction she peered at Amelia, squinting at her in such a way that Amelia wasn't sure if she needed glasses or was simply surprised at finding a Goth in the village.

It was definitely a shortsighted issue, as when she'd focussed, she gave Amelia a sunny smile. Her large blue eyes shone. Even her bubbly blonde curls bounced along with the daisy in her hat as an expression of general joy.

'Thanks a bundle,' she said. 'I would have been in a right pickle if you hadn't come along at just the right moment. You are Dee's granddaughter, aren't you?'

'Yes, I'm Amelia,' smiled Amelia, thinking that this sleuthing business was a lot easier than it was made out to be in books. 'Actually, I'm pleased to have bumped into you. I've been wanting to ask you about something.'

'Really?' Blossom leant forward so that the daisy on her straw hat tilted towards Amelia. 'What?'

Amelia paused. *Hmm, I can't really launch in with, 'Did you have anything to do with Granny's deceased clown? After all – he was a clown, and you're a clown; there must be some connection. And what exactly were your movements on the day in question?' even though that's what I want to ask.*

The silence must have lasted for longer than Amelia had realised as Blossom felt the need to prompt her. 'Amelia? What do you want to ask me about?'

Thinking fast, she replied, 'Being a clown – I want to make it my career.'

Blossom regarded Amelia with wide blue eyes before hesitantly saying, 'Well, not many clowns are fortunate enough to be able to make it their full-time occupation. It tends to be more of a sideline.' She looked embarrassed, almost ashamed as she leaned her head forward so that her curls hid her eyes while she confessed, 'I'm an actuary to pay the bills. I work for Ken Pilbersek. You might know him better as Joseph Popov.'

She said his name with such awed reverence that for a moment Amelia wondered if there was another Ken Pilbersek in the region. The only one Amelia was aware of was a rather grey and grumpy middle-aged bloke whom she could not imagine invoking awe in anyone.

As Amelia tore her thoughts away from Ken to the dead clown in hand she realised that Blossom was scrutinising her, her eyes roaming over her from top to bottom. Eventually, she said apologetically, 'And you'd probably have to have a bit of a think about the whole *black* thing you've got going on.'

Amelia glanced down at her Doc Martens, studs and ripped tights. They were rather a contrast to Blossom's dazzling pink dress.

Solemnly, Blossom continued, 'You see, a clown is always a clown, whether you're in costume on stage, or just going to the local shop. A clown has a duty – a calling, if you like – to make the world a happier, brighter place.'

'Oh!' was all Amelia could think to say.

Perhaps I should have stuck to my first line of questioning and gone straight for the corpse issue.

Blossom suddenly went pink and crinkled her pert freckled nose. 'Oh, dear! I am sorry. I do hope I haven't squashed your dream.' She grasped Amelia by the hand and fervently added, 'Don't lose hope. There really is no need to look quite so crestfallen. Tell you what, why don't you come home with me? I've got some pink frosted cupcakes just waiting to be eaten and we can discuss it more over a nice cup of tea.'

Amelia smiled and agreed which seemed to please Blossom. So wheeling the bicycle between them, they walked down the road, past Ken's modern house and several other dwellings until they reached Blossom's cottage.

Her home was tiny but perfect. The little windows on either side of the low crooked front door reminded Amelia of bright harvest mouse eyes. In front of the house, there was a jumble of vivid flowers. They were planted in a variety of containers – a watering can, a bucket, and a small wheelbarrow. Bird feeders were hanging from every available branch and a myriad of small birds fluttered as they walked past.

Blossom propped her bike against the wall. There was a prolonged pause whilst she tried to find her keys. 'I know they're in here somewhere,' she muttered as she rattled her raffia handbag and out came lollipops, tissues, lip balm and numerous other things, but no house keys. She searched her bicycle basket and her pockets, but all to no avail.

Helpfully Amelia stated, 'It's alright, they're here.'

She indicated a key in the red front door. It was hard to miss; an enormous yellow sunflower dangled off the key chain.

Blossom laughed and pushed the door open. She picked up a few brown envelopes that the postman had left on the doormat and shoved them carelessly on a pile of similar bills on the sideboard. Amelia noticed that several of them had red writing, obviously overdue.

Amelia was instantly struck by two thoughts: *Who doesn't pay their bills online?* And then, *So Blossom is in debt! Could that be a motive for murder?*

The inside of the cottage was dark, but full of colour, from the pink walls to every cluttered surface; Blossom evidently liked to collect eye-catching comic china figures, so grinning frogs smiled out from troops of tumbling clowns while a piggy orchestra played a variety of instruments.

The front door led straight into the kitchen; the house was only one room wide so Amelia could view the garden beyond with more flowers and a potting shed painted to look like a fairytale cottage.

It was not until they were seated at the kitchen table sipping extremely strong coffee from mismatched mugs that Amelia was able to get onto the corpse – or so she hoped.

'So what makes you want to be a clown?' asked Blossom as she smiled and looked encouragingly at her guest.

Amelia scanned the room for inspiration. On the walls, above the clutter there were brilliant balloon posters and vibrant cushions on every chair and sofa; there was an abundance of visual stimulation but nothing to provide Amelia with inspiration.

'Have you always felt that there was a clown inside you longing to get out?' suggested Blossom hopefully, with her head on one side.

Amelia's black lips twitched. The studs on her choker seemed a bit too tight.

'You're very brave. Lots of people try to suppress their inner clown,' said Blossom warmly.

'Is that what Andrew Bernier did?' blurted out Amelia with more desperation than discernment.

'What?' Blossom sat back in her chair and blinked.

'Andrew Bernier – he turned up in Granny's veg patch, dressed as a clown.' There was a pause, before she added unnecessarily, 'Dead.'

'That man was no clown.' Blossom's voice was flat and her eyes narrowed.

'You knew him?' Amelia leaned forwards in her chair; she was alert for any clues.

Blossom had paled, the flowers in her hat drooped and she clenched her pink coffee cup so hard her knuckles showed white. Her voice shook with emotion. 'He was not a nice man.'

'You came across him whilst working as a clown?'

'I told you – he definitely wasn't a clown.' She swallowed and looked as if she was fighting to hold back tears. 'He was actually extremely rude about me being a clown. He was rather cruel about it. I met him professionally, but there was nothing very professional about him.'

'He was an actuary?'

'An accountant specialising in tax law. He …'

Amelia prompted, 'He …?'

'He liked to use the information he got to his own advantage.'

'In what way?'

Blossom was no longer wide-eyed and friendly; there was a coldness in the way she was regarding Amelia that sent a chill down her spine. After an arctic minute, she said icily, 'I think you ought to be going now.'

'But we haven't had our pink frosted cupcakes,' wailed Amelia, genuinely sad to miss out on the frosted delight she had spotted on the sideboard.

Ignoring Amelia's plea, Blossom rose to her feet.

Reluctantly, Amelia stood up too. 'Just one more thing. Where were you on the morning that Andrew Bernier was found in Granny's chard?'

'What?'

'It's a bit like the old *Where were you when JFK was shot or when Princess Di died*? Everyone can remember.'

'Well, not me. Now, Amelia, please leave.'

Chapter 6

Shortly after Amelia left, Zara noticed the time and exclaimed, 'Must dash, I've got two viewings this afternoon.'

She departed, leaving Dee to finish the clearing up from lunch. It didn't take long and Dee rather enjoyed handling her precious china and generally putting her home in order.

Housework is very grounding, she thought as she checked herself in the mirror before going out. *I wonder if it's an energy-flow thing? A bit like feng shui?*

A glance in the looking glass confirmed what she had always suspected. *Life's little challenges, be they mundane or murder, are so much easier to face when one has a good haircut.* She ran her fingers through her short shiny pixie bob. *Thank goodness I had just been for a cut and tint before all this unpleasantness happened.* She checked her well-cut beige slacks. *These linen blends one can get these days are so good at not creasing but feeling light. It used to be so dispiriting when one looked like a used, crumpled tissue two seconds after donning a summer frock.* Her eyes skimmed over her tan ballet flats. *Should I invest in some other sort of footwear? I seem to live in flats. Where is the line between having a signature style and just being boring?*

Leaving such philosophical questions to one side she adjusted her cream silk blouse and green jade necklace. *The jade does bring out the colour of my eyes,* she thought, happily remembering the excellent trip to Japan where she picked up the necklace along with a favourite teapot. *Besides which, without the pop of colour, I fear I would look rather, well, beige.* She moistened her lips with some salve and headed out of the door to do a spot of sleuthing.

She was better prepared with an excuse to question Ken than her granddaughter had been when approaching Blossom. As she marched up to Ken Pilbersek's red front door she was armed with a notebook and pencil, her opening gambit already mentally rehearsed.

She knew a little about Ken; he lived just down from her on the same road and she knew that he was generally grumpy. Mrs Jenkins, that well-known nosy cleaner and village gossip, had once mentioned that Ken Pilbersek came from a long line of actuaries, where numbers and statistics were the family's lifeblood and that his urge to clown was his way of rebelling while still having a stable income.

Very sensible, thought Dee. *Self-expression is all very well but life without the wherewithal to pay for heating would be very wearing.*

She brought her attention back to the present. The front of his house was a picture of order. Two round bay trees in classic square tubs flanked the step. The neat garden of pruned roses could have come straight out of a magazine. The hedge between his garden and the village was low. The only things that were not ordered with military precision were the numerous birds that hovered around his neat collection of feeders.

The house was a new build but, unlike Mrs May's bungalow, Ken's home was tastefully in accordance with the rest of the village. It was built in the same traditional cream-coloured stone of the more historic buildings but whereas the medieval homes had tiny windows, his were large.

She rapped firmly on the door. After a moment or two, it was opened by Ken Pilbersek. He was quite a bit taller than Dee but then most people were. His grey hair was cut short and he was slim apart from the hint of a middle-aged potbelly. He was wearing his slippers and a nondescript shirt and trousers. *So obviously there is no clowning around in his near future.*

He did not look pleased to see her; his steely eyes were narrow and his thin lips pursed.

Dee beamed at him with more enthusiasm than she felt.

'Good afternoon, Mr Pilbersek. I'm doing an article for the local paper on the cultural significance of clowns and their role in today's society. Obviously, as you are a renowned authority on the subject, I was hoping you wouldn't mind me interviewing you.'

There was a pause as he surveyed her.

Her jaw was beginning to ache from her bright smile so she was relieved when she noticed a softening in the hardness of his eyes and even the merest twitch of a smile around his mouth. 'Renowned authority, eh? Why don't you come in and have a coffee?'

Dee was pleased to note that even actuaries who like to clown are not immune to flattery.

He led her into the front room which, like the garden, was neat and tidy. Even the pot plants were lined up in an orderly fashion. There were old-fashioned white lace head protectors on the sensible brown sofa and armchair.

He indicated a seventies Formica chair at a matching table in front of the large window. 'You sit yourself down there and I'll just go to the kitchen and make us some coffee. Won't be a jiffy.'

Settled on a rather uncomfortable seat at the table, Dee looked out at the front garden and the village beyond. She felt rather exposed; while Ken's table had a good view of this bit of the village's goings-on, it gave Dee the unpleasant impression of being in a goldfish bowl.

He returned with a tray. In a neat Wedgwood cup and saucer, he served her coffee that was strong enough to take her breath away.

He took a sip and sighed with satisfaction. 'So Ms FitzMorris, what would you like to know?'

'Call me Dee. And could we start with your clown name?'

'My character is Joseph Popov.'

She scribbled in her notebook. 'And why did you choose that name?'

Ken leant back in his chair. 'Well, obviously the Joseph is from Joseph Grimaldi – commonly known as the father of modern clowning. Did you know he was the first clown to wear white face paint and paint red lips?'

Dee did know this – she had after all watched the documentary series on Netflix, but she simply said 'Really?' and scribbled some more. 'And Popov?'

Ken Pilbersek smiled. At least, Dee took the unaccustomed wrinkling around his eyes and the quiver of his mouth to be an indication of happiness. 'Oleg Popov was, in my opinion, the greatest clown of our generation. A master of physical theatre – mime, if you like. I was lucky enough to see him perform in 2006 at the thirtieth anniversary of the International Circus Festival at Monte Carlo.'

Dee hoped she looked suitably impressed.

'Do you know, he was seventy-five years old and still able to command a standing ovation?'

'Gosh! That's really something,' said Dee eagerly, while she tried to move the conversation on. 'And today – are there many clowns? I mean is it possible that one's neighbour in the village might be a clown and one knew nothing about it?' She was about to go on and say something along the lines of, *Could, for example, hypothetically, someone who was a tax accountant with an antisocial boxer dog be a clown? And more to the point, have you any idea why he turned up dead in my chard?* All this and more was on the tip of her tongue but she didn't get a chance to say any of it as Ken Pilbersek was in full clown mode.

'Of course, you will want to say something about the history—'

'The history?'

'Of clowns. They originated as the rustic fool in all manner of plays, shown around the world ... but it was Joseph Grimaldi who in his performances as Joey, in the pantomimes at Convent Garden in the early 1800s ... shouldn't you be writing this down?'

'Sorry?'

'Shouldn't you take down the dates and the details?'

'The dates and details?'

'Yes – for your article.'

'Oh! Yes. 1800s.' Dee jotted with her pencil as he continued his monologue.

'His role was to aid Harlequin in his quest for ...' His voice trailed away.

Dee looked up to find that Ken was gazing wistfully out of the window. Curious, Dee glanced outside. She could see Amelia talking to Blossom Bim Bam. Well, to be quite accurate, Blossom seemed to be trying to eject a reluctant Amelia from her premises. Blossom's hair was wild beneath her straw hat. She was obviously flustered but that gave her a rather attractive glow.

Ken swallowed and continued, '… to aid Harlequin in his quest for the love of …' He sighed and glancing once more in the direction of Blossom, added, 'Columbine.'

Interesting! thought Dee.

Sounding suitably innocent she enquired, 'Julia Fryderberg is a fellow clown isn't she?'

Ken snorted, but his eyes remained transfixed on where Julia, otherwise known as Blossom, and Amelia still seemed to be negotiating Amelia's departure. 'Hardly! She wastes her time on children's parties, rather than truly exploring her art – her calling. I mean, what sort of name is Blossom Bim Bam?'

'You don't do children's parties?'

He cleared his throat and took a steadying slurp of coffee. 'Well yes I do, but it's quite different.'

He looked at Dee with exasperation tinged with annoyance and she feared that this interview was not going as well as she had desired. She could only hope that Amelia's chat with the said Blossom Bim Bam had been more productive than hers was with Ken. However, judging by the way that Amelia and Blossom were now both on the pavement outside Blossom's diminutive cottage, and that Blossom was making flamboyant shooing gestures with her arms, Dee doubted it.

Chapter 7

What a waste of time that was! thought Zara as she arrived back at Little Warthing.

Her first appointment after lunch had been disappointing and that was putting it mildly. A wife, keen to downsize now the children had left home, had dragged her reluctant – not to say truculent – husband along to view a neat two-up, two-down with a manageable garden. He had complained and made snide comments throughout and now Zara's nerves were on edge.

She looked at her watch; she had forty-five minutes before she must be back on sparkling form. Her second appointment of the afternoon was showing a family their perfect new home. She knew her success at selling properties was down to two things: firstly her ability to assess who her clients were and so be able to gauge what they required from a home, and secondly, her vivacious nature.

The failure of the first appointment had been because she had only met the wife before. *If I'd had so much as thirty seconds with the husband beforehand, I would have known that that lovely neat home was not for him!*

The next clients she was about to meet were taking a second look at the rather splendid farmhouse she had found them. It would be ideal for them with their growing family and unnecessary number of dogs. And, more to the point, the commission would pay for Amelia's second year at uni.

What she needed now was to clear her head.

It wasn't even as if I had gone into that empty nesters' viewing full of serenity – lunch was not exactly restful.

Not for the first time, she wondered why both her daughter and her mother had the ability to make her feel she was losing all sense of reality.

What is called for is a refreshing coffee at The Old Chapel café and a perusal of the latest Vanity Fair.

She walked straight to her favourite coffee shop. The Old Chapel only had three outside tables, but as luck would have it, one of them was free.

At the far table, two young mothers with toddlers were chatting and enjoying the sunshine. At the middle table sat a gentleman who was hidden behind a large broadsheet newspaper. Zara glanced in his direction. *What a refreshing change it makes to see someone reading a paper rather than peering at a phone.*

A kind waitress took her order and within minutes she was sipping her red bush tea and listening to the birds singing. *This is heavenly.* Zara took out her magazine and was happy.

She was unaware that the gentleman behind the paper was noting the way the sun caught the saffron highlights in her hair and glinted off her gold bracelet. Nor did she realise that he was admiring the lines of her classic emerald dress as it elegantly enhanced her slim figure. She crossed her legs, showing off her attractive calves and ankle, drawing attention to her heels with just a hint of seduction.

Her magazine failed to hold her attention, so she closed her eyes and simply enjoyed the feel of the sun on her face – but not for long.

'Zara! How lovely to see you. May I sit down?'

She recognised the voice. Without opening her eyes she uttered a cold firm, 'No!'

He disregarded her words and sat. Annoyed, Zara opened her eyes and coldly regarded Justin Harper, otherwise known as The Vicar.

'We used to be such good friends …' He sounded genuinely grieved. Those beguiling blue eyes were alight with emotion but quite what emotion it was Zara couldn't gauge.

She steadied herself. *I'll not fall for him again!*

'That was before I discovered that you—'

What she was about to say was lost in a cacophony of wails as one of the toddlers fell over.

Once calm was restored, Justin commented, 'I believed what we shared was something special.'

At his words, flashbacks played out in Zara's mind as clearly as scenes from a film. She could see them walking arm in arm through autumn woods surrounded by glorious golden leaves, the air crisp and cold on her cheeks. Then as autumn turned to winter she could see them sipping brandy, wearing cosy sweaters in front of a crackling fire, while the rain lashed at the windows and they listened to Rachmaninov.

She could recall the thrill and excitement of waiting for him to pick her up for a dinner date and the house full of red roses.

But then she remembered the betrayal and heartache. Coldly she enquired, 'Special? Is that what you call it?'

'Yes! Wouldn't you?'

'Hardly! A relationship built on lies and manipulation is exploitative at its best. You took shameless advantage of my vulnerability. You know how difficult it was for me to even contemplate being in a relationship again but you were relentless.'

'Losing your husband in that terrible car crash was tragic … but it was nearly a decade ago and he would want you to be happy.'

Zara stiffened. When she spoke, her voice was icy and composed. 'Don't you *dare* to presume you have a clue about what he would want. As for happiness, the only person who you ever want to be happy is Justin Harper.'

She looked away from him and carefully resumed reading her magazine.

Conversational silence hung in the air, the birds continued to sing and the toddlers to chatter. Zara gave every impression of being unconcerned by Justin. Such was her disregard, it seemed she did not even care if he stayed or left.

With hawk-like eyes, Justin was regarding her intently. He moved his long limbs stiffly – they were obviously uncomfortable under the small table. Gently he tried another approach. 'I'm sorry your mother is having all these difficulties.'

Instantly alert, Zara snapped back, 'You knew him, didn't you?'

'Who?'

'Andrew Bernier – the clown corpse.'

'In my calling, I know a lot of people.'

'I'm going to ignore *your calling* as I suspect your only calling is to serve yourself. Didn't he do your tax returns?'

Justin muttered, 'Not exactly.'

Zara continued, 'And with your so-called *calling* not being under the wing of any recognised religious organisation, I would imagine your taxes are interesting, to say the least.'

'Interesting?' he queried.

'Irregular.'

'Zara, Zara, my dear child, I don't know what you mean. Actually, Bernier and I parted ways some time ago. I fear he was a troubled soul.'

'He was probably troubled by where your obviously lavish income comes from. You're not even a legitimately ordained minister and yet—'

Justin Harper cut across her. 'Must we talk of such worldly matters?'

'Yes!' she replied firmly. 'Your dodgy organisation, God's Gateway, is about as worldly as it gets.'

'Sister, I'm sorry to see you so troubled.'

'I'm not half as troubled as you will be when the police catch up with you.' She glanced at her watch. 'I have an appointment.'

She rose and strode purposefully away ignoring Justin's, 'Bless you.'

Chief Inspector Nicolas Corman, sitting at the middle table, lowered his newspaper and regarded Zara's departing back with interest. His curiosity was piqued; he wondered when he would see her again.

Dee was not a regular at the Flying Pheasant but she liked the Rossillina family, and that evening her Lavinia Lovelace romance was failing to hold her attention, so when she got a text from Sophie, her friend who ran the Sophie and Son deli, suggesting they meet up, she willingly obliged.

Corpse In The Chard

Sophie's text had mentioned she'd be in the garden at the back of the pub. Dee was pleased, it would be nice to be outside as the showers had cleared and it was a glorious evening. The sun was still low as it was only very early summer but at least it was out and shining after all those long dreary winter nights. The sky was clear and blue with just a wisp or two of cloud. The sun was casting long shadows but was giving little warmth.

We'll need the outdoor heaters burning – so bad for the environment but ...

While she was walking over to her local, she was distracted by the hauntingly beautiful song of a blackbird and paused to enjoy the melody and inhale the evening air. *This time of the day has a scent all of its own; later in the summer the air will be heavy with roses, stocks and jasmine but now there is just a hint of rose, mingled with honeysuckle.*

She entered the pub garden from its back gate. The garden was large and dotted with a variety of tables which had bench seats attached. In summer each would have a large sun umbrella but at the moment there was a greater need for free-standing heaters. Dee always admired the simple stylish planting – it was low maintenance, being largely swathes of blue geraniums with the occasional taller plant for colour and interest. Now in the evening sunshine, there was a gentle hum of bees stocking up on nectar and pollen. The flower borders' colour scheme was blue and pink and was well looked after by a local firm of contractors. Dee particularly liked the frizzle bantams that scratched and clucked at one end of the garden. Their homes were little miniature cottages and never failed to enchant visiting children. Originally they had been free-range but after a couple of unfortunate incidents with patrons' dogs, the bantams had been confined to a spacious run.

The garden was surprisingly busy; there was a carnival atmosphere as locals and tourists made the most of being outside and catching up with friends after so many nights tucked up in their homes.

She spotted Sophie the moment she walked in – she was on one of the larger tables and surrounded by the younger element of the village; her own lean and lanky son, David, and Alex Rossillina, with her mane of dark curls, vivacious laugh and wheelchair, and her younger brother, Marcello.

Sophie stood up and waved; blonde and long-limbed like her son, she looked good in her jeans, white shirt and navy blazer. The blazer had a military twist with epaulettes, cuffs and buttons. Dee suspected that Sophie's invitation had been her way of showing support and she greatly appreciated the gesture.

'Hi there! I got you the usual.' Sophie indicated a golden cider. The 'usual' in Little Warthing in the spring and summer was invariably the local cider; light and crisp, it was universally enjoyed. 'I texted Zara but I haven't heard back.' There was just an appealing hint of an American accent in Sophie's speech.

'She's got a viewing or a listing – I forget which,' explained Dee, sitting down next to Sophie and nodding to the others. She gave David a grin. He was exceptionally tall and had a gentle smile that showed off his very white, straight teeth.

'Are you home for the holidays?' she asked.

'Yeah, school's out for the summer.'

It seemed strange to Dee as she felt they were still half in spring. *But then Americans do things differently – like calling university 'school'.* He sounded very transatlantic but she knew that would change after a few weeks with his English friends. *He must be musical as he has an ear for accents.*

David continued, 'I'm looking forward to catching up with all my mates here, including Amelia.'

'She's coming here later,' said Alex, shifting her wheelchair to one side with a whirl of its engine.

David nodded. 'And the other two I want to see are Jake and Tristan.'

Dee mused that one of the many lovely things about living in the same village for decades was that one knew multiple generations of different families. Jake was the son of one of her contemporaries, Sebastian Rivers; he'd had his first and only child around the same time Dee had become a grandmother and now Jake and Amelia were studying psychology together. The Rivers family, father and son, lived in decaying grandeur in their family home just outside the village.

Tristan was in a very different situation. He lived and worked in London but having lost both his parents he made his base with godparents and distant relatives, the terrifying Vivian Plover and her amiable, bumbling husband Christopher. Tristan was charming, good-looking and troubled, and Dee was very fond of him. She suspected that life with Vivian wasn't very restful which would explain why since he was young he had always spent a lot of time at Dee's.

Alex said, 'Tristan is down this weekend for the tennis tournament. I'm competing in the mixed doubles.'

The heater near their table made some spluttering noises and went out. Marcello stood up and started to fiddle with it. His mother Gina, whose voluptuous curves were only just contained in her red dress, gave him a grateful smile as she walked past with two lasagnes for the neighbouring table.

David looked at Dee and said, 'Mum says you've had a bit of trouble.'

There it is again – that blending of American culture with English – the American warmth and directness combined with English understatement.

Dee laughed. 'If you call someone turning up dead in my garden *a bit of trouble*, then yes.'

Alex hunched over and gripped the control knob on her wheelchair.

'Who was it?' asked David.

'Andrew Bernier,' supplied Sophie. 'I'm not sure if you would ever have come across him. He lived a few roads over; you might have seen him walking his boxer.'

David looked thoughtful then shook his head. 'No, doesn't ring a bell.'

Alex was fidgeting with her glass. She spilt a bit of cider on her hand, swore softly and, biting her lip, rubbed her hand on her trouser leg.

Marcello stopped struggling with the heater and looked at his sister. 'Bernier? Isn't he the bloke you had all that bother with at work, Alex?'

Everyone looked at her and she flushed and swallowed, but Marcello had already lost interest. 'Hey, Mum! I can't get this to work.'

Gina, empty tray in hand, walked up. 'I'll get your father to come out – he has a knack with these heaters.' She glanced at Alex. 'You alright, love? You look a little—'

'Fine, I'm absolutely fine!' snapped Alex, looking down.

Marcello added, 'I was just asking her about Dee's corpse. I'm sure—'

Gina cast Alex a worried glance then brusquely turned on her son. 'Actually, can you get your father? I've people to serve.'

Compliant and with no hint of rancour Marcello obliged, leaving Dee to ponder Alex's sudden silence and Gina's curtness.

More was to come as Francesco, apron tied around his waist, hurried out. He strode up across the grass with the air of a chef who had ten starters and three mains to prepare and who didn't have the time to fix broken heaters. Small and wiry, his movements were fast. With a flick of the wrist, he had the said heater roaring into life.

As he was turning to go he was distracted by Justin Harper's unmistakable elongated figure coming through the garden gate. Justin was smiling benignly at the world in general, he held his Grecian nose high and was wearing one of his habitual well-tailored suits.

His expression did not waver as Francesco strode over to him with his face taut and his fists clenched. Francesco, a good foot shorter than Justin, squared up to him and hissed, 'You're not welcome here.'

Justin looked down his nose at Francesco and smiled, he raised his eyebrows and in a mild tone said, 'Do you really think it's wise to threaten me?' Then, with great dignity, he turned and left.

Gina stopped taking an order from an elderly couple with a terrier who were sitting at a corner table. She walked up to Francesco and touched his sleeve. Leaning into him, she murmured, 'Leave it – there's nothing more you can do now. Better go back to the kitchen.'

Marcello had watched all this with wide eyes and an open mouth. When both his parents were safely out of earshot he looked around the table and enquired, 'What was that all about?'

'Why can't you just shut up!' sighed Alex as she abruptly turned her wheelchair and headed inside at speed.

Dee, Sophie, David and Marcello observed her departure in silence then Dee rather weakly and with obviously forced jollity changed the subject. 'I've been counting ladybirds.'

Paul was determined to maintain his washboard abs. He wasn't exactly vain but he was deeply aware of all the young army officers coming through the ranks. In an effort to keep middle age at bay, he went for a run whenever he could.

He knew he was getting older; he was greying slightly at the temples but he liked to think that just made him look more distinguished. His jawline was still firm and he was able to deploy a devastating look with his intensely blue eyes. Straight nose, full lips, firm chin – yes! He was far from looking his age.

Admittedly when he went for a run now, he needed to wear knee supports but lots of top athletes wore them and it was without doubt that he went on runs not jogs. Keeping in shape was so much easier now the days were getting longer; running through black, cold drizzle was not a lot of fun.

He was nearing the end of his exercise and looking forward to a shower and a quiet supper with his husband, Robert. Tonight it was to be tender lamb chops – he'd been marinating them with garlic and rosemary and they smelt delicious. He was going to serve them with sautéed spring peas, shallots and mushrooms – he could hardly wait.

He turned a corner and in the distance, in the shadow of the grand old church, among the gravestones, he spotted two men having an animated – not to say acrimonious – discussion. He didn't think he knew the taller, lankier one; he was sure he would have remembered anyone with hands that large on the end of those long stick-like arms. The man was wearing a dog collar which puzzled Paul as he thought the village was between vicars. His confusion grew as he realised the other figure was Robert.

Robert looked agitated and Paul wondered if he should stop. As swiftly as he had the thought, he reasoned that Robert was a grown man quite capable of looking after himself. He suppressed the knowledge that he was motivated more by thoughts of his dinner than his lover.

As he ran past he did have a moment of self-reflection. *Perhaps I should be more solicitous of Robert – after all, losing his mum was a blow and then what was there about the will? There had been something about probate? Tax? Hence that Bernier chap being involved – but wasn't there something else? Something about her leaving lots of money to the church? No! Not the church – some vicar.*

Paul hadn't really paid much attention when Robert had talked about it and as he opened his front door and headed upstairs for a shower, he forgot all about the subject.

Robert, as he strode away from the graveyard, didn't have the luxury of being able to forget about his recent altercation with Justin Harper or his mother's will.

He ran a sweaty hand through his thick blond hair. He felt hot, his heart was pounding and he was experiencing slight dizziness and nausea. He couldn't go home in this state. Paul might be a bit oblivious but even he was bound to notice that Robert was not quite himself. He'd walk slowly around the village to cool off and pray he didn't bump into anyone he knew.

He strolled on, oblivious of his surroundings and totally consumed by his own thoughts.

Oh, Mum! What a pickle!

His mum, soft and sweet-smelling with a penchant for pastel colours and cashmere would have been heartbroken if she'd been able to see the mess she'd left after her death for Robert to sort out.

You always said I was the only man you needed in your life! Why did you have to choose your last year on this earth and Justin Harper to change your mind?

His mind flashed back to his childhood, happy seaside holidays with his mum in beautiful sundresses with her matching straw hats and glamorous sunglasses. They had both loved making sandcastles together. Her laughter seemed to fill every corner of his life. When he was older, they started visiting fine restaurants and they never missed the latest West End musical or comedy. She'd been his greatest supporter and financial backer in the early days of setting up his interior design business. He knew he'd inherited – or was it learnt? – his sense of style from her.

He sighed as he remembered their home, cosy, warm and always changing as she embraced the latest trends.

She never really liked Paul beyond his good looks. She loved going out with Paul on one arm and me on the other but that didn't happen often as Paul never really got the point of musicals. What was it she once said to me? Ah yes! 'Paul's too in love with himself to be able to give you all the love you deserve'.

And now she was gone and he was left with happy memories but a nightmare of a will and probate.

I should have paid more attention when she started talking about the wonderful young man she'd met at the golf club. I thought she was just having a touch of religious fervour – at her age, it was to be expected.

The walk was helping to calm his heart rate and get his ideas in order.

Now my lawyer and accountant say there is nothing they can do about the will.

He clenched his fist.

I shouldn't have done it! After all, I had no solid proof that Bernier had been involved beyond introducing Mum to Justin but when I confronted him he was so ... so cocky. He thought it all a tremendous joke ... I don't know what came over me. I just saw red! I don't think I've ever lost my temper like that before which would have been bad enough but why, oh why, did Justin Harper have to witness the whole thing?

To his surprise, Robert found he was at his front door. He took a breath and walked in. There was a wonderful smell of rosemary, garlic and lamb.

Paul was at the little round table in the bay window. He didn't look up from his phone. 'I've eaten,' he said. 'Couldn't let it spoil.'

Chapter 8

Nicholas Corman didn't have long to wait before he saw Zara again; the opportunity arose when he went to Dee's home to ask her some more questions. He took the car and Josh to Little Warthing.

'So Gov, why exactly are we here?' Josh enquired as they drove into the picturesque village.

Nicholas winced at Josh calling him 'Gov' and shuddered as he saw Josh brush down his jacket; with a careless hand, he sent a snowstorm of greasy crumbs from his latest snack all over Nicholas' pristine car interior.

'As I've already told you – we're following a tip-off from a member of the public. We are making further enquiries.'

'Yes, but it wasn't exactly a tip-off was it?' said Josh. 'I mean it's not really new evidence or anything. It's just that the member of the public happens to be a retired police chief, so we have to drop everything and come running.'

He was right, which for some reason annoyed Nicholas even more.

Josh hadn't been privy to the unexpected call that had come through to Nicholas on his mobile as he walked through the back office of the police station. He'd had the phone on vibrate, which was just as well as he wouldn't have heard the ring above the normal hub of chat, heavy feet and chairs scraping on the floor. He held the phone to his ear.

'Corman!' His name had come out as a bark, not a question, leaving Nicholas confused as he didn't recognise the number on his screen or the voice.

'Obvious that you need a hand with this case – a bit beyond you, eh?'

'Excuse me?' said Corman.

'Nothing to be ashamed of. Only to be expected in a youngster like you.'

Nicholas glanced around the police station. This had to be a prank call. He scanned all the people in the immediate area but everyone was busy, there were no little groups of giggling officers huddled around a phone.

He stood still. He was tempted just to put the phone down but instead, he drew himself to his full height and said, 'Who is this?'

'Peter Wilson. Police Chief Peter Wilson.'

Now Nicholas knew where he was and whom he was dealing with. He noted that Peter Wilson had not used the words 'retired' or 'ex' when giving his previous job title.

'We need to get this matter cleared up immediately as it doesn't look good for me having a murder right on my doorstep. I knew Bernier well – excellent chap, we were members of the same golf club – but I'll tell you all about it when I see you. I also have some vital information to give you regarding that FitzMorris woman, linking her unmistakably to Bernier on the night of the murder. A reliable eye-witness account is what you need my boy. This case will make your career, thanks to me.' He cleared his throat which reminded Nicholas of the rasping sounds that a fat toad makes. 'But that's far too sensitive a matter for me to divulge over the phone. We will need to meet privately. Firstly though it's got to stop!'

'What?'

'Speak up, boy!'

'What has to stop?'

'Why, that Dee FitzMorris woman and her granddaughter going round the village stirring people up and asking questions. I won't have it, you hear! I can't have my neighbours upset! Bad for my reputation. They are only doing it to cast confusion and doubt. Dee FitzMorris just wants to create uncertainty in people's minds about her own guilt.' He cleared his throat again. 'I'll tell you what you are going to do, get yourself down here right now. I'll be on my lawn watching out for you. You come to Little Warthing and put the fear of God into that woman.'

'If you have relevant information pertaining to the case you should come into the station and make a statement,' said Corman.

'Don't be ridiculous, boy! I need to catch the twelve-thirty train to London – I have tickets for Lord's this afternoon. I'll just have time to check you do as you're told then I'll need to be off.'

The phone had clicked into silence leaving an outraged Nicholas to march into his superior's office and complain. Far from his superior sharing in his fury, he had looked worried, murmured something about Peter Wilson being very well-connected and suggesting that Nicholas hurry along to Little Warthing as there would be hell to pay if Mr Wilson missed his train.

As Nicholas parked his car on the side of the small road where both Dee and the pesky ex-copper lived, he glanced up, and sure enough, there was retired Police Chief Peter Wilson waiting and observing from the safety of his front garden. His home, a modern bungalow, was stark and the garden totally barren of flowers and foliage, with just a pocket handkerchief of a lawn cut with the perfect stripes of the hallowed turf.

Does that man not realise he's retired? Don't the words 'wasting police time' mean nothing to him? And more to the point, who gave him my personal mobile number? And why does he have a ponytail when he wears a suit?

'Cor, speak of the devil; there's the old codger now,' declared Josh unnecessarily. Peter Wilson was both very tall and extremely bulky which made him hard to miss on his deckchair in the middle of his modest garden.

'Have a bit more respect,' said Corman.

'Why does he always wear that daft tie?'

'That daft tie, as you call it, is his pride and joy. He never goes anywhere without it. It marks him out as an illustrious member of the MCC.'

'The what?'

'The Marylebone Cricket Club, which is the most prestigious cricket club in the world. It takes connections and thirty years to become a member.'

'I still think it looks daft. I mean, who wears yellow and orange unless you're a clown?'

'It's yellow and red – or egg-and-bacon as they call it.'

'Why's he so interested in the case?'

'Once a policeman, always a policeman. Besides the MCC isn't the only club he's a member of.'

'Eh?'

'He was a member of the local golf club along with Mr Bernier. In the tip-off phone call that I've just had, he mentioned what a fine fellow Bernier was.'

They opened their car doors and were assailed by loud music.

'Cor! What is that racquet?' asked Josh.

'Meatloaf. Bat Out of Hell,' Nicholas replied coolly.

'I'm surprised no one has reported him.'

'They have. Many times.' Nicholas was about to add a few words on the old boys' network and a retired police chief having connections when Josh moved onto a new topic.

'Still, if we're here, there's a chance we might see Amelia FitzMorris again.'

Nicholas sighed, acknowledged Peter Wilson with a nod, and as he had been instructed went straight past the retired police chief and up to Dee's front door.

He knocked firmly and heard footsteps.

'Chief Inspector, how lovely of you to drop by. The kettle's just boiled,' Dee declared as she opened the door. 'Josh, how wonderful that you could come too. I'm afraid Amelia isn't here at the moment.'

Not for the first time, Chief Inspector Nicholas Corman felt he was not in control of this investigation. 'Ms FitzMorris, we are here on official business.' He was aiming to sound professional but feared he just came off as pompous.

Dee's smile was only slightly dampened. 'But surely you can still have a cup of tea?' she declared as she showed them into the open-plan kitchen at the back of the house. Light flooded the room. The French windows were flung wide providing a view of Dee's impressive garden with its blossoming fruit trees and abundant borders. Gentle summer scents floated in on the breeze; Nicholas detected traces of lavender, roses and lime trees.

Before he could respond, Zara strode in calling, 'Mother, I'm just between viewings. Any chance of some tea?'

Dee cheerily replied, 'We're in the kitchen, dear. Josh and the nice Chief Inspector are here. They are being frightfully official so we're just working out the correct beverage for formal visits.'

It struck Nicholas that Zara always strode, she never dawdled. She was a woman of purpose, not to mention one with excellent dress sense. He was just admiring how becoming she was with her auburn curls and what he was beginning to think of as her trademark green dress, when he realised she was looking at him.

'Inspector,' she cooed, her voice taking on a husky pitch and her eyes an extra sparkle.

Nicholas swallowed and he felt decidedly unprofessional and even less in command of the situation than before. He brought his full authority to bear in his voice in an attempt to regain his composure. 'Ms FitzMorris.'

'Which one?' asked Dee brightly.

Josh sniggered.

'You.' Nicholas hoped he spoke firmly rather than it coming as a desperate snap. 'We have had complaints—' He paused and corrected himself. 'Reports.'

'Really? Who from?' asked Dee, as she handed him a cup of Earl Grey, her face full of happy curiosity.

He pressed on. 'Er, thank you. It has come to our notice—'

Zara butted in, waving a plate of homemade flapjacks under his nose. 'Biscuit? It will be that retired policeman, Mother. He's never liked you, especially after that last unpleasant incident.'

'You're probably right, dear. Here, have a side plate – they're rather crumbly – and Josh, do take two.'

Nicholas pushed on. 'It has come to our notice that you and Amelia have been asking questions around the village.'

Dee looked the picture of innocence. Zara's eyes flashed and she swung round, hands on hips to confront her.

71

'Mother! How could you? I clearly said you were to leave this to the police.'

Despite all his deep-set, post-divorce prejudice against militant women, Nicholas could not help thinking Ms Zara FitzMorris looked rather magnificent flushed with outrage.

'I am an adult, dear, and as such you can not tell me what to do.'

'You may be an adult, but what about Amelia? Leading your own granddaughter astray – you should be ashamed of yourself.'

Josh, leaning against the kitchen counter, tea in one hand and flapjack in the other watched with interest.

'Really dear, you make me sound as if I'm encouraging her to a life of sin. Besides which, she is also an adult – a young adult admittedly, but still of an age to make her own decisions.'

'Well, if you won't listen to me, perhaps you'll listen to the police.'

She glared at Nicholas and Josh for support. Nicholas' gaze went from the impressively outraged Zara to her placid mother. He took in Dee's calm demeanour and composed expression, and had a stark and accurate realisation. *She has no intention of listening to either of us.*

Dee was happily wondering how soon Zara, Nicholas and Josh would leave. She had a lot to do. Zara's mention of the retired police chief had reminded her that she hadn't questioned him yet. Then there was the vicar. Zara's cryptic comments about him had been playing on her mind. He certainly would bear further investigation.

Chapter 9

To say that the police visit had no impact on Dee was not quite accurate. She had had a lot of time to think about things since their call. After much contemplation, she realised that their latest call had left her with the impression that they were not getting on very fast with solving the murder, which spurred her on to want to get to the bottom of the burning question: who is the murderer? Curiosity was underpinned by some less pleasant emotions.

She sighed, firstly there was the change in how the village, in general, was treating her and then there was Zara. Dee's normal buoyant persona was in danger of being pricked as effectively as a pin popping a pink helium balloon.

Little Warthing was no longer a friendly place. It had ceased to be a refuge from the outside world. She dreaded running out of milk and having to go down to the village shop. *Is this a good time to become a vegan?* And now there was the problem with Zara. Her stomach knotted as she thought of their last conversation after Josh and Nicholas had left. It would have made Dee feel less bad had Zara just been angry but she was more worried and worse still, frightened.

She had sat at the kitchen table, her shoulders hunched and her eyes brimming with tears. 'Mother, this isn't a game! You could get hurt – killed, even! I wish you would just grow up.'

Dee blocked out her own response which involved the words *over-controlling*.

Of course, they'd had spats in the past – what mother and daughter hadn't? But this was different. The angry silence had never lasted more than an hour or two but this argument had happened in the morning, and now it was nearly five. Zara hadn't rung or texted and Dee couldn't make the first move.

The issue for Dee was that she knew Zara would not make up with her unless Dee agreed to stop sleuthing, and she was not prepared to do that.

Her mind was full of questions. *If I am to find the murderer I need to gather more information – ask further questions. I really didn't get very far with Ken and his association with clowns and I gather he had professional dealings with Bernier to boot. Amelia wasn't able to glean much from Blossom before she was shooed away. Then what were all those goings-on at the Flying Pheasant? Alex definitely went a bit odd at the mention of Bernier and what about Francesco and Justin Harper? And talking of Justin Harper, I need to discover in what way he was involved with Bernier and while I'm about it I might probe into whether Justin is as corrupt as Zara suggests. I wonder if our resident retired copper Peter Wilson would be able to give me any helpful clues? After all, I'm sure with his professional background he picks up on things we may have missed.*

She took out her notebook and decided that she'd start by asking Ken Pilbersek a few more questions. She draped a camel cashmere cardigan over her shoulders against the growing chill of the late afternoon, found her notebook and applied some tinted lip balm.

'Bye, Cat,' she called as she pulled her front door shut. She hadn't even made it out of her drive when she was stopped.

Mrs Elizabeth May was lying in wait for her. 'You're brave!' came the bold statement from the other side of the fence, where Mrs May stood on her front step. She had bright yellow rubber gloves on and a fierce scrubbing brush in her hand. A halo of acrid scent from a steaming bucket of bleach surrounded her.

'What?' mumbled Dee, taken off-guard. *Why did I speak? I should have just ignored the woman. Water off a duck's back and all that. What were my morning affirmations again? Oh yes!* Feeling hot and rather unbalanced she mentally asserted, *I am strong, I am capable, and I cultivate inner peace.*

'I said, you're brave going out in the village. It's not as if anyone wants to see you.' Mrs May's voice had risen by a decibel or two so her words rung out. As the volume grew so did the tone of triumphant venom. Dee stole a sideways glance at her neighbour and noted that her lips were as tight and grey as a poodle perm.

Dee put her shoulders back and marched firmly towards the road, still mentally repeating, *I am strong, I am capable and I WILL jolly well cultivate inner peace even if it kills me! Thank goodness there weren't any affirmations this morning about love or forgiveness as that really would have been a bit much.*

Mrs May continued, but more loudly, 'Not after you found that fool, dead in your garden.'

Fool? Odd term for an accountant. Still, best not to engage.

As Dee walked down her road she attempted to be present in the moment but instead of being grounded, it was more like a thought-fight. *I can feel the pavement beneath my feet – bloody woman! Why does she have to be so horrid – I enjoy the sensation of the breeze on my face – she's so ruddy aggressive – I focus on the bird song, I am at one with nature – I'd like to take her stinking bucket of bleach and tip it over her ridiculous perm.*

Realising that mindfully being present in the moment wasn't working, Dee slipped into gratitude.

I am grateful to be living on such a quiet street. I am grateful for my home, I am grateful that Little Warthing is such a beautiful village – of course, it would all be far improved if that odious woman didn't live here.

Fortunately, by this time, Dee had arrived at Ken's house. She may not have had inner peace but she did have her notebook.

Ken Pilbersek was clipping his box hedge. Well, more accurately, he was standing over the hedge with a large pair of shears in his hands, but his eyes were fixed on the other side of the road. A quick peek by Dee confirmed that he was looking at Julia Fryderberg, aka Blossom Bim Bam, who was in front of her tiny cottage. She was obviously flustered as she tried to pump up her bicycle tyre.

Ken was gazing with unashamed admiration. *Blossom's curls and gay dress are appealing – anyone can see that – and perhaps her general air of 'muddle' brings out my protective side.*

Dee made a polite cough. He looked up startled, and then blushed, giving his marble features some life. 'Ah yes, Dee, I, er, I …' he blustered, then gathered himself. 'It occurred to me that you might want to put in something about the rustic fool.'

'What?'

'In your article. The origins of clowns are thought to stem all the way back to medieval days when the village players would have someone perform as the rustic fool. It was to lighten the mood of the morality tales.'

Dee was not sure how to respond; she stared at Ken and he, looking down at her from his greater height, with his clippers in hand, blinked.

Realising that he was waiting for her to say something and forgetting that well-known saying, *'fools rush in, where angels fear to tread'*, Dee blurted out, 'That's odd. That's the second time this morning someone has mentioned fools. You knew Andrew Bernier, didn't you? Would you describe him as a fool?'

Ken stiffened and Dee wasn't at all sure she cared for the way he was gripping his shears. He was holding them so tightly that his knuckles showed white. Menacingly, he thrust their point towards her.

'So you've heard about our dispute.'

'Yes!' Dee lied. She was frantically wondering what he was talking about but she hoped that by pretending she already knew everything, he would spill the beans.

'The world is a better place without him in it,' declared Ken coldly. Dee must have looked shocked, as he regarded her and then justified his words. 'He was corrupt to the core, but I couldn't prove it. Ruddy ridiculous that it wasn't him who suffered, it was …'

His voice trailed away but his eyes remained fixed on his neighbour.

'Blossom?'

'I thought you knew.' Fortunately, he was too busy looking over Dee's head, his eyes moist with emotion, to Blossom and her bicycle pump, so he didn't fully register Dee's admission of ignorance. 'It was only natural that she checked with our company accountants as to whether Mrs Reading had a life policy.'

'Eh? Mrs Reading? Robert's mum who has just died?'

Ken nodded in acknowledgement and continued, 'And for him to ferret out her little slip with her tax return and use it against her – the man was neither a gentleman nor a clown. After all, anyone could have made a mistake over the car and that work trip-come-holiday.'

He looked away from Blossom and at Dee, totally mystified she nodded as it somehow seemed appropriate.

It must have been the correct response as he continued, 'Anyway, back to the article – Zanni.'

'Zanni?' queried Dee, while trying to work out what he had been talking about. *Was Bernier corrupt? It was Ken who suffered? Robert's mother – Mrs Reading? Life policies? Tax? Car? Holiday?*

'Yes! Did you know the word Zanni actually comes from the name of an Italian clown?'

He looked at Dee presumably so she could admit her lack of knowledge and his superiority but Dee was still in sleuthing mode. Instead of meekly shaking her head she said, 'Where were you on the morning, or even the night before, Bernier was found in my chard?'

Ken's eyes flashed, and Dee felt uncomfortable about the way his mouth twitched. Her heart began to beat faster and she grabbed her notebook tighter.

'What's that got to do with your article?'

'Oh, well, nothing really. I was just thinking about clowns.'

He gave her a long appraising look.

Dee felt herself going hot. The hairs on the back of her neck prickled. She looked from him to his shears. 'Gosh. Is that the time? I really mustn't hold you up any longer.'

She backed away, reluctant to turn her back on him in case he took it as an opportunity to thrust his shears between her shoulder blades. When she judged there was a safe distance between them she scurried away, very aware he was watching her.

I feel Miss Marple would have handled that better. At least I found out that they had a dispute, so there's a possible motive for murder and he didn't establish an alibi. He has to be a suspect; after all, he'd be a dab hand at clown makeup and he certainly looked pretty threatening with those shears. I can't wait to talk it through with Amelia.

But what now? What I really want to do is to stride over to Blossom's place.

She risked a furtive glance in that direction and confirmed that Blossom was still there, bicycle pump in hand. Dee also noted that her pink fit-and-flare dress had daisies on it that matched the daisy on her hat.

I could ask her what Andrew Bernier had to do with Mrs Reading's life policies and slip in a question about cars, holidays and tax. It would be so easy to offer to help her with her bicycle as an excuse to go over – judging by the way she is struggling she could certainly use a hand.

But Dee could feel Ken's cold eyes boring into the back of her head and she suspected that any infringement on Blossom's property would result in her being pursued by him and his clippers.

She peered up and down the road and there was Alex coming towards her from the direction of the girl's home at the Flying Pheasant. Dee presumed she was on her way to the tennis club as she had her racquet in its case, slung over the side. Dee knew Alex kept a second, lighter and specially adapted wheelchair at the courts. It was non-electric with its wheels slanting in for ease and speed of movement when she played tennis.

Alex is just the person I need to see – after all, she is an accountant and I need more information about life policies, besides which I need to find out what cars and holidays have to do with tax.

By this time Alex was within hailing distance so Dee said, 'Hello, off to play tennis?'

Alex smiled, nodded and said, 'I'm in a tournament tomorrow so a bit of practice won't go amiss.'

'Mind if I tag along, just as far as the club? I would like to pick your professional brains about some financial issues a friend is having.'

'Sure!' replied Alex and Dee felt a twinge of guilt as she looked at her smiling face. The little sun that the early summer had afforded had already burnished Alex's olive skin into an attractive tan and she looked very young with her long dark curls tied back in a ponytail.

'You work at the same company as Ken and Blossom don't you?'

Alex nodded, skilfully avoiding a bump in the pavement.

'Your company does life policies, doesn't it?'

'Yeah, all the general stuff like life policies, car insurance and household, too.'

'So as an employee, you could gain access to someone's records?'

Alex looked thoughtfully at the heavens and considered. 'Yes, I suppose it would be possible but you could get into a lot of trouble unless you were meant to be doing it professionally. You know there are lots of client confidentiality issues.'

She looked earnestly at Dee, who tried to hide her elation with another question. 'And would it be possible to hide that someone had a life policy or two?'

Alex creased her brow and bit her lip as she pondered the point. 'I guess so.' She looked at Dee. 'A friend you say? You want to know all this for a friend?'

Dee nodded innocently.

'A trustee could probably not declare it.'

'A trustee? Sorry, I'm awfully vague about this sort of thing. What is a trustee?'

'Someone who looks after an estate, which is just a fancy term for someone's assets.'

'But why would a trustee want to hide a life policy?' asked Dee.

'This isn't really my field of expertise but I would think they could take the money as fees.'

Dee nodded. 'Another friend is having a spot of bother, which

I don't quite understand, to do with a car and a holiday and tax. Could you please explain how that is possible?'

'Gosh, Dee, you do have a lot of friends with financial problems.'

Dee gave a weak laugh and shrugged.

'Well, with the car if they had it for work but used it outside work they would need to declare that on their tax return.'

'And the holiday?'

Alex paused as she gave the matter some thought before saying, 'I've heard of someone who got in trouble because they had a work trip to Mexico and then tagged on a holiday.'

Dee blinked and tilted her head. 'Well if you've gone all that way, surely it's only sensible to have a holiday?'

'Absolutely, silly not to, but then you must declare it because you need to pay something in relation to the flight.'

'You are a mine of information, thanks!'

Dee really wanted to ask Alex why she had behaved so strangely when they'd all been chatting in the pub and Bernier's name came up.

Of course, Alex can't be a suspect. She might be able to work out how to kill someone but with her wheelchair, she wouldn't be able to dress a corpse as a clown and dump them in my veggie patch.

They trundled along a little further, past pretty gardens, most newly mown, and up to the courts. The sound of rhythmic twanging as balls hit rackets reached them above the hum of traffic noise and the melody of birdsong.

It was then that a little voice murmured in Dee's ear. *Alex couldn't, but Francesco and Gina could, and they would do anything for their little girl.*

An image popped into Dee's mind of Francesco, inflamed with anger and with his fists clenched as he confronted Justin Harper.

They were at the courts now and it was here they met Robert, smelling fresh and his hair still damp from a shower. Her was wearing crisply-ironed chinos and a pink shirt and on his shoulder, he had a navy kit bag with a racquet attached.

He greeted them both warmly then said to Alex, 'Tristan is looking for you in the clubhouse.'

Alex said her goodbyes and hurried off.

'Not working?' enquired Dee. She knew that for Robert, running his interior shop and business, weekends were generally his busiest time.

'I'm between clients. It was a bit of a push time-wise but I really needed to blow off steam and for me, tennis works wonders.'

Dee lightly touched his sleeve and looked up at him with concerned green eyes. 'Is work stressful at the moment?'

He shrugged. 'Not really. Are you walking home? We could go together; I'm heading back to the shop and your place is on the way.'

She agreed and they started strolling back. She felt more relaxed than when she had been gathering information from Alex. Robert was an old friend and easy company. The sun was warm and the few clouds that were in the sky were appealingly white and fluffy. The village was well-blessed with trees, especially elegant beeches. At this time of year, the trees all had their leaves, which were translucent with youth. The walk from the courts on the outskirts of the village to Dee's home near the church was exceptionally picturesque. As with many villages, there was no real border between farmland and habitation. It was meadowland, awash with buttercups, and grazing cows lived happily alongside a row of cottages. It seemed to Dee that there were pleasant reminders of early summer everywhere, from the birds singing, to the warmth of the sun on her face, to the abundance of wildflowers on either side of the pavement.

Her happy enjoyment of the present was tainted by her growing awareness that her walking companion Robert was abnormally quiet. Usually, he had a host of amusing comments and would laugh readily at anything. Dee stole a glance at him, he had well-defined features and thick fair hair, but today there was a tightness around his jaw and he scanned the ground in front of them rather than throwing his shoulders back and holding his head high.

'So if it isn't work, what is stressing you? Is it anything to do with your mother? After all, you two were so close and her passing is relatively recent. It would be only natural if you were finding things a bit much.'

Robert looked over at Dee with his kind blue eyes. 'I like the way you're so direct.' He smiled. 'Most people are embarrassed about death and avoid the subject. I've had one or two people deliberately cross the road rather than have to chat with me. And yes you're right I am missing my mum. It comes in waves; I'll be absolutely fine for a day or so, then a customer will come into the shop wearing Mum's favourite scent and I'll be fighting back the tears, or a song from a musical will come on the radio and I'll have such a vivid memory of her singing it that I'm caught off balance.'

Dee didn't say anything but just gave his arm a little squeeze.

He seemed relieved to have someone to talk to. 'It's the practicalities I'm struggling with.'

'Clearing out a loved one's home is always hideous,' acknowledged Dee.

'That hasn't been too bad, Mum was a great one for keeping things in order and she'd prearranged with me that her bevy of godchildren should get the majority of bits and pieces I didn't want. No, it's various legal bits that are keeping me up at night.'

They were on Dee's road now; she was nearly home.

'I saw that lovely girl, what's her name? Lots of freckles, and lives over the other side of Little Warthing Woods. She was thrilled that your mother had left her lots of golf clubs and bits.'

Robert laughed. 'That would be Jane. Mum did love her golf and she was very fond of Jane; they used to meet up at the golf club regularly.'

'I believe golf is a wonderfully social sport, though I've never played it myself.'

Dee noticed that Robert had slightly stiffened; his stride was less fluid and his fists were clenched. 'Slightly too social if you ask me. Mum met Andrew Bernier there.'

At the mention of what Dee thought of as her corpse, she became alert. 'Andrew Bernier? I didn't know your mother knew him.'

'It would have been far better if she hadn't,' said Robert bitterly.

Dee was just about to ask a few questions, like, 'You didn't kill him did you?' when Robert curtly said, 'Let's not talk about him.'

It was just then that Blossom, cycled past, having evidently succeeded in fixing her tyre. The voluminous pink skirt of her dress flashed an attractive bit of leg as she pedalled. She was in a hurry but managed to give them both a wave. The gesture made her wobble but she corrected herself without anything falling out of her bicycle basket.

'You know Blossom?' asked Dee.

'Blossom? Oh, you mean Julia Fryderberg. Yes, but only slightly; she works at the insurance company where Mum had all her policies. She was very sweet, really concerned when Mum died.'

Again Dee had a few burning questions but she was thwarted by the willowy figure of Justin Harper crossing the road up by the Flying Pheasant. At the sight of him, Robert stopped walking and his eyes narrowed.

'There's Justin Harper,' commented Dee, hoping to prompt Robert into some sort of an explanation for his reaction.

He swung round to face Dee and actually clasped her hands. 'Dee, you must be careful, he is not a nice man and he likes to prey on older women.'

Dee might be a pensioner and a grandmother but she did not like to think of herself as an older woman, especially not one that a good-looking younger man might prey on.

'He is very personable,' she stated.

She felt Robert's grip on her hands tighten. His eyebrows were drawn together and his forehead creased as he urgently whispered, 'Don't be fooled!' Fear more than anything else radiated from his blue eyes as he urgently stared into her green ones. 'That man is wicked, dangerous and ruthless.'

Dee was confused, a bit afraid but mostly curious. She began to ask, 'Did your mother—?' But her words were lost in by a deafening blast of Vaughan Williams emanating from Peter Wilson's front lawn.

Robert dropped her hands and hurriedly mumbled, 'I must go, I'll be late for my next appointment.'

His brisk strides left Dee far behind.

As she walked more slowly towards both her home and the deafening musical racket her mind was racing. *Surely Robert couldn't be involved in Bernier's death? I don't understand his reaction to Justin Harper. I've never seen him so angry. I've known him for years and before a few minutes ago I would have said he was incapable of being aggressive. I'm collecting so much information I may need a bigger notebook.*

The route to the tennis club meant that Dee's home was closer than Peter Wilson's, *but,* she thought, *I may as well take advantage of him being in his garden.*

Deafening music or equally loud cricket commentary was a sure sign Mr Wilson was in his front garden on his deckchair. Dee walked past her own home and Mrs May's, and was pleased to note that the lady of the house was not in evidence.

Another few steps and sure enough, there he is, sitting on his striped deckchair with his old-fashioned radio beside him.

'Good evening!' smiled Dee over the gate. She was in full charm offensive; one thing all the FitzMorris ladies could do was be charming. She pushed aside the thought that he looked like a bloated toad oozing out of both his collar and deckchair.

This will be quite easy – like taking candy from a baby. After a few pleasantries about the weather, I can admire his ponytail, suit and choice of music and while he is feeling flattered I can ask a few pertinent questions about dead clowns. Easy peasy, lemon squeezy, as Blossom Bim Bam might say.

Dee was not to know that Peter Wilson was in a filthy mood and that even an archangel would be unable to elicit anything but a scowl from him this evening. He had missed his train and so for him, there had been no heavenly afternoon of cricket at Lords. He held the petite and smiling woman in front of him personally responsible; had he not had a civic responsibility to wait and check that that Corman fellow paid her a visit, he would not have missed his train. The fact that in London, unlike the Cotswolds, the rain stopped play, did not lessen his hostility.

Dee was about to comment on the sunshine, when Peter Wilson spoke in a deep, thunderous voice, with only the hint of toad about it. 'Bernier was a marvellous chap. I knew him from the golf club. He always loved talking to me, couldn't get enough of my stories, found them fascinating.'

Dee wasn't sure how to respond but she was pleased the conversation was immediately on topic.

With a smirk, he added, 'I see you had another visit from the police.'

'Yes,' said Dee, trying to think of a way to get back to Bernier.

Mr Wilson looked extremely satisfied; his jowls seemed to ease over his collar and his beetle eyebrows were raised. 'I may be retired, but I still have a hotline to those who matter.'

'How nice for you.' Dee was still aiming at charm, but unfortunately, the tone of her words came out as barely polite. She didn't like the way he was looking at her. He was gloating and she had a feeling of foreboding, rather like a midge gets when a hungry amphibian is eyeing them up for a tasty snack.

'I hoped to catch Corman when he was leaving your house,' he said, 'but I must have missed him. He probably left when I was answering a call of nature.'

This is not how I planned this conversation. Where is he going with this? I just hope he doesn't mention his prostate.

'You see, there are things I need to tell Inspector Corman in person rather than over the phone. I had thought it could wait but I changed my mind.'

'Really?'

Peter Wilson nodded. 'You see, I ... saw ... you.'

He left suitable pauses between the words, so each one had time to penetrate Dee's panicked brain. She swallowed hard, afraid she was about to be sick.

He couldn't have seen me. It was three in the morning. Everyone was in bed.

'You thought you'd got away with it, didn't you?' Peter chortled. 'You thought that no one had seen you – or rather, you and the deceased together. What you failed to realise is that a policeman, retired or not, is always on duty. Even at three in the morning. Besides which, I have trouble with my prostate.'

Dee was at a total loss as to what to do. Then help arrived, in the most unlikely form of the alleged vicar. Tall and serene, he greeted them both. 'Dee. Mr Wilson.'

Dee's first thought was why *is this man always grinning?* Her second was, *Hallelujah!*

Seeing her chance to escape, she declared, 'Vicar! You're so punctual. Let's go to my house for that cup of tea I promised you.'

If he was surprised by her sudden friendliness he didn't show it, nor did he appear to notice her agitation. He simply followed her as she hurried down the road to the sanctuary of her own home.

She almost cried with relief when she was back in her kitchen; it was filled with evening sunshine and plants. She walked over to the French windows and let in both her fat cat and the sound of a melodious blackbird. She paused for a moment, closed her eyes and inhaled deeply. Her legs felt wobbly and her palms were sweaty. Her mind was in turmoil; Peter Wilson's words haunted her. *I wonder what prison food is like? And who would look after Cat? It's so unfortunate that Cat and Zara loathe each other.*

She would have liked to take the time to ponder over what she had learnt from Ken, Alex and Robert, but she had a guest and needed to get the kettle on.

Ten minutes later, Dee and Justin were siding at the kitchen table. She had her glass teapot in front of her and the dried camomile flowers were slowly turning the boiled water a pleasing yellow colour. Justin had declined the wine Dee had offered and was having a small cafetière of coffee. Cat, who was looking especially fine with her long white coat and even longer whiskers was purring coquettishly at the vicar and gazing adoringly up at him with green eyes.

Dee took a sip of her camomile tea; as ever she found it wonderfully restorative. Another sip and her equilibrium was almost restored. In fact, she was so far back to her normal self that she remembered there were one or two things she wanted to ask Justin Harper, including whether or not he really was a vicar.

She regarded him, wondering where to begin. Those dazzling blue eyes were quite mesmerising. It was difficult to concentrate on anything else. *There is something very appealing about a good-looking man who seems to want to give you his full attention.*

Cat was purring, winding in and out of the vicar's long legs. Dee couldn't think what to say.

Sensing her hesitation, he prompted her. 'I'm so sorry you're having a troubling time. Would you like to tell me about your problems?'

'You mean Andrew Bernier turning up dead in my chard whilst dressed as a clown?'

He nodded, his ever-present smile taking on a sympathetic edge. 'What would you like to tell me about Andrew Bernier?'

'Nothing, but I would like to ask you about your relationship with Andrew Bernier.'

Was there a twitch in that smile of his?

'Sorry?' he said.

'According to Zara, you have quite a lot to be sorry about. For starters, she doesn't seem to think you are a legitimate vicar.'

Justin Harper's smile froze.

'She also said she thought you had some dealings with the deceased … she mentioned that he acted as your accountant. She also said that your finances are dodgy.'

Dee couldn't remember if Zara had said anything about Bernier and Justin's finances but it seemed to be a good conversational point.

His smile remained stiff but still in place. In a quiet cold voice he said, 'My, your daughter has been chatty.'

Dee got up from the kitchen table and went to put the kettle on for a second pot of camomile. It was then, and only then, that she realised she had made a mistake. Too late, she recalled Zara's words, 'Mother, this is not a game. You could get hurt.'

And what was it Robert had said about my guest? 'Wicked, dangerous and ruthless'?

Cat had stopped purring.

Dee sensed evil.

She had her back to Justin Harper, but some primal instinct told her that he had silently crept up behind her and was now looming menacingly over her. With mounting dismay, she realised she had nothing to defend herself with but some camomile tea. Slowly she turned to face him.

He was so much taller than her that his mere physical presence was intimidating. Dee cowered against the countertop. Her heart was pounding as she forced herself to look him in the eye. His jaw was clenched but it was his sinister grin that Dee found to be terrifying; there was no hint of humanity in it.

Dee's throat was dry and she didn't think she could scream.

When he spoke, his voice was soft, even friendly. 'In my line of work, people sometimes disappear. Their loved ones never see them again. And sometimes, just sometimes, they turn up in unexpected places like a vegetable patch.' He bent his head down so it was only an inch away from Dee's and she could smell his cologne over his coffee breath. 'I think you might look rather good as a clown.'

She swallowed. 'So, is that 'no' to another cup of camomile?'

He inhaled loudly and was about to say something more when they heard the front door open.

'Mother, it's me! I can't bear us being at odds so I came round to make up.'

Zara reached the kitchen and saw her mother pressed against the countertop with the vicar looming threateningly over her.

She regarded the scene for a second, and then with a forcefulness that defied her tiny stature, proclaimed, 'Justin Harper. You are to step away from my mother and leave this house this instant.' With one immaculately manicured hand, she took her phone from her designer handbag and calmly added, 'I have the police on speed dial.'

He locked eyes with her. They stared at each other, for what seemed to Dee like an age, and then he took a step back and, still smiling, left through the front door.

Dee staggered back to the table and, with wobbly knees, allowed herself to sink into a chair. 'I'm so pleased you came. I've been having a rather trying day. Can I make you a cup of camomile tea, dear?'

Chapter 10

Nicholas Corman tried and failed to brush something sticky off his left trouser leg. He glanced at Josh in the passenger seat. Oblivious to the discomfort he was causing, Josh continued crunching on some toffee confection.

Life would be so much more restful if only reality matched my model train set.

Nicholas sighed as he thought of the ordered perfection he had created in his spare room. There, the trains ran on well-dusted tracks, the gardens were always in full bloom and there was not a trace of sticky toffee crunch.

'That old Peter Wilson must really have given you an earful for us to be back here so soon,' chortled Josh between mouthfuls.

'A bit more respect if you please.'

'So what exactly did he say then?'

Nicholas left out the bits about Mr Wilson having missed his train and had told him that on consideration his information was far too important to wait, so against his better judgement he would have to give it over the phone and he only hoped that Nicholas wasn't totally incompetent. Instead, he informed Josh that Peter Wilson had seen Dee FitzMorris in a heated argument with the deceased at three in the morning on the day he was murdered.

It was with a heavy heart that Nicholas Corman drove through the early evening to Dee's home. He was despondent for two reasons: firstly, Mr Wilson's call had ruled out the pleasant evening Nicholas had planned to spend with his Flying Scotsman model train and secondly, he liked Dee FitzMorris and he didn't relish the idea of taking her down to the nick.

Once they were parked in Little Warthing, Josh was quick to stride up to Honeysuckle Cottage and knock. Amelia opened the door. She was wearing a dashing stiff black tutu along with a studded leather corset. The harsh black was striking against her cascading red locks and porcelain skin.

What is wrong with a nice floral dress? thought Nicholas with a sigh. Suddenly he felt very old.

Josh seemed to have lost the ability to speak. He just stood there, his mouth slightly open, staring.

'Who is it?' asked Zara as she too came to the door. She had opted for something floral; it was form-fitting to just the right degree, hinting at elegant curves.

Nicholas swallowed. 'Um – er – is your mother in?' he stammered.

Dee appeared and seeing who it was at the door, she beamed. 'Chief Inspector and Josh; how lovely to see you both.'

'Can we come inside?' asked Nicholas, aware of Mrs May peering through the fence. Safely in the cottage, he got straight to the point. 'Ms Dee FitzMorris, we need to take you down to the station for questioning.'

Zara immediately asked, 'Why?'

And all Nicolas could think of was, *Why have I never noticed how attractive her voice is?*

He managed to state, 'New evidence has come to light.'

'What new evidence?'

Nicholas regarded Zara. *She is so dignified; poised.*

Dee spoke up. 'It will be from retired Police Chief Peter Wilson. I probably should have said something.' She was pink and more than a little flustered. 'You see, I had words.'

'Who with, Mother?'

'The clown. I mean, Andrew Bernier – the corpse. Of course, he wasn't a clown – or a corpse then! Well, I suppose if I was to be honest it was more than words. We had a sort of scuffle. I was only protecting myself. It's so important for women to learn a bit of self-defence, don't you agree, Inspector?'

'Granny, you've got a black belt in Taekwondo – that is hardly basic self-defence.'

Dee looked at her granddaughter. 'I don't think you're helping, dear. Anyway, I had reckoned without Mr Wilson's prostate.'

Nicholas was totally confused now; his eyebrows went up and his tone was uncertain when he enquired, 'Retired Police Chief Wilson's prostate?'

'Yes,' smiled Dee helpfully. 'He has problems with it so he was up at three in the morning and saw me with Andrew Bernier, having words ... well, a fight really.'

'But Ms FitzMorris, why were you up and out of the house at that time?'

Dee looked up at him, surprised that he needed to ask. 'I'm part of the night-watch team at the woods.'

'Sorry?'

'I thought I told you already. We log things; survey the wildlife. Amateur naturalists helping the professionals do their work. Of course, there's not a huge amount going on at three in the morning, but I was aiming to get there for dawn – that's when all the action kicks off. Have you ever experienced the dawn chorus in the woods, Inspector? It's really wonderful. Would you like to come with me next time?'

Nicholas felt they were straying from the point.

Fortunately, Zara asked the next obvious question. 'But Mother, what were you fighting with Andrew Bernier about?'

'His dog, Brutus.'

'His dog?'

'Yes, dear. Brutus. Well, more precisely about what Brutus leaves behind. I'd never before been able to actually catch him at it. Then, at last, that morning, voila! I caught him red-handed; not a doggy-poop bag in sight! But when I confronted him he got angry – violent actually. Inspector, I know I shouldn't speak ill of the dead but really Andrew Bernier was a deeply unpleasant person.'

Nicholas spoke in what Dee termed his *official* voice. 'We need to continue this down at the station.'

Undaunted, Dee continued. 'Really I'm only surprised someone didn't strangle the man years ago.'

'How did you know he was strangled?' asked Josh, clearly excited at this slip.

Dee smiled. She liked Josh's open-faced good looks. 'Just a figure of speech.'

Amelia was looking thoughtful. 'But if he was strangled, surely you have forensic evidence indicating the size of the murderer's hands, fingerprints even.' She gave Josh a stern look and he blushed. 'Common sense should tell you that Granny is hardly built to be strong enough to strangle a grown man!'

Defensively Josh blurted out, 'He was strangled with a tourniquet and he wouldn't have put up a fight. He must have been given sleeping pills.' As an afterthought he added, 'But there was extensive bruising under all that greasepaint – looked as if someone had hit him.'

'How interesting!' exclaimed Dee.

Amelia smiled – a slow appraising smile that Nicholas was not at all sure he liked. 'Oh dear, Josh, I'm afraid you're in trouble with your boss.'

All eyes turned to Nicholas. He felt uncomfortable.

Josh was looking from Amelia to Nicholas and then back to Amelia; his forehead was wrinkled and his mouth was slightly open.

Amelia explained, 'I believe you're not meant to give away information like that to suspects.'

Determined to regain command, Nicholas put his shoulders back, and with all the dignity of a man who believes in the order and serenity of model railways, said, 'Ms FitzMorris, you will now accompany us down to the station.'

Zara took a step closer to him; she possessed what he could only describe as *presence*. He was reminded of great Shakespearean actors who command attention the moment they come on stage, before even uttering a word.

When she did speak it was with complete authority. 'Inspector, this is ridiculous. Justin Harper was here a little while ago. He threatened my mother and more or less confessed that he was the murderer. Why are you not arresting him?'

Nicholas glanced at Zara. Her eyes shone like emeralds and her chin jutted upwards, exposing her white throat.

Calmly he said, 'We are not arresting your mother. We are simply taking her down to the station for questioning. And with regard to other suspects, we are following several lines of questioning.'

Zara regarded him coolly. Nicholas swallowed. Unbidden, the image of Queen Elizabeth I holding court came into Nicholas' mind. Zara FitzMorris was redheaded and regal.

'Mother, you were right.'

'Was I dear? About what?'

'This is far too important to leave to the police to investigate.'

Nicholas felt a flash of annoyance. *She might be majestic, but this is too much!*

'Ms FitzMorris I must caution you against interfering in police business.'

'Chief Inspector Corman, I wish I could leave it to you but if the best suspect you can come up with is my mother, then I really have no alternative.'

Serenely she turned to her daughter. 'Amelia, I hope you don't have any plans for the next day or two as I may need your help.'

It was after ten-thirty that evening that Nicholas and Josh sat down to food or what passed for it in the police station canteen. There was a lingering smell of fried onions but Mrs Phipps, who usually manned the cashier desk, had clocked off hours ago. Instead of her heady repertoire of egg and chips, bacon and chips or burger and chips all served with a side of fried onions, Nicholas and Josh had to make do with a curly sandwich served from a vending machine. Despite being halfway through eating it, Nicholas was still perplexed by what the filling was. As a nod towards a balanced diet, he'd chosen a green apple which was also served from a vending machine.

Nicholas gave up trying to eat, let alone enjoy, his meagre repast. He looked across the grubby table to where Josh sat. His subordinate never looked tired, regardless of how few hours sleep he'd got. He always appeared as sleek as a Siamese cat. Of course in Josh's case, it was an oriental cat with a penchant for junk food; he was currently munching his way through a sugary doughnut. The doughnut had been Josh's equivalent of Nicholas' apple; a necessary addition to the sandwich to provide a balanced meal.

They were the only ones in the canteen but outside were the normal sounds of a siren wailing and the early drunk-and-disorderly culprits shouting obscenities.

Questioning Dee had made Nicholas feel sullied and leaving her in a police cell was despicable; he did not feel it the conduct of a gentleman. He tried to direct his mind in a different direction. With his shoulders slightly drooped and eyelids heavy, he murmured, 'Does Ms Zara FitzMorris remind you of anyone?'

Josh nodded, spraying the table and Nicholas with sugar. 'Yes. Ginger Spice. I was watching the retro channel and thinking that she was the spitting image.'

Nicholas dusted some sugar from his sleeve and sighed. 'I was thinking of someone rather more regal. Elizabeth the First.'

Josh looked up from his doughnut. 'Don't know the chick – which band does she gig with?'

Nicholas looked to the heavens and sighed again.

Chapter 11

A few days later all three FitzMorrises were back at Dee's house. The plants were looking wilted; evidently, Dee hadn't been watering them. The bird feeders were empty. When Amelia had pointed out the meagre pickings Dee was providing for her birds, she had gone outside to rectify the lack.

From her vantage point, sitting at the kitchen table, Amelia watched her granny doling out seeds and fat balls under the branches of the twisted apple tree. The blossom was nearly over and the last few petals swirled around Dee like delicate pink confetti in the breeze. Amelia glanced away and noticed that there were no fresh flowers on the table, just some sad lilies sitting in milky water, beginning to smell rank.

'Granny was only at the police station for a night, but she's …' Amelia broke off, at a loss for how to describe this new Dee.

Zara stopped watering her mother's neglected pot plants with the brass watering can with its elegant long nozzle and nodded. 'Crumpled.'

Dee came back into the kitchen. She gave them both a weak smile.

'So Granny, what do you think of my new image?' asked Amelia with forced enthusiasm. She stood up and stepped proudly into the middle of the room. She twirled around – gone was the sombre black. She now sported a forest-green tutu and matching corset. The black nail polish and lips had been ditched for a more natural look.

'Very nice, dear,' said Dee flatly. Her mouth barely twitched and her eyes were dull. She seemed shrunken.

'Camomile tea, Mother?' asked Zara.

When Dee shook her head, Amelia and Zara exchanged a look that clearly said, *This is serious!*

'So, Mother, are you going to yoga later?'

'I don't think so, dear.'

'Are you sure? You missed Taekwondo last night and you mentioned that you haven't been doing your morning forms and stretching exercises – you don't want to stiffen up.'

Dee didn't react.

Amelia tried this time. 'What about if I go to the woods with you tomorrow? I'll sleep over tonight and—'

'No, thank you, dear.'

Zara regarded her mother and declared, 'We need to get this unpleasant affair sorted out as soon as possible.'

Amelia nodded. Dee absently stroked Cat and said nothing.

Zara persisted, 'I've been thinking about it. There are two people we need to investigate. Firstly, Justin Harper and secondly, Andrew Bernier. We know remarkably little about the victim. Perhaps if we knew more about him we could prove who wanted him dead.'

Amelia was nodding away in agreement. 'So Mum, if you tackle Justin Harper, I'll find out all I can about Bernier.'

In a rather feeble voice Dee said, 'That all sounds lovely, but before you go could one of you please nip to the chemist? I have a dreadful headache and I'm out of paracetamol.'

'I'll go. I feel like some fresh air,' volunteered Amelia, heading straight towards the door.

For Amelia, it was a relief to be out in the sunshine. Granny's normally happy home felt dead and oppressive. The village was at its best at this time of year, with its picture postcard houses and neat front gardens overflowing with bright flowers. The delightful scent of newly mown grass hung in the air. Neither Mrs May nor that curmudgeonly retired police chief were outside their respective homes, which made the saunter even more enjoyable.

When she reached the high street she turned left and started walking up the hill to the old-fashioned pharmacy. As she passed the deli, Sophie and Son, with its smart blue sign, she noticed David working behind the counter. They waved at each other and she walked on, dodging some German tourists eating ice cream cones.

She reached the pharmacy. It was not your normal sterile chemist. This could have stepped straight off a Victorian film set. Rickety stone steps led up to the open door. An old-fashioned painted sign declared it to be 'Perkins' Pharmacy'. The inside did not disappoint; it had maintained the traditional apothecary drawers and its Dickinson atmosphere appealed to her romantic soul.

She skipped up the steps and blinked as her eyes adjusted to the gloom within. Instantly her happy mood was dampened. Mrs May was there. She heard her before she saw her.

'I've come for my Zolpidem,' hissed Dee's neighbour as she leant over the wooden counter.

The young assistant scurried off. Mrs May swivelled round and glowered at Amelia; her wizened face screwed up with disgust.

If there was anything that being a FitzMorris taught you, it was to be charming in the face of rudeness. As Granny always said 'It's so gratifyingly annoying to whoever is being unpleasant.'

Amelia smiled and said, 'Hello.'

Mrs May harrumphed and turned her back. The young assistant returned and grudgingly, Mrs May took her prescription, while grumbling, 'You took your time.' Pills in hand, she left without acknowledging Amelia.

Amelia gave the assistant a smile. The poor girl deserved a bit of kindness after that encounter. They exchanged the normal few words about the wonderful weather and she procured the paracetamol. It turned out that the girl had been at school with her but was two years younger so this led on to some pleasant chit-chat about the latest school news. Amelia was feeling lighthearted as she waved her new friend goodbye.

Unfortunately, she left the pharmacy only to find that Mrs May had not headed straight home. She was no more than twenty yards away, by the historic red post box from Queen Victoria's time.

Grey and sour Mrs May was loudly berating Blossom Bim Bam. The milling tourist had paused in their sightseeing to stare at the spectacle.

Poor Blossom looked near to tears. Even her bright daisy print dress could not alleviate how unhappy she appeared. She was simultaneously offering Mrs May futile apologies and rummaging through an overstocked wicker basket.

The only one who seemed oblivious to Mrs May's wrath was a white fluffy dog who happily wagged his tail and looked lovingly up at Blossom.

'Petal isn't my dog. I'm just looking after her for my aunt. I'm sure I put the poop bags in here.' She rummaged some more in the basket.

At the mention of poop bags, Amelia noticed a small chipolata of a doggy poop by the letterbox. It had obviously caused Mrs May offence way out of proportion to its size.

'As if you expect me to believe that!' scoffed Mrs May. 'People like you should be punished. No sense of responsibility. You're a fool, just like Andrew Bernier. He thought he could behave just as he liked and look what happened to him!'

Amelia clenched her jaw and thought of several choice words she would like to say to bullying Mrs May, but instead of escalating the situation she took a large paper tissue out of her pocket and handed it over to Blossom. 'Here, use this!'

Gratefully, Blossom made eye contact with Amelia then scooped up the offending pile and dropped it into a nearby bin. The gesture, far from pacifying Mrs May, seemed to enrage her even more.

'Don't think you've heard the end of this!' She pointed an accusing finger at Blossom. Petal yapped, excited at this new game.

'I really am most terribly sorry,' stammered Blossom.

'Come on, let's go home,' said Amelia, firmly taking Blossom by the elbow and guiding her down the hill and towards home.

The tourists began to disperse, realising that the show was over.

Amelia and Blossom walked back down the hill, conscious of Mrs May's malevolent eyes watching them.

'You're a fool, Blossom Bim Bam! And Amelia, that grandmother of yours is another fool. Justice will be done, you'll see ... then you'll be sorry.'

'I do find her a little ... unpleasant,' whispered Blossom, stepping closer to Amelia for protection. Petal, the dog trotted happily beside them on the end of her pink lead.

'She's more than a little unpleasant. I wonder why she's so poisonous? In the good old days, she would have been burnt as a witch!'

Blossom smiled. Her shoulders unclenched and she started to relax. She took a refreshing breath of the early summer air laced with the scent of roses.

'It's hard to remain unhappy for long on such a glorious day,' she commented. Then, regarding Amelia, she added, 'I like your new persona. That forest green really makes the most of your wonderful hair. Being a woodland nymph is a much better look for a clown. Your whole Goth vibe never would have worked at kiddies' parties. The kids probably would have loved it, but their mums wouldn't have been keen.'

Amelia explained, 'I felt like I needed a more uplifting look. Things are a bit on the gloomy side with all this Bernier business.'

They were rounding the corner and nearly back at Dee's house.

'Yes, I've been feeling bad about our last conversation.' Blossom had dropped her head, her blonde curls tumbling around her face and she bit her lip.

'No need. I was too pushy. I just want to find out as much as possible about Bernier. The sooner we can sort this murder business out, the sooner Granny's life can get back to normal.'

They paused outside Dee's house.

'How can I help?' asked Blossom. She was beaming. Her yellow curls reflected the sunlight and her bright daisy dress was the finishing touch to the happy picture she now presented.

'Well, what can you tell me about Bernier?'

Once again Blossom's mood changed as swiftly as the sun going behind a cloud. She frowned and bit her lip again. Petal looked up at her and pulled on the lead.

'He was very dubious in his business practices. Poor Mr Pilbersek got into awful trouble when he tried to have a discreet word with the Financial Reporting Council.'

'The Financial Reporting Council?'

'They're a sort of internal governing board for accountants and actuaries. It wasn't an official word, you understand; he just wanted to put the local chairman in the picture.'

Amelia leaned into Blossom. 'What happened?'

Bosom wrinkled her forehead and her freckled nose. 'It totally backfired. It turned out that Bernier was a tremendous friend of the chairman; they both belonged to the same golf club. He was like that.'

'Like what?' asked Amelia, her eyes were sparkling and she couldn't help grinning as she realised that she was finally getting somewhere.

Blossom didn't notice her glee. She gazed into the far distance, her mouth a flat line and her voice bitter. 'He was a total weasel if you were an ordinary person, but he was very good at getting in with anyone important. He could be very charming when it suited him.'

'More like smarmy?' suggested Amelia.

Blossom looked at her and smiled. Petal, bored of standing still, yapped.

'I better get you home, is it din-dins time?' enquired Blossom in the high-pitched, patronising voice usually reserved for babies. Petal wagged her tail and turned around in a circle. Blossom was about to walk on then paused. 'There was something else ...'

'Yes?'

'I probably should confess.'

'You killed him?' asked Amelia eagerly. She really did feel she was getting to the root of things.

Blossom's mouth dropped open in horror and she stared at Amelia with large blue eyes. 'No! Nothing like that! But I did sort of bend the rules, and Bernier found out and was, well, rather nasty about it.'

'How?'

Blossom wrinkled her forehead and put her head on one side and said, 'How did I bend the rules? Or in what way was Bernier rather nasty about it?'

'Both!'

Amelia was nodding and looking at Blossom keenly; Petal picked up on the energetic vibe and started yapping with more vigour.

'Shhhh, Petal!' Blossom smiled as she looked down at the little white fluff ball. Petal took this as praise and continued barking while exuberantly turning circles. She spoke over the din. 'You see, strictly speaking, I shouldn't have done it.'

'Done what?'

'Well poor Mr Reading-Wright or is it Mr Wright-Reading? I never can remember. Anyway, the one with the lovely interior shop. He was so upset when his mum died and he happened to mention that he was surprised she hadn't had a life insurance policy. I sort of looked it up even though I shouldn't have done and then ...'

She was biting her lip again and looking at the ground. Petal picked up on the change of mood and stopped barking.

'And then?' urged Amelia.

'Well, it all got rather messy. I told Mr Pilbersek and he said I wasn't to worry, that he'd deal with it. You see there was a chance that Mr Bernier, as a trustee of Mrs Carter's will, hadn't declared the policy. He might have taken it under the cover of fees.'

'Which is illegal?'

'Highly! Mr Bernier must have got wind of what I knew as the next thing was he'd somehow found out that I had,' – she went rather pink – 'an anomaly on my tax return to do with a work car and a trip, and he started making veiled threats as to what would happen to me if I said anything.' She sighed. 'When I confessed to Mr Pilbersek he was very understanding – he's going to do my tax returns from now on as I do tend to get muddled.' She stared wistfully into the middle distance.

'Was it then that he had a word with the chairman of The Financial Reporting Council?'

Blossom nodded. 'He didn't want to do it officially as dear Mr Pilbersek didn't want to get me in trouble.'

'But instead of Bernier being investigated, it turned out that he was buddies with the chairman – I think they were members of the golf club. So poor Mr Pilbersek looked bad and Bernier got off scot-free.'

Blossom gave Amelia a sad smile. 'Exactly!'

Petal was growing restless. Blossom glanced at her before adding, 'I must get this little one home but there's something else you should know about Mr Bernier.'

'What?'

'He was passionate about salsa dancing. He went to the Cuban club in town every Tuesday and Friday. There's bound to be someone there who can tell you more about him. On another note, I feel bad you never got your cupcake when you were at mine the other day. Would you like to come home with me and we can have tea and cake after I've fed Petal?'

Amelia smiled, patted Petal and replied, 'No thanks. I need to give Granny her headache pills and tell Mum to break out her dancing shoes!'

Robert did not feel good about himself; in fact, he had a sensation of disgust. Self-loathing seeped through his body. *To think I've come to this! Mum would be turning in her grave!* He would hate for any of his friends to know that he had sunk to being a stalker; he certainly wouldn't be telling Paul.

So here he was, on a Monday morning, sitting in his car. He had pulled up in a lay-by, with Warthing Woods on one side and Justin Harper's bungalow on the other.

The forest was green, a refreshing change from the bleak bare branches of winter, but Robert took no notice of its distant beauty. He was intent on a spider just outside his window. He'd been staring at it for at least ten minutes. The spider was industriously spinning a web over last year's crumpled brambles and a discarded McDonald's carton. The vivid red fast-food logo was an ugly intruder in an otherwise bucolic scene with a blue sky, and wildflowers pushing their way through the lay-by's thick grass. The spider's actions were earnest and futile.

Robert would have liked to pretend that he was here by chance, that he'd just been passing and pulled in but he'd actually been rehearsing this in his mind for days. To be completely accurate, he had played through this scene not so much during his days as his nights. His days were so filled with clients and fabrics that there was no time for his thoughts to stray. It was during the long lonely nights, when he lay sleepless and alone, next to Paul, that his judgement deserted him.

At night his mind ranged free and dangerously out of control over memories and regrets. He could still not quite believe that his mother had left all that money to Justin Harper.

Justin Harper! Of all people! Had it been one of her old friends from the golf club who'd fallen on hard times I could have accepted that. Or some up-and-coming young person, like the girl she'd left her golf kit to, that would have been fine, but Justin Harper seems like a betrayal.

Anger swelled in his chest. He swore under his breath and clenched his jaw. His grief counsellor had mentioned anger was often part of the grieving process but Robert had the impression that it was rage at the situation rather than at an individual. Disbelief was another stage of grieving – well that was accurate. He couldn't believe his mum was gone and he was in this situation.

He could not recall ever being filled with such hatred. He longed to crush Justin, to physically beat him until his face and body were a bloody pulp. Robert realised that at the thought he'd clenched his fists so hard that his nails were biting painfully into his palms.

He'd been wrong, this wasn't the first time his mind and body had been controlled by molten wrath. He'd felt like this about Andrew Bernier. Smug, fat, little Bernier who had scoffed at Robert's distress, his grief and confusion at the will and the lack of a life policy. He could not understand why his mother had chosen such an obnoxious man to be a trustee – he didn't have Justin's false charm or striking blue eyes.

But he's dead now.

Robert felt calmed by the knowledge and took a deep breath but no sooner had he exhaled than another troubling image loomed in his mind.

He'd gone to Bernier's office certain he'd be able to sort everything out. It was in the local market town, not far from the insurance company where Julia, Ken and Alex worked, but his office was very different from their sleek modern building.

As he drew up to the side street with its terrace of shops, Robert had felt confident in his ability to be calm and logical. Bernier's workplace was up a narrow staircase. There was the hint of cat pee overlaid with air freshener. The staircase was poorly lit by a single naked light bulb hanging from a wire. The office was above a fish and chip shop and the smells and sounds of the fryer and the people filtered through the thin stairway walls.

A scrappy paper sign on the chipped door said: *Andrew Bernier ACCA.*

Robert had paused, not sure whether to knock or not. In the end, he opted for a light tap and was answered by a brisk, 'Come in.' He'd swallowed and opened the door.

The office was painted the same uninspiring brown as the stairs. There was a single window that overlooked a wall. Papers, files and books spewed over two metal bookshelves and onto the floor. Bernier's desk was as cheap and grubby as his suit.

It was the smile Bernier gave him that began to unravel Robert's composure.

The man is pleased to see me!

It wasn't the professional grin of acknowledgement, it was the gleeful smirk of a playground bully.

And despite all Robert's good intentions, within minutes he'd found himself embroiled in a schoolboy fight where words quickly escalated to fists.

He was unclear as to the exact sequence of events but he thought Bernier had made some scoffing comment about Robert's mother being 'an old biddy'.

Things had turned physical when Bernier had stood up and taken hold of Robert's arm to show him out. Robert had looked at the chubby fingers clawing his cashmere sleeve; this was coupled with Bernier's patronising, 'If you are unable to be civil I really must insist that you leave.'

Robert had felt a burning in the pit of his stomach, a tightness in his chest and a red mist over his eyes and the next second his fist smashed into Bernier's doughy jaw.

In hindsight, Robert had been amazed that the noise hadn't brought people from the fish shop running but unfortunately, the clash hadn't gone unobserved.

When Robert, fury spent, had looked up from the floor and Bernier's inert body, there had been the shiny shoes and pressed suit trousers of Justin Harper. Silently, with ice-cold eyes Harper had gazed on Robert's sin.

Justin Harper, of all men, now had a hold over him.

There was a movement outside his car which snapped Robert back to the present.

He glanced over to where he'd caught sight of someone. It was the back entrance to Justin Harper's garden.

There he is and now's my chance!

Gina needed to get out of The Flying Pheasant. To be more precise she had to get away from Francesco. She required space to process everything.

Francesco has always had a temper, but this … And Dee – poor Dee. She's a shadow of her old self.

She had lied to Francesco saying she had some errands to run in town but actually, she was heading to Warthing Woods. She craved solitude and nature.

In Francesco's world, and I guess in mine, to some extent, an activity has to be practical to be deemed worthwhile.

Worthwhile or not she was pleased when she pulled into the lay-by near the woods. The weather was good but she knew the paths would be wet and in places muddy so she had brought her boots.

Soon she was strolling under a soothing canopy of green. Sun dappled through the leaves. Here and there the last of the bluebells pooled in small puddles of blue. A squirrel raced through the branches far above her head and in every direction there was birdsong. She inhaled the restful smell of earth and leaves.

For the first time since Francesco had had that terrible fight with Bernier, Gina relaxed. With each step, she took her shoulders began to ease and the tightness in her chest lifted making her breathing smooth.

Perhaps I should get a dog of my own, then I'd have an excuse to get out like this every day.

Francesco had a dog, a black Labrador, which he used for field trials. Gina fancied something small, a lapdog of some description.

But it was no use, she couldn't just enjoy the trees for long before the same old worrying thoughts started popping into her mind. *Bernier! If only he hadn't started to harass Alex.* The thought of Alex in tears, her face red and blotchy made her throat hurt. *Alex, of all people, crying. I haven't seen her cry since she was seven.*

That had been a few weeks ago before Alex had passed her final exams and got a great new job at the insurance company. It had been when she was doing an audit at some company Bernier was involved in. Gina didn't quite understand what had happened but Alex had done something wrong with the accounts. *Anyone can make a mistake! But oh no! He pestered her, bullying her.*

She'd moved on, got this wonderful job and all seemed well. Gina and Francesco had been so happy for her. They'd never made a big thing about her disability but it was there – it was always there; the pain, the doctors' appointments, the slights and unhappiness when as a teenager she'd have a crush on a boy and he wouldn't give her the time of day. They were so proud of the way she'd tackled all her challenges. By anybody's standards, she was doing well.

Then Bernier had to come back into the picture, hinting, implying he could ruin things for her at her new company. Gina's heart raced as she thought of it and her head began to ache. *But Francesco shouldn't have confronted him! If only he could control his temper!*

It had been a relief when Bernier was dead. As Francesco rightly said the world was a better place for Alex now that Bernier wasn't in it.

If only it had stopped there!

Gina found herself back at the car. She took her boots off. All the health benefits of the walk had been obliterated by her own futile thoughts. *It would all be okay now if only Justin Harper hadn't witnessed everything.* Now *he* was the one hinting and making vague threats.

She got into her car but before she drove away, there he was: Justin Harper. Her breath caught in her throat, and she gripped the steering wheel so hard her knuckles were white.

There he is, all alone! He hasn't seen me and there's no one around! How easy would it be to simply eliminate him from the picture? Then our lives could go back to normal.

Chapter 12

This isn't what I imagined when I joined the police force, sighed Chief Inspector Nicholas Corman as he regarded himself in the mirror; form-fitting – not to say tight – black trousers, patent dancing shoes, black silk shirt and neat waistcoat. As the finishing touch he put on a fedora, tilting it at a jaunty angle over one eye. Wishing he could stay at home and finish dusting his model railway, he left his house.

The Cuban Club was exactly as he'd imagined it would be. Soul-stirring music throbbed out of the door; its hypnotic rhythm had one's toes tapping before one had even crossed the threshold. Twin red, white and blue Cuban flags flanked the doorway.

Once inside, his eyes were assaulted by bright pink, cobalt blue and vivid yellow.

I presume the interior decorator was trying to recreate the colours of Cuba.

He was not impressed by the colour scheme, but he was rather taken with the excellent collection of black-and-white photographs. They were stylish depictions of all things 1950s – mainly iconic cars.

He made his way through the milling crowd. He noticed the bar with its bewildering number of cocktails on offer, in a multitude of glasses. There were small fizzy pink drinks, tall ice-clinking tea-coloured offerings, and dangerous black suggestions in martini glasses. All boasted an overflowing bounty of lemon peel or fruit at their brims. Conservative by nature, Nicholas opted for a clean fresh mojito. He took a sip and winced – it was strong. Scanning the room he wondered where to start his undercover investigation.

His eyes were drawn to a lady leaning nonchalantly with her back against the bar. Self-possessed calm exuded from her while several men hovered avidly around her.

She looked vaguely familiar.

No! It can't be!

Even as he denied it to himself he knew that flame-coloured hair. He swallowed and openly stared.

It is!

Nicholas watched, entranced, as a young man in ripped white jeans and a vest that showed off his muscly arms confidently strode up to her. He held out his hand. She took it and, to the backdrop of trumpet and maracas, they took to the floor.

They faced each other, then on the beat, he took a step forward and she retreated. He held her in his arms. Her sleek black jumpsuit moulded against his lean body. Established in the rhythm snake-like they swivelled their bodies. He twirled her and she yielded. Nicholas, with an involuntary spasm, tightened his grip on his glass. The music pulsated; he could feel the vein in his temple throbbing. They danced until the final beat, which they concluded intertwined.

Nicholas regarded the two bodies fused together in passion and he didn't like it.

Before he had time to think through his emotions, he strode onto the dance floor. As he got closer to her he realised that every atom of him ached with a longing to hold her.

As the first notes of the next song rang out, he held out his hand to the lady. She regarded him for a second, her green eyes penetrating his grey ones. Electricity crackled between them and then she took his hand. Nicholas pulled her to him.

Her old partner was momentarily surprised, but then shrugged and left.

Eyes still locked, Nicholas firmly led – his hand on her waist, hers draped on his shoulders. For the first eight beats, they assessed each other and how they moved together. With an easy grace and growing confidence, they began to branch out. The music pulsated through their bodies. They backed away and danced freely, mirroring each other's movements. Unashamed, Nicholas' dance partner raised her arms above her head, flicking her long hair. Without hesitation, he caught her left hand and twirled her towards him.

For a beat, he held her close to him. Her scent washed over him and his heart skipped a beat. For an instance, she moulded against his body, and then he flung her from him while keeping a firm grip on her hand.

For the next eight beats they twirled and intertwined in a complex pattern until the final bar where, triumphantly, he spun her into a dip. Then, and only then, did they speak, a little breathlessly and their eyes still riveted on each other.

'Ms FitzMorris.'

'Inspector. I presume you are here looking for more information on Bernier.'

He nodded, losing himself in those green eyes.

She spoke again in those soft, husky tones, 'Could we continue this conversation ...'

He realised he was still holding her almost horizontally, his face only inches away from her as he leaned over her. He suddenly felt rather hot. 'Er, um, yes. That is, let's talk at the bar.'

He righted her and followed as she strode, not towards the bar as he'd expected, but towards a table where a rounded middle-aged lady sat in a flamboyant turquoise dress. Its frills and plunging neckline were at odds with her staid librarian glasses.

'Mavis, this is the friend I was telling you about.' Zara nodded at Nicholas. He flushed at Zara calling him her 'friend' and then pulled himself together.

'Nicholas, Mavis was Bernier's regular dance partner and she has some important information.'

Mavis smiled over her pink cocktail evidently pleased at being the centre of attention, but then self-consciously schooled her features into a picture of suitable sadness. 'Such a shame what happened to poor Andy. I still wake up at night all of a quiver over it. I mean, one doesn't expect it. Not here. You know it's the sort of thing you only see on the telly, isn't it? As I was saying to—'

'Yes, quite,' cut in Zara impatiently. 'Why don't you tell Nicholas about Justin Harper?'

'I didn't hear his name.'

'Fine. Just tell Nicholas about the very tall chap with long limbs and dazzling blue eyes who Bernier – Andy – was scared of.'

'That's right.' Complacently, she took a sip of her cocktail.

They both looked at her expectantly.

Nicholas leaned forward. 'Mrs, er, Mavis, could you possibly tell me more?'

'Well, like I said to your missus …'

Panic assaulted Nicholas. *I should correct her! Obviously, Ms FitzMorris and I are not – could not – ever! But if I interrupt this Mavis lady, I'll never hear her information.*

His thoughts raced. He had a sudden vision of Zara as his wife – probably admiring his Flying Scotsman. The club instantly became infernally hot.

His attention came back to Mavis who was still speaking.

'So like I said, Andy was a one. Always flashing his cash and making out like he was some sort of a gangster. He liked to boast how people thought they were clever, but one flash of their accounts and he could ferret out their misdoings. He said there wasn't an accounting dodge he couldn't find.' Her voice was full of admiration. 'He was always dead cocky. Then a day or two before he was killed, as I was arriving at the club I saw them.'

She took another long sip of her drink.

'Who did you see?'

'Andy of course, with this tall lanky chap, in the alleyway.'

'Did you hear what they were saying?'

'No, but you could tell from their body language that it wasn't a friendly chat. Andy was cowering, obviously scared witless and the other bloke was leaning over him, menacing, like. And what's more, my poor little Andy didn't feel like a quick salsa after that.' She wiped an absent tear off her cheek.

Nicholas was about to thank her and leave when she gave a sort of hiccup.

'Yes?' Zara encouraged.

'Well, if that tall chap was Justin Harper, I can't help thinking I might have been partly responsible for what happened.'

She had both Nicholas' and Zara's full attention. Simultaneously they leant towards her across the table.

'How so?' enquired Nicholas, his voice hushed and soothing. It was a favourite tone of his that he deployed to get maximum information out of children and other witnesses.

'Well, you see … it was through me that he met this Justin Harper fellow.'

'I thought you said you didn't know Justin Harper.' Zara's voice was sharp.

'I don't, not personally—'

'I don't quite follow. If you don't know him how could you have any responsibility?' Nicholas coaxed. He'd spoken quickly. He was keen to keep the conversation reassuring. Experience had taught him how to draw people out and he could see that Zara was irritated and about to say something sharp.

'You see. It was like this … the girls and I were—'

'The girls?' Nicholas was confused.

'That's what we call ourselves. There's a group of us that play golf every Wednesday at the local club and then have lunch afterwards at the clubhouse. They do a lovely salad.'

'I'm sure they do, but what's this got to do with Harper and Bernier?'

She looked a bit affronted at the interruption and gave Zara a dismissive glance before having another sip of her cocktail and settling her ample behind more comfortably on the chair.

'Well somehow Justin Harper came up, and it turned out they all knew him.' She giggled and gave Nicholas a broad wink. 'Rather well, actually!' She leant back and smiled. 'Things got a bit heated after that! He must be quite something as all the ladies were unaware of his friendship with the other!' She chuckled again. 'Then Sylvia – that Sylvia Greg who used to have the boutique on the high street – anyway, she mentioned the large donation she'd given him for his mission, whatever that might be …'

Both Zara and Nicholas were sitting forwards, eager to hear more.

Their star witness took another rather large sip of her drink. 'Well, will you look at that! I've finished my drink!'

'I'll get you another one!' Nicholas hastily declared, leaping to his feet.

He soon had her replenished with another lethal-looking pink concoction.

'Cheers, love. Now what was I saying?'

Zara reminded her, 'Sylvia Greg had mentioned she'd given a large donation to his mission.'

Mavis sipped her cocktail, smiled and continued. 'As it turned out, they all had.' She gave a raucous laugh at the memory. 'Large amounts! And there they all were thinking they were his one and only donor, if you know what I mean.' She gave Nicholas another wink.

Zara cut in. 'But what has this got to do with Bernier?'

Reluctantly Mavis turned away from Nicholas and addressed Zara. 'He'd been at the bar the whole time. I hadn't noticed him but he'd overheard everything. He came over, all charm, like, and asked to be introduced. He was very interested – rather too interested if you get my drift.'

'I'm sorry Mavis, but I still don't quite get what you're driving at.'

Nicholas looked the picture of puzzlement, which Zara correctly guessed was a pretence to elicit more information.

Mavis gave him another patient smile. 'Bernier was a great salsa partner but he wasn't the type who you'd want to know your secrets – especially not financial ones.' She toyed with her pink cocktail. 'Blackmail might be too strong a word but he certainly was not above, hinting, shall we say.'

Triumphantly, Zara declared, 'There, you see! I told you Justin Harper did it. He more or less confessed to my mother, after he threatened her.'

'Ms FitzMorris, this is not conclusive proof.'

'If you're not going to bring Justin Harper to justice, I will!' she declared, before standing up and heading for the exit.

He was going to remonstrate with her but instead, he just watched her go, overawed by how impressive she was when angry. He could not help noticing that she was wearing stockings with a line that ran up the back of her shapely legs. Her heels clicked and her hips swayed as she strode away from him.

Chapter 13

'I don't want to be difficult dear, but I really don't feel like doing this,' Dee sighed.

As she feared, Zara was having none of it. 'Don't be ridiculous, Mother. This is just the sort of outing that will perk you up and put a bit of oomph back in your life. You know you've been moping around for days now. You need to get out of the house. Amelia, have you nearly finished your grandmother's makeup?'

'Almost,' smiled Amelia brightly, sponging Dee's nose. 'This is rather fun. After all, it's not often all three of us go out at night together. I think we look fab – all three of us in black!'

Zara glanced at herself in the mirror. 'My old black jumpsuit is certainly coming in handy.'

'It does suit you, dear, but I'm not certain that all of us going out together is a good idea—'

'Do stop making a fuss, Mother. You know you'll enjoy it when you get there.'

'But Zara, do you really think it's wise?'

'Of course it is.'

'But what if we get caught?'

'Oh Granny, now you're just making excuses! Anyone would think you don't want to spend time with Mother and me.'

'Of course I do, it's just that I'm not sure breaking into Justin Harper's cottage is a good idea.'

'We've been through this before, Mother. The man has disappeared. I've looked everywhere for him, contacted everyone I know and no one has seen hide or hair of him. We need to get some evidence to prove him guilty and you innocent. Now let me look at you.' She surveyed Dee and nodded her approval. 'Good job, Amelia. You've totally blacked out Granny's face. Who'd have thought your Goth makeup would come in so useful? Now all we have to do is tuck our hair into our berets and we're good to go.'

With the utmost stealth, they slid out of the front door and headed towards Zara's car.

'Remember, everyone, that secrecy is vital,' whispered Zara as she clicked her car open. Dee and Amelia silently nodded. Like three highly trained ninja warriors, they slipped into the car. They fastened their seatbelts and Zara opened her window to let the air in.

'Good evening Dee, Zara and yes, Amelia.'

With a jolt, all three spun around to see Mrs May with her thin lips contorted into a smirk and her bony hands firmly on her hips.

'Mrs May! I didn't see you there,' blurted out Dee.

She was going to add something about it not being surprising, as Mrs May had probably been lurking in the shadows – after all, grey against black is virtually invisible.

Zara revved up the engine and nonchalantly declared, 'Lovely evening! But we can't stop to chat, I'm afraid. We're late for a party.'

'A drinks party? At this hour?' Unashamedly she looked from one camouflaged face to another.

'It's a "come as a cat burglar" gig; they're all the rage!' chipped in Amelia as they roared off.

'You don't think she suspected anything do you?' enquired Dee doubtfully.

'No! We are just three generations of a family going out together,' said Zara firmly, while clicking the indicator and taking the turn towards the woods and Justin Harper's house.

With more than a hint of sarcasm, Amelia added, 'After all, what's suspicious about that?'

They drove for about five minutes before Dee spoke again. 'Zara, how come you know where Justin Harper lives?'

'Oh. Um, well that's really not important, Mother. What's far more critical is that we find some concrete evidence to clear you of murder and implicate him.'

'But what if he's in?'

'Highly unlikely. I've made thorough enquiries and he has vanished.'

'But what if he reappears tonight at his home?'

Zara shrugged. 'Then we just say we're … trick or treating.'

'In spring?' asked Amelia.

'Exactly – local tradition,' said Zara, putting her foot down. In a few minutes, they arrived and she pulled the car into a lay-by close to the woods.

Dee looked around. 'Why have we stopped here, dear? This is where I always park the car when I do my dawn bird-watching.'

'Justin's bungalow is in the middle of three. He has terribly nosy neighbours but if you park here you can go through the back garden and no one will see you.'

'Just how well do you know Justin Harper, Mum?' enquired Amelia as she released her seatbelt.

'Shh! We must be as quiet as possible.' hissed Zara, getting out of the car and leading the way over a rickety style and along a narrow footpath.

'When we get there, what sort of evidence are we looking for?' whispered Dee.

'Anything really … papers linking him to Bernier, clown makeup?' replied Zara.

'A signed confession?' added Amelia.

'Darling, your growing habit of sarcasm is most unbecoming! Remember, sarcasm is the lowest form of wit,' hissed Zara.

They had reached the backs of the bungalows. Zara gently creaked open a small gate that led into Justin's small orderly back garden.

'Oh, dear! I've just thought of something – there might be an alarm or movement-sensitive lights. And we mustn't actually break into his house, that would be illegal.' Dee sounded both breathless and worried.

'There isn't any security system and we don't have to break in as I know where he keeps the spare key,' Zara reassured her.

They reached the back door and Zara bent down, moved a small flower pot and triumphantly held up a key.

Dee looked at Amelia through the darkness and softly stated, 'I really want to ask your mother a few questions about this, but I don't think this is the right moment.'

It certainly wasn't the moment, as at that second the three FitzMorris ladies were startled and dazzled by a bright light shining directly at them. Amelia let out a small scream and instinctively Dee seized her arm. Boldly, Zara placed her body between them and the threatening spotlight. Defiantly she blinked into the blaze. Her hand outstretched, she stood ready to defend her family.

'Ms FitzMorris!' declared a familiar and exasperated voice as the flashlight was lowered.

'Oh, Inspector! How lovely to see you!' exclaimed Dee. 'I was frightened it was that horrid Justin Harper.'

'Now why would you think it might be him? After all, this is only his home.'

'Really, this is turning into the most wearisome evening. What's with all the sarcasm? First Amelia and now the Inspector,' muttered Zara.

'Excuse me?' asked the Inspector.

'Oh, nothing. Now, if you'll excuse us, we really ought to be going. Come on Amelia, Mum ...' Zara said airily, as she started leading the way back down the path.

'Not so fast.' Nicholas blocked their path. Josh, standing slightly to one side, looked vaguely bemused. 'What exactly are you doing here? And why do you look like three cartoon cat burglars?'

Dee helpfully answered, 'Well Inspector, Zara couldn't find any trace of Justin Harper and, as you know, we think he murdered Andrew Bernier – so we thought we'd just pop over and—'

Josh butted in, gazing admiringly at Amelia all the while, 'Yeah, that's why we're here too. We're on a stake-out.'

'Really? How brave!' purred Amelia.

Her sarcasm was lost on Josh who swayed slightly before he replied, 'Oh no, not really. It's all just part of the job.'

'Be quiet,' commanded the Inspector.

'Right-ho, Boss.' Josh sounded deflated.

'Ms Zara FitzMorris, I'm waiting for an explanation.'

Confidently, Zara replied, 'It's really quite simple, Inspector.'

'Yes?'

'Trick or treat?'

Chapter 14

Less than forty-eight hours later, the FitzMorris ladies were back; they parked in the same lay-by at the rear of Justin Harper's cottage. It was still dark but dawn was near.

'I don't care what you say, Zara. I think, under the circumstances, the Inspector was very good about it. He could have made an awful fuss,' declared Dee, as she unfastened her seatbelt.

'Granny's right,' yawned Amelia. 'I'm sure he could have charged us – instead, we just got a good telling off.'

'That's quite enough talking about that,' Zara said crisply while turning off the car headlights. 'Let's focus on the matter at hand. I'm so glad you've finally agreed to come to the woods, Mother. It's high time you resumed your life again. Goodness knows how long it's going to be before this nasty affair is sorted.'

'Yes dear,' sighed Dee as she checked she had her binoculars, notebook, pencil and flashlight. Content that she was kitted out, she surveyed the party. 'Amelia, I love the way you've dressed the part. You do look rather dashing; a sort of cross between Disney's Tinkerbell and a pantomime Robin Hood.'

'I was going for a woodland nymph,' smiled Amelia, smoothing down her petal tunic.

'Very apt, dear. Now follow me. We need to set up camp at the hide; it's in the middle of the woods. I'm afraid it's a bit of a trek away, down several muddy tracks.'

They clambered out of the car; glad of their coats as the air was cold and damp.

Dee led the way into the woods. Their eyes were rapidly becoming accustomed to the poor light but nonetheless, their torches were useful in showing the path in front of their feet.

Once they were under the canopy of the trees it was darker. Dee strode on, down one path, then another, with tall trees towering above them on either side. They veered off the main path onto a narrow winding track. Silently they picked their way single file avoiding the tree roots that criss-crossed the way. It had rained in the night, which brought out the fresh woody scent of damp earth and rotting leaves. Unfamiliar rustles and creaks whispered in the air.

'So what exactly are we going to do, Granny?' whispered Amelia.

'We go to the hide and wait.'

'Wait for what?'

'Dawn. Then we record birds or anything else we see or hear.'

'What? And that's all we do?'

'Yes. There's no need to sound so bored. It's actually very exciting. The information is sent to a clever lady who is researching woodland habitat and to help her we have to include the time, date and weather.'

'I'm sure it will be great, Granny. I've never been birdwatching before.'

If Dee was aware of the sarcastic note in her granddaughter's voice she ignored it. 'Well, this is more like bird-listening. Actually—'

She abruptly stopped mid-sentence, cut off by the thunderous sound of someone crashing through the undergrowth to their left. All three of them froze. Instinctively, they stared in the direction of the danger. Heavy breathing coming from the thicket of undergrowth had their pulses racing. The threat was coming closer.

'What should we do?' hissed Amelia

'Stand very still,' hissed back Dee.

There was an edge of terror in Zara's whisper and Dee felt Zara's hand grab her arm and grip it painfully as she declared, 'I think we should run for it.'

'Don't move!' commanded Dee quietly.

There was a cracking of branches and a wheezing sound. Despite Dee's own words it took all of her self-control not to run.

Just when Dee felt she could stand it no longer, a cumbersome badger broke out on the path in front of them. Oblivious to the terrified FitzMorris family, it blundered on, a black and grey blur against the undergrowth. The FitzMorrises gave out a collective sigh of relief.

'Was I the only one who thought the clown murderer had tracked us down to the woods and was intending to add to his tally?' asked Amelia as she plucked a twig from her hair.

'It was a bit … unnerving,' agreed her mother.

Dee was already back in citizen scientist mode as she checked the time and jotted the badger sighting down in her notebook. That done, she looked up and commented, 'We're nearly at the hide. It's just around the corner.'

They rounded a curve in the path and came to a small clearing where there was the hide. It was a nondescript little hut with a viewing hatch. Dee took out a key, unlocked the padlock and opened the door. In the dim light inside, Zara could make out a couple of ancient fold-down garden chairs and she noticed the walls were covered with posters helpfully labelling British fauna and flora. It smelt musty.

They settled themselves down and Dee got out her notebook, then Amelia took a sharp intake of breath and seized her mother and grandmother by their respective arms.

'What's that?' gasped Amelia as she nodded through the viewing hutch to the dark woods beyond.

'It's a robin, dear. They're normally the first birds to start singing. They're early risers, pre-dawn like blackbirds and thrushes.'

Exasperated, Amelia spluttered, 'Not that – *that*!' She pointed through the viewing hatch.

Zara and Dee looked.

'What's what?' asked Dee.

'That, over there!' exclaimed Amelia pointing with more urgency.

Dee and Zara looked again.

'I can't see anything but trees and shadows,' confessed Zara.

Dee was still peering out of the hatch. 'Um, yes. I think I see what you mean … where that odd eerie dark shadow falls under that old oak tree? It does look a bit like a figure.'

Zara stared over to where Dee was also pointing. 'Yes, now I see it – I suppose it's just a trick of the light.'

'It's a figure. Someone is there,' insisted Amelia.

'Don't be ridiculous, darling. After all, who would be lurking under an oak tree at this hour in a deserted part of the forest miles away from anyone?' Zara said.

Amelia looked at her mother. 'I'd rather not answer that.'

They stared some more.

'It's not moving,' whispered Dee. Her mouth felt dry and the hairs on the backs of her arms were rising.

'Shall I call out?' asked Amelia.

'No! We don't want to frighten the wildlife.' Shock overcoming Dee's apprehension she was determined to keep focused on being a good citizen scientist.

'In that case, shall I tiptoe up to it and get a closer look?' suggested Amelia, who was already moving towards the door.

'Good idea, but we'll come too. I'm sure when we get within a few feet of it there'll be a perfectly innocent explanation,' stated Zara calmly.

'Bound to be!' agreed Dee, swallowing hard.

They crept out. Dee's heart was beating uncomfortably fast and all her senses were on heightened alert so when a small mouse ran in front of her, she nearly screamed.

They inched towards the menacing shadow under the stately tree.

Dee screwed up her eyes in an attempt to see more clearly. 'I think it's a scarecrow tied to the tree,' she whispered as they got a little closer.

'It's an awfully long scarecrow. It must be well over six foot,' commented Amelia.

'And who would put a scarecrow here of all places? I thought the idea was that you wanted to attract birds not frighten them away!' added Zara.

'More to the point … why would you make a scarecrow look like a clown?' There was a catch in Dee's voice.

Zara thrust her hands on her hips and swung around to face Dee. 'Oh, Mother! You haven't! Not again! Please tell me you haven't just found *another* dead body!'

'I don't know why you're blaming me, dear. After all, you are here too. And Amelia saw it first … so strictly speaking, she found it,' Dee gabbled defensively.

While her elders squabbled Amelia ran her torch up and down the figure. 'Granny … does he – it – look familiar to you? Mum, have a closer look. What do you think?'

Dee and Zara both peered up at the figure. Thick rope secured its torso to the gnarled tree trunk. Its head lolled drunkenly to one side, with a fiendish grin painted on its lifeless face. Long arms hung at its side with oversized white gloves swaying at the ends.

Zara cocked her head to one side. 'You know, I think you're right. It does look familiar. Could it be—?'

'Yes! It is! It's Justin Harper,' Dee declared.

'I suppose that means he's not our murderer,' Zara sighed.

'No need to sound so disappointed, Mum!'

'Amelia, I've told you before; sarcasm is not appealing – and of course, I'm disappointed. He was our chief suspect. Now we have to go back to the drawing board. Speaking of which, bagsy I'm not the one to tell the Inspector!'

Chapter 15

Nicholas was not totally surprised when he was awoken at 5.22 in the morning by a contrite Dee.

'Good morning, Inspector.'

He yawned and groggily queried, 'Dee FitzMorris?'

'Did I wake you?'

Nicholas glanced over at the alarm clock that he preferred to use rather than his phone. It was solid and roused him with a bell. He liked to think that it was a bit like being roused by the respectful murmur of a butler, à la Downton Abbey. So much more civilised than being brutally forced into wakefulness by the shrill demands of a phone alarm.

'Dee, it is only a bit after five.'

'Oh, I did wake you. I'm sorry – I'll ring back later.'

Nicholas could hear that this statement was met by a chorus of high-pitched objections from whoever was with Dee.

'I should probably mention that I've found another clown.'

Nicholas sat bolt upright in bed in his blue cotton pyjamas with red piping, a present from his mother.

'Dead?' he enquired hesitantly.

'Very.'

'Oh.'

'The good news is that we know who it is – it's Justin Harper.'

'Why is it good news that Justin Harper is dead?'

'No, I didn't mean that. I just thought it would save you a lot of work as there is no need to identify him.'

Nicholas took the location, established Zara and Amelia were with her and gave her instructions about not touching anything before he ended the call.

A couple of hours later he was in one of the interrogation rooms back at the station, with Zara FitzMorris sitting across the table from him, a recorder to hand and a smart WPC stationed by the door.

Only Zara FitzMorris could sit on a plastic chair in a stark police investigation room and give the impression she was sitting on a regal throne, thought Chief Inspector Nicholas Corman.

He couldn't stop humming. It was one of those tunes that gets into your head and keeps buzzing around on a loop. It was rhythmic and fast. For some reason it made him feel happy.

'Would you like some coffee?' he asked.

'I refuse to answer any questions without my solicitor,' replied Zara curtly. She was regarding him coolly.

He smiled. 'I think you can safely say if you feel like a cuppa without legal representation.' He was rewarded with a softening of her gaze. He laughed. 'Your mother asked for camomile tea.'

'Do you have any?'

'Not at the moment, but I believe she has charmed Josh into popping down to the Co-op and picking some up.'

Zara was smiling properly now. He like the way it brought warmth to her green eyes.

Encouraged, Nicholas continued, 'Look. Despite all the evidence to the contrary, I don't really think you or your mother are capable of these murders – but, the more information you can give us, the sooner we can get this sorted.'

There was a pause. Zara was obviously thinking.

'You are not being questioned as a person of interest; you are here to give a statement.'

There was another pause, lengthier this time. He didn't think that now was the moment to raise her own dubious relationship with Harper. He knew from overhearing Zara and Harper at the coffee shop that previously they had been romantically involved. Her animosity towards the man had been obvious with her accusations about him threatening her mother, and then there was the little matter of him finding her in Justin Harper's garden, in the middle of the night, camouflaged in black. Yes – he would have to investigate her but right now …

She was looking steadily at him. Eventually, she spoke.
'Inspector ...'

'Yes?'

'You're humming that song again.'

'Am I? Sorry – I seem to have it stuck in my head.'

'No need to apologise ... It's a good song.'

'It is rather, isn't it?'

'Where did you learn to salsa like that?'

'What?'

'The song you are humming is the song we danced to at the Cuban Club.'

Nicholas swallowed. He felt rather warm. He had a sudden vivid recollection of what it had felt like to hold Zara FitzMorris in his arms. He gave the WPC a furtive glance.

'My mother,' he stammered.

'Your mother?'

'She ran a ballroom-dancing studio.'

'Oh, that explains it.'

Their eyes were locked together.

'I can foxtrot too,' he blurted out and immediately felt foolish.

Zara serenely replied, 'How useful.'

It seemed to Nicholas that it took forever to get the FitzMorrises' statements. Dee kept apologising for getting him up so early and for all the fuss, bother and extra work she was giving him by finding another body. Amelia, on the other hand, was keen to explore the psychological angle; she kept asking him questions about what kind of childhood trauma could lead someone to not just murder but then paint them up as a clown. He felt he was not equipped to answer her query and he also was rather annoyed as he was pretty certain he was the one who should be asking questions. The final straw was when Amelia managed to procure a notebook and pencil from Josh so that she could take notes for a potential special essay for her degree. She seemed to believe that getting extra credits outweighed any police protocol.

By the time he had finished, he felt quite drained.

While Nicholas was prepared to pause in his investigation of Zara, Mrs May and retired Police Chief Peter Wilson were not.

The moment they heard the news from the girl behind the counter in the local Co-op, they were intent on discussing how Zara was no better than she should be and the general lack of morality shown by the whole FitzMorris clan.

They rendezvoused on the pavement outside the shop, Mrs May clutching a tin of tomato soup to her withered bosom and Peter Wilson with his lunch of sliced white bread and processed cheese in a battered plastic bag that he'd had for years. It was early in the morning so there were not many tourists around. The tourist coaches tended to arrive between ten and eleven after which, until they departed at two, there was barely enough room on the pavement for anyone to loiter, especially anyone as bulky as Peter Wilson.

'Of course, I'm not surprised,' said Peter, rolling his weight back on his heels and looking sagely up in the blue cloudless sky.

Mrs May shuffled a little closer, her lips parted. She leant into him. 'You're not?'

Peter Wilson rolled his weight back onto his toes and gave her a knowing look. 'During my years on the force I came across many a criminal family.'

An unpleasant smile spread across Mrs May's face that evolved into a sneer. She wetted her lips and through a bark of a laugh said, 'And from your long experience you think the FitzMorris women …'

He nodded his head slowly. 'Could be. It's not uncommon to have three generations all tainted with the same evil tendencies.'

Mrs May's bland eyes danced as she explained, 'That Zara certainly knew the poor murdered soul better than most – there was a time she was with him a lot. I saw them together, friendly like, more than once.'

Peter nodded. 'So you noticed that too.'

Mrs May felt a warm happiness radiate through her and she walked home with a spring in her step.

Peter Wilson walked back to his place at a more ponderous pace. *Now is probably the time to give young Corman another call and put the lad on the right footing – give him the heads up about Zara and that Harper chap.*

Up the high street, in the smart deli with its blue awning, Sophie and her son heard the news at about the same time but they felt none of Mrs May's glee.

Sophie put down her cheese knife and stared at Vivian Plover, while her son, David, stopped arranging red tomatoes on the vegetable table.

Both Sophie and David were as clean and shiny as their deli. In their crisp blue aprons, they exuded an air of all-American wholesomeness that went with the sparkling white teeth and the Levis. The unexpected revelation took them by surprise.

Vivian seemed unaware of their consternation and continued talking in a monotone. 'I never cared much for the man but still one wouldn't want anyone to come to an end like that – so undignified. Oh, and I'll have a jar of pickled walnuts too; the Lord Lieutenant is coming for supper and he's rather partial to them.' Vivian's lips hardly moved as she spoke, her red lipstick a thin, emotionless line. Her starched floral dress crackled as she reached into her wicker basket to check her shopping list.

Her husband, Christopher, stood a diffident two paces behind her. He had the same resigned expression in his soulful eyes as his chocolate working cocker spaniel, who was sitting on the pavement, patiently watching them through the window.

Sophie reached across the expansive glass counter to pluck a neat black jar from the shelf and ring it up. 'And you say poor Dee found him?'

'Well, I think it was all of them. Zara and Amelia were there too. But I'm not sure about 'poor Dee' – I've always been a bit suspicious of the way she's always smiling. And I'll have a few slices of prosciutto and some salami and olives.'

Christopher cleared his throat. 'I think that's a bit much.'

'Not really, there will be ten of us for supper.'

'I didn't mean the meat – I don't think Dee's suspicious, she's just got one of those jolly dispositions.' Christopher had spoken with the utmost politeness but Vivian swung around and gave him a 'Just you wait until I get you home!' glare that made both Christopher and his watchful spaniel shrink.

Blossom told Ken over her cubicle at work. She spoke against the background noise of low office chat and louder laughter as a group of accountant executives clustered around the water cooler.

'Oh Mr Pilbersek, the police found the body in the woods.' She looked up at him breathlessly, a pink highlighter in her hand.

He overlooked the astringent smell of the pen and the glitter that had somehow gotten on her work suit and placed a strong calming hand over hers. Leaning close, he whispered, 'Miss Fryderberg.' He swallowed. 'Blossom. Don't worry, I'll deal with everything.'

She bit her bottom lip. 'Oh, Mr Pilbersek, you've never called me Blossom before.'

He flushed, withdrew his hand, stood up straight and in a business-like tone said, 'Miss Fryderberg, is there anything else troubling you?'

'Well, yes.'

'What is it?'

'I'm totally out of my clown makeup – my white face paint and my red – and I'm booked for a party tomorrow afternoon.'

Ken swallowed again. He looked into Blossom's wide shining blue eyes and murmured, 'Why don't you pop round to mine after work today? I've got plenty.'

Blossom blushed. 'Oh! Mr Pilbersek!'

Robert and Francesco both heard it from their cleaning lady.

Mrs Jenkins, pail and mop clashing against the door jam, burst into Francesco's kitchen at the Flying Pheasant. The kitchen was a monument to chrome and modernity and Francesco took pride in the efficient way he ran it. His domain was as lean and wiry as his physique and he knew the food he produced was sublime.

'Heard the latest?' she asked.

Francesco looked up from reviewing that day's menu; the watercress was good so he was going to use it in a soup and there'd be plenty for a duck salad with segments of blood oranges.

Francesco's attitude towards Mrs Jenkins fluctuated. At times he felt warmly towards her; her bulk and energy reminded him of his mother. At other times he just found her annoying. He regarded her, her big smile, ample bosoms and strong arms.

She took this look as encouragement. 'Well! That Dee FitzMorris has only gone and found another one.'

He didn't need to ask what she was talking about, he already knew, but for form's sake he said, 'Another what?'

'Corpse!' she declared with triumph.

All Francesco could think about was how pale and withdrawn Gina had become. All the life and gaiety had drained out of her and she no longer sang Verdi as she pottered around the pub. He missed the deep vibrancy of her voice and the passion of the soaring notes but most of all, he longed to hear her untroubled laughter once more.

Later on, Mrs Jenkins moved on to cleaning Paul and Robert's house. She didn't really like cleaning for them; for a start, they were usually out and she did like to have someone to chat with while she worked. Secondly, their home was always so neat, there was nothing for her to get her teeth into. For Mrs Jenkins, there was satisfaction in transforming dirt and squalor to pristine order.

For once she was in luck as Robert had popped in to pick up a sweater.

'Have you heard the news?' she asked, shouting over the hum of the cordless Dyson.

Robert shook his head, his crushed-raspberry sweater in his hands. Mrs Jenkins thought he looked pale; there were dark smudges under his eyes.

'You not sleeping, love?' she asked, turning off the Dyson and cocking her head to one side.

Robert shrugged. 'Oh, you know.'

'Oh, I do! My Mr Jenkins, God rest his soul, had a rare old time with sleep or rather with not sleeping, he'd toss—'

'Excuse me, Mrs Jenkins, but I'm meeting a client in half an hour, so I must rush.'

Mrs Jenkins looked affronted as she blurted out, 'Fine, far be it from me to hold you up, I just thought, you being acquainted with Justin Harper, you'd want to know that he's turned up dead as a dodo and dressed as a clown!'

She finished triumphantly and clicked the Dyson back on.

For Robert, the room began to spin and he leaned against a chair. *Will this nightmare never end?*

Chapter 16

While Nicholas Corman had felt drained by the day's activities, the FitzMorrises were invigorated. Giving their statements had taken less time than the intrusive forensic tests but now it was all done and they were free for Zara to drive them back to Little Warthing. It was late afternoon by the time they reached Dee's home but the sun was still shining and there was some warmth behind it.

'Nothing like finding a corpse in a coppice to chase away any sense of tiredness. We've been up since before dawn and yet, I'm totally revved up,' commented Amelia as they parked outside Honeysuckle Cottage.

'I'll make us all some camomile tea. That should calm us down,' said Dee as they got out of the car.

'How extraordinary! Just look at that!' hissed Zara glancing towards Mrs May's bleak bungalow with its excess of concrete and scarcity of greenery.

There was Mrs May. Her bloodless, waxen features were set in hard lines as she regarded the FitzMorrises. Her tight grey perm was as rigid as her posture. Hands on her hips, she was the embodiment of disapproval, which was to be expected.

What was quite out of the ordinary was the cosy way she was having a tête-à-tête with Peter Wilson. Standing very close to her, he joined her in sending the three FitzMorris ladies his condemnation. He glared at them, a look that did not match his MCC tie, potbelly and ponytail. Unbeknown to Dee and co, this was round two of the May-Wilson conference, a sort of 'après the Co-op rendezvous'.

'I thought the only person Mrs May disliked more than you, Mother, was her other neighbour, Peter Wilson.' Zara spoke in an undertone, grinning at the incongruity of seeing the two together.

Dee gave both her neighbours a bright smile and wave, whilst under her breath she whispered, 'That's what I thought too, dear. How very odd.'

Amelia who was still wearing her green corset with its petal skirt looked from Mrs May to Peter Wilson. Her saffron locks had come loose from the sensible ponytail she had worn for birdwatching so that her curls fell in a luxuriant cascade over her narrow shoulders.

She shrugged and said, 'Not really, it's simply a case of "my enemy's enemy is my friend." Now, can we hurry up and get inside? I need something to drink.'

'Just give me a second, dear, and we can have iced camomile tea and honey in the garden,' soothed Dee, reaching for her house keys from her bag.

It was more like ten minutes than the one second promised before the three of them were relaxing in the comfy chairs Dee kept set up around the table. This spot was ideal; sunny, but not too sunny. Lavender and catmint fragranced the air and many bees hummed happily. Honeysuckle and a budding rambling rose climbed up a handy tree. Dee had left a water hose on the path and there was a large watering can nearby, but otherwise the garden was neat and tidy. Colourful garden birds flitted in and out of the trees. Nearby someone was having a barbecue and mouthwatering smells of meat sizzling over charcoal wafted in the air.

The camomile flowers floated between the ice cubes in their glasses. Being sweetened by honey, it was the perfect antidote to dead bodies.

Dee regarded Amelia. 'You know, dear, I may have said it earlier but that whole green pixie look is really most fetching.'

Amelia smiled and slipping her sunglasses on, added, 'You're not the only one who thinks that!'

'Oh, do tell, darling!' Dee urged, leaning forward.

Amelia tilted her head back and with the suggestion of a smile said, 'Let's just say that Josh was finding it difficult to focus on my statement.'

Dee nodded. 'Statements are tricky things, The sweet girl taking mine got quite agitated when I was saying how we heard the robin singing shortly before we found Justin dead, but that it wasn't long after that, that the blackbird and song thrush joined in.'

'Why did she get agitated over that?' enquired Zara, as she leant back in her chair and tilted her face towards the sun. She had refreshed her makeup and run a comb through her hair but she was still in her khaki combat trousers and black top, so she looked rather like a Lara Croft who'd been to finishing school.

'Well, she didn't seem to think it was relevant. But, as I explained to her, we were all there to record the birds, not to find dead bodies.'

'Robins aside, Justin's murder really is unfortunate,' murmured Zara without opening her eyes.

'Especially for Justin!' quipped Amelia with a grin.

'Well yes, I suppose so, but it puts us in a very awkward position,' continued Zara.

'Really dear? How so?' enquired Dee politely, taking a sip of her iced tea.

'Not to put too fine a point on it, I'm afraid that with Justin's demise, you – Mother – are the only viable suspect for the two murders,' Zara explained with a hint of an apologetic tone.

'Oh,' was all Dee said but her mind was whirling.

That's hardly accurate! The village is positively buzzing with suspects: there's the fiery-tempered Francesco – actually the whole Rossellini family have had issues with both Bernier and Harper. Then much as I hate to contemplate it, dear Robert seems to be going through some mental turmoil that's making him behave totally out of character and he has reasons to want both corpses out of the picture. Then there is the clown link ... Can it really just be a coincidence that the dead bodies were made to look like clowns and we already have two clowns residing in this very village? And finally – she gave her daughter a surreptitious glance – *you, Zara FitzMorris, seem to be glossing over your own link to the latest murder victim. The police are bound to be as curious as I am as to exactly what your relationship with Justin Harper was.*

They contemplated their drinks. The camomile flowers had turned the water a pale yellow while the ice had caused a misting of condensation on the outsides of their tall glasses. A blackbird was singing on a nearby tree and the bees continued humming. Other than that, there was silence until Zara took command.

'Given that we don't really have any suspects,' she said, 'let's start with what we do know.'

Dee looked innocent, without a hint of her thoughts of, *that's what you think!*

The silence resumed, broken only by a squirrel with a fluffy tail making a dash along the top of the hedge; evidently, Zara and Amelia couldn't think of anything that was useful in solving murders and clearing Dee's name.

Eventually, Zara declared, 'Clowns!'

'What, dear?' asked Dee while dubiously watching a cabbage white butterfly fluttering towards her veg patch.

'The one thing we do know is that there is some link to the murders with clowns,' continued Zara, looking between her mother and her daughter.

Dee blinked and focussed her attention away from the pesky butterfly and back onto Zara. Curious, she asked, 'So?'

Zara explained, 'We need to work out what the significance of the corpses being made up as clowns is. This is one for our resident psychology student.'

The women looked at Amelia. In her present get-up, she looked more like a pixie than a psychologist with the ability to profile murderers.

Amelia paused, considered, took a sip of her drink, and then said, 'The murderer is probably someone who feels deeply inferior to others. By making the bodies of the victims the object of ridicule in death, the murderer probably gets some sense of superiority.'

'What a load of utter bunkum!' The retort was unequivocal and came from Mrs May's side of the fence.

They looked up to see her perched on a stepladder, shears in hand, supposedly trimming her hedge. She was obviously more intent on eavesdropping than gardening.

Unperturbed by Dee, Zara and Amelia all looking daggers at her, Mrs May continued, 'The clown represents the rustic fool. It is to emphasise to society, as a whole, that they are a figure of fun.'

Zara was mentally composing a few scathing words, focussing on the phrase 'nosy parker', but Amelia beat her to it. 'How interesting! I'm sure you have lots of ideas about suspects too.'

Mrs May tucked her chin in and nodded, a gesture designed to suggest both wisdom and mystery.

Amelia lavished a broad smile on Dee's neighbour and asked, 'Why don't you come and join us?'

Mrs May raised her thin eyebrows and regarded her with incredulity. Surprise was soon replaced by joy and she glowed with happiness; well, she didn't look quite as crab-faced. Dee gripped the table to steady herself and Zara gave an audible intake of breath.

'Alright!' nodded Mrs May as her head and her shoulders disappeared from the top of the fence.

'What on earth are you thinking of?' Zara hissed.

Amelia complacently took another sip of her drink and replied, 'Keep your friends close and your enemies closer.'

'My, you are full of old-world wisdom today,' Zara commented flatly, while Dee hurried into the house to open the front door and get more tea.

Unruffled, Amelia smiled. 'What are you always saying to me about sarcasm?'

Zara simply smiled too and they awaited the arrival of Mrs May. She soon appeared following Dee out of the house. Mrs May glanced towards the infamous veg patch and smiled before sitting down at the table.

Without any introduction, she drew herself up to her full height, inhaled deeply and directed a stare at Amelia which was dripping with judgement. 'You should be careful about drinking so much camomile tea.'

'What?'

'It can be dangerous if you are pregnant.'

'What! I'm not pregnant!' spluttered Amelia.

'Well, you easily could be if you go around wearing such suggestive outfits like that nymph thing you've got on now. I heard what you said about that young police officer.'

Amelia's body stiffened, lost for words. She stared at Mrs May and her mouth fell open.

Zara happily handed her a tissue to mop up the spray of tea and whispered, 'What were you saying about keeping your friends close?'

Mrs May had already turned her attention to Dee. 'And as for you! Call yourself a birdwatcher? Of course the robin is always the first bird to give song in woodlands.'

Amelia rallied. She leaned forward across the table and in full sarcasm mode said, 'You are a mine of information! Is there anything you don't know about?'

'Not a lot! I was, after all, a librarian for many years.' Mrs May's flat grey exterior took on an aura of self-satisfaction; her pointy chin jutted up, she thrust out her meagre chest and gave Amelia a dismissive nod.

'So, do you know about embalming?' enquired Dee brightly, whilst pouring everyone more iced camomile tea from a glass jug.

'Anyone can find out how to embalm. You just have to look on the internet. There's a realm of information about Egyptian rituals that have obsessed crime writers as well as more modern methods. But I'm not surprised you don't know anything about such basic information, after all, you're not that bright, are you? I nearly fell off my ladder in amazement when not one of the three of you could come up with a viable suspect!'

'So, who do *you* think did it?' enquired Amelia, eyeing Mrs May over her sunglasses.

'Well, that retired Police Chief is suspicious for a start!'

Dee stopped doling out the tea and jerked her head up. 'What? Peter Wilson?'

'You were being very chummy with him just now, especially if you suspect him of double homicide.' Zara's tones were as icy as the tea. She leant back elegantly in her garden chair and regarded Mrs May.

'The man is ancient ... and quite infirm,' stammered Dee.

'He's younger than you! Don't be fooled by his potbelly. He's six foot four of pure muscle and determination. Besides, he's been a lot fitter since he had his knees done.'

'Oh I have heard that knee surgery can be wonderful,' mused Dee, 'but even so, I can't see what his motive would be.'

'I can,' said Zara speculatively. 'Bernier and Harper were both law-breakers or, at the very least, law-benders. Peter Wilson spent years upholding law and order; it would hardly be surprising if it went to his head.'

Amelia added, 'Or to use the psychological term – if he's gone a bit crackers.'

Mrs May nodded enthusiastically. 'Obviously, there's something a bit odd with him with his MCC tie, his ponytail ... and then there's that radio!' At the mention of the radio, Mrs May's voice rose and her washed-out countenance took on a waxen hue. 'If it's not heavy metal, it's the cricket. No consideration for others! The number of times I've been on to the council about it – but he's untouchable. Ex-police chiefs are above the law!'

Dee raised a concerned eyebrow at Mrs May, while Amelia made a mental note that the mere mention of the dreaded radio was obviously a trigger.

As Dee regarded her grey and uninspiring neighbour, she was reminded of a misty memory. There was something in those grey furtive eyes that reminded her of a scene from far away in the distant past. Dee recalled sitting like this, in the warmth of the early summer sun. It was many years earlier and Dee was in her smart grammar-school uniform. She was with her friends and they were all giggling and whispering confidences to each other, the way teenagers do. A smaller, younger Mrs May sat a bit away, totally alone in her secondhand uniform which was both too big for her and grubby. When Mrs May had mentioned they'd been to the same school, Dee had had no memory of her but now this ghost of a child came to haunt her.

'More camomile?' suggested Dee.

Zara opted instead for deflecting Mrs May onto another subject before she self-combusted. 'Any other suspects?'

'Well ... there's that grumpy old clown.'

'Ken Pilbersek?'

'Yes. He's another one who's obviously not normal. A grown man dressing up as a clown! Even stranger that he thinks of clowning as an art form. Sees himself as an artist – the inheritor of a rich cultural history, not just someone to make children laugh.'

Amelia nodded, 'And of course, he's got a thing for clowns and would have loads of makeup and costumes to hand.'

'And what's more, he's had dealing with Bernier and Justin Harper,' agreed Zara.

'Oh, I do hope it's not him! He's so good about feeding the birds and I think he's got a crush on the nice Blossom Bim Bam,' mused Dee.

'Blossom? You mean that Julia Fryderberg?' Mrs May sounded aghast. 'I don't know what there is about her that you think is nice! She's a menace on that bicycle of hers. And she's so chaotic! Not to mention how irresponsible she is, taking that mutt out without even having a doggy-poop bag to hand. I wouldn't put it past her to be the murderer. All that smiling and singing and those ridiculous bright happy floral dresses! It's too good to be true if you ask me!'

Zara coolly regarded Mrs May. 'You've left out the most obvious candidate.'

'Who?'

'Why, you, Mrs May!'

Mrs May's cold grey eyes narrowed as she regarded Zara and her thin lips flattened. Eventually, she sneered, 'Don't be ridiculous! Look at the size of me! Do you really think I could haul a tall chap like Justin Harper up a tree?'

'How did you know he was up a tree? And how did you know he was a clown, for that matter? The police have not given a press release report yet,' asked Zara sharply.

'I had to get a tin of soup from the village shop this morning.'

'That would explain it – who needs news reporters when we've got a village shop?' agreed Dee.

Amelia leapt in with another question. 'But if you're saying you couldn't have done the murderers because of your size and build, how come you were so happy to accuse Granny? She's positively elfin!'

'Unlike your grandmother, I don't do yoga, hiking or martial arts. And I certainly don't have a black belt in Judo!'

'Taekwondo,' corrected Dee.

Mrs May seemed to lose all interest in them and this conversation. Rising to her feet she said, 'Anyway, unlike, you all, who obviously have nothing better to do with your day than to sit around gossiping, I have jobs to attend to.'

Without so much as a 'thank you for the tea', she swept out. Cat, sunbathing in a particularly lush patch of catmint, flicked her tail and gave her retreating back a look of disdain.

Chapter 17

For the next day or two, Dee avoided finding any more dead bodies and generally kept herself away from clowns.

Then came Saturday.

The day had started off gently enough; she began by drinking red bush tea, from one of her mother's beautiful bone china cups. The tea was from Fortnum and Mason's and had a delightful hint of vanilla. She took time over her yoga and then her Taekwondo forms, focusing on her deep tranquil breaths. With each inhalation, she celebrated her connection to life. She felt satisfied with the world at large and all the chaos of the clown bodies seemed far removed from her.

Breakfast was a bowl of crunchy homemade granola with red, juicy strawberries and ruby raspberries followed by a leisurely bath scented with peppermint oil. Later, having indulged in an hour or two of reading a Lavinia Lovelace romance, she felt her need for brocade and gallant gentlemen had been assuaged so she decided it would be pleasant to do a few jobs. First thing in the morning she'd thrown open all the kitchen doors and windows allowing the air and sunshine in. Now she gazed around her kitchen with its many green plants, an inviting bowl of fruit on the side and the elegant arrangement of lilies on the kitchen table. Their fragrance added to the scents borne in by the breeze.

As she looked at the table she was flooded with happy memories. It was sturdy, made of reclaimed pine, and she'd had it since Zara was a child. *So many happy meals! That table has witnessed a lot of laughter and a few tears.*

She felt the urge to show the table some love, so reached into the cupboard under the kitchen sink and took out a small round tub of beeswax and a soft cloth. As she firmly polished the table's knots and grain she could see Zara, in pigtails, excitedly telling her about a triumph on the hockey field, then later, it was Amelia, with her milk teeth recently lost, earnestly explaining that now she had learnt to ride a bicycle she planned to run away and join a circus. Dee smiled as she polished on, enveloped in the clean, homely smell of the beeswax. In a way Amelia's wish had come true, the three of them had taken off for many travel adventures, all of which had been planned at this very table, with maps and guidebooks strewn across its top.

Apart from family memories, this table contained the echoes of so many joyful meals with their friends Sophie and David, giggling over culture clashes, since they lived half the time in the States and half in the Cotswolds. Then there was that delightful November evening, when, with a storm raging outside and a power cut inside, Robert and his mother had sung duets from current West End shows by candlelight; even Paul had found it amusing. She stopped mid-circular stroke – there it was again, an intrusive twinge of fear in the pit of her stomach.

Perhaps I need to cultivate acceptance and acknowledge that until these murders are solved I can't have true serenity. But what if the murderer is a friend as well as a neighbour?

She hastily thrust aside the thought along with the beeswax and went outside. As ever, simply being in her garden gave her pleasure and she happily pottered around, plucking off a deadhead here and pulling up a weed there. She watered her herb garden and mused about her family.

I'm so pleased Zara appears totally unaffected by Justin's death – obviously, their relationship was a flash in the pan rather than anything deeper. And Amelia was, mercifully, unmoved by the sight of dead bodies – in fact, she was interested rather than horrified so perhaps a career in criminal profiling would suit her.

She stopped watering and looked up at the blue sky. *A walk is definitely in order. I'll loop up past the playground and tennis courts then drop back down into the village via the high street. Who knows, I might pop into Robert's shop and say hello – although with it being Saturday afternoon it may be heaving with tourists. Still, I can always wave through the window.*

She checked herself in the mirror and quickly decided that her neat navy trousers and top looked rather too austere. She popped upstairs and added some bright beads she'd picked up in Kenya and an equally colourful woven bag that had come from a beach in Thailand. Satisfied that she no longer looked dull, she ran a comb through her sleek bob, applied some lip balm, bid farewell to Cat, and left.

Outside her front gate, she glanced up and down the road. There were a few cars but what struck her most was the absence of bullying neighbours.

Well, that's a mercy – no Mrs May or Mr Wilson, lying in wait to pounce on me.

She strolled in the direction of the playground, all the while admiring the froth of white cow parsley beside the path. She inhaled its heady scent, *a real herald of summer.* A blackbird burst into song and Dee smiled at another sign that summer was coming.

After a few more moments of walking a thought struck Dee. *How unusual, here I am almost at the playground and I haven't bumped into a single person I know.* She paused to let a large group of elderly Germans pass. *Naturally, there are plenty of tourists, phones in hand and bemused expressions on their faces. But I've not seen anyone I can pass the time of day with.* She stepped off the path to allow a harried-looking tour guide with a bunch of raucous French teenagers to hurry towards the church and no doubt a history lecture that none of her charges would listen to. *Although it's probably for the best not seeing anyone I know as I'm really not feeling robust enough to deal with snubs and cutting comments.*

She pushed to one side unpleasant thoughts and focussed on the pleasures she had in store. Dee liked the playground, or to be more precise she liked the energy of the people who visited it. The joyful sounds of children laughing on the swings and roundabout always made her feel happy.

She crested the hill and squeaked the metal gate open. As village playgrounds go, this was a fine one; there were woodchips under the swings and monkey bars and thick black matting under the rope climbing frame. The sun glinted off the slide and the swings squeaked as they swung back and forth. The equipment was swarming with children, running, laughing and climbing while a group of teenagers who thought they were cool watched on from a distance. On the nearby benches, mothers, equipped with plasters and snacks, chatted as their babies lay in their strollers and kicked chubby legs. The food had drawn the attention of two especially intelligent birds, a canny pair of jackdaws who watched with keen blue eyes, ready to snatch any titbit dropped.

Dee gazed at the happy scene then her eyes were drawn to a little knot of older children. They were at that in-between age, perhaps nine or ten; too old to be under their mothers' constant supervision but too young to be permitted to hang around with the hallowed teenagers.

About five of these in-betweeners had formed a circle around a small white dog that was wagging its tail, delighted by the attention. Completely trusting that everyone in the world loved it, the bright-eyed bundle of exuberant fluff was going up to one child after another for cuddles. Dee walked up to get a closer look.

'Your dog, Missus?' enquired a freckled boy of about eight.

'She's ever so sweet,' added an older girl with blonde curls; while the little dog exuberantly turned circles.

Dee smiled and shook her head. She recognised it as Blossom's Petal complete with its pink collar.

Did Blossom say something about Petal belonging to an aunt? Anyway, no need to go into that now.

Dee cleared her throat and said cheerily, 'No, she isn't mine, but I know who she belongs to.'

'We just found her here, all alone – lost,' commented the boy by way of conversation.

'You obviously took very good care of her,' Dee assured them all and they looked suitably gratified. 'Now, what can I use as a lead?' she wondered out loud.

'Half a sec …' said the freckled boy. He turned out his trouser pocket and, along with a half-chewed toffee, pulled out a length of string. With great expertise, he tied it to the collar.

Dee thanked them politely and headed into the village with Petal trotting happily at her heels. Walking downhill and spurred on by Petal's enthusiasm, her return trip was made in a far shorter time than her leisurely stroll up to the playing field.

As they approached Blossom's home, the diminutive mutt started pulling excitedly and Dee hoped the string knot would hold.

When they reached the front of Blossom's tiny cottage, Dee admired the eclectic collection of pots and flowers that surrounded the front door. Somehow the profusion of colourful flowers planted in a surprising variety of containers, from painted watering cans to old rubber boots, whilst far from chic, looked inviting.

Dee knocked on the door and the dog yapped, but no one came. She knocked again, louder this time. The dog seemed to take this as an instruction to bark with more enthusiasm.

Still there came no response.

She was just wondering what to do next when a voice behind her stammered, 'She's not in. I've tried knocking.'

Dee swung round to see Ken Pilbersek. He was not in his normal dowdy clothes but instead wearing a bright yellow checked suit with a giant daisy pinned to his lapel. His sparse greying hair was replaced by a vibrant red wig. His frown and pencilled brows were at odds with his painted red smile and nose.

'Joseph Popov, I presume!' quipped Dee.

Ken either did not get the Dr Livingstone reference or he didn't find it funny. Either way, he didn't smile. Instead, he shook his head and muttered, 'I can't imagine where she can be.'

'Oh I'm sure it's nothing to worry about; she's probably at a children's party and this little rascal got out of the house while her mistress was out,' Dee said soothingly.

Ken glanced at the dog who fixed him with its black button eyes and wagged its tail so hard its whole body wriggled. Ken didn't look impressed. 'No! You're wrong! It's not her dog; it's her auntie's. Blossom is just watching it while her auntie has a holiday in Skegness. And she isn't at a children's party! She was meant to be but she didn't show up! That in itself is very unlike her. She may be scatty in many ways, but she would *never* let kiddies down.'

'How do you know she missed a party?' asked Dee.

'I got an emergency call.'

Dee had a vision of Ken in a clown version of The Bat Cave perhaps reading a paper when suddenly a call came through on the hallowed red phone and Ken nobly leapt into action – without a cape but with his trusty red nose. 'What? On a sort of clown hotline?'

Ken was rattling the door handle and looking through the letterbox, he gave Dee a sharp, 'Yes!'

Dee was still puzzled. 'But I thought you didn't do children's parties.'

'I don't as a rule but I couldn't let the honour of the clown community come into disrespect, much less let Blossom down.'

Dee felt quite moved. 'So you did it for her?'

He stopped fiddling with the door and with eyes creased with makeup and emotion, nodded. 'Yes!'

Dee persisted in optimistic mode, 'Perhaps she's just gone somewhere. The library perhaps – I know she's very keen on reading.'

'She goes to the library every Wednesday on her way home from work – it's their late-night opening. And besides, as I've already told you, she would *never* have forgotten she was booked for a child's birthday.'

In a patient tone, Dee said, 'People do make mistakes; perhaps she double-booked … doesn't she also volunteer at the old people's home?'

Ken was restlessly looking around the garden as if Blossom might be hiding behind the painted wheelbarrow. 'Yes. It's a waste of her talent, but they all love her. She gets everyone singing.' He looked misty-eyed, or at least Dee thought he did. It was difficult to tell with all the makeup. 'Anyway, she can't be there now; she goes every Tuesday and today is Saturday.'

Dee was beginning to have an uneasy feeling in the pit of her stomach and her heart was beating strongly. 'Oh, dear! I hate to say this, but perhaps … something has happened to her. She might have collapsed or had an accident. Let's go around the back and see if we can get in.'

She led the way around the side of the cottage and with difficulty they picked their way, stepping over a hose pipe, a rake and what looked like a toy pink tricycle. Their path was further impeded by an overgrown spotted laurel that had to be pushed past. The back of Blossom's home was much like the front; bright and chaotic in a happy sort of way. Although the back garden was only about half the size of Dee's, it was crammed full of bright flowers and even brighter pots. There was a small white round table and two ill-assorted chairs. It was shielded from the sun by an enormous umbrella covered in a daisy pattern.

The garden shed had been made to look like a little fairy cottage with a painted window, complete with a flower box overflowing with blooms. Against the shed Blossom's bicycle leaned. Ken pointed at it.

'See! Her bicycle is here – she must be in the house!' He spoke under his breath while tugging at his collar.

Dee felt herself begin to perspire and when she spoke her voice was more rushed and high-pitched than normal. 'I'll try the back door,' she said, darting over towards the French window which served as a back door into the house. Petal scampered excitedly beside her.

She tugged at it but it didn't open. Turning to Ken with wide eyes and a pounding heart she said, 'It's locked.'

'Let me try.' Ken pulled, but to no avail.

Dee peered through the window hoping to spot Blossom dozing on the sofa and pushing away her fears of a clown killer on the loose in the area. *Blossom has to be alright, she's so young – so very much alive.*

Eventually, she sighed. 'I don't like the look of this!'

Ken joined her. As he gazed through at the empty kitchen, he slowly shook his head and said, 'Nor do I. I don't like the look of this at all. Nothing matches. There are letters and bills all over the sideboard. Some of them might be important! And look, she's left the vacuum out. She really does need someone to take care of her!'

Dee regarded him coolly. 'That's not quite what I meant.' The pup was tugging at the string and whining. 'What is it, dear? Are you trying to tell us something? Do you know where Blossom is? Can you show us?' Dee spoke encouragingly in that slightly high-pitched voice reserved for babies and animals.

Ken glowered at her, which looked odd with the clown makeup on. Sourly he said, 'She's a cockapoo, not Lassie!'

The pooch obviously had not understood, because at that moment she pulled away yanking the string lead out of Dee's hand. She ran yapping over to the garden shed and started to paw at the door.

Both Dee and Ken gave chase. Dee reached the shed first and tried the door.

'It's padlocked,' pointed out Ken.

Dee looked frantically around the shed for another way in. 'And we can't peer through the window as it's fake – only painted on.'

Desperation mounting she heard, above the thumping of her own heart, a slight sound, she froze. 'Listen, Ken. Do you hear something?'

Ken threw Petal a look and said sourly, 'Only that mutt yapping.'

'No, I'm sure I can hear something coming from inside,' persisted Dee, pressing her ear against the door.

'Will you be quiet!' commanded Ken and, surprisingly, Petal was instantly silent.

He too put his ear to the door and after a second he excitedly murmured, 'Perhaps you're right.'

By now Dee's mind was as chaotic as Blossom's kitchen. 'What should we do?'

Ken stood straight, put his shoulders back, and raised his red nose in the air. With great poise and command, he declared, 'I will break the door down.'

In a twinkling of yellow-checked suit and daisy, he charged at the door, shoulder first. There was a cracking of bolts, and a splintering of wood and the door fell to one side.

And there inside was Blossom. She was bound and gagged and tied to a garden chair, her demure yellow-flowered dress a sharp contrast to the ropes wrapped tightly around her body and at her ankles. She had evidently been en route to the children's party as she had her full clown makeup on. There were pitiful tear tracks down her cheeks from her weeping. A red-and-white spotted handkerchief was acting as an effective gag. Gently, Ken untied it.

With watery eyes, she stared up at him. 'Oh Mr Pilbersek, I was so frightened!'

Ken gazed at her tenderly and swept her still-bound body into his arms. 'I'm here. I'll look after you,' he crooned, their matching red noses only inches apart.

Petal rushed up to Blossom and enthusiastically started to lick her.

Relief flooded through Dee. Her knees felt weak and she was quite dizzy but she knew what needed to be done. 'Let's get Blossom into the house and get her a nice mug of camomile tea. Where's the key to the back door? I'll pop the kettle on whilst Ken unties you.'

'Coffee!' said Ken, while fending off excited licking kisses from the dog.

'Good and strong, please,' added Blossom through her tears.

'I'll make it for you, love, just the way you like it,' murmured Ken, fiddling with a knot at her left ankle.

He reminded Dee of a clown knight errant, vowing allegiance to his fair lady clown.

'The key …?' prompted Dee.

'It's not locked; it just sticks. I've been meaning to get it fixed for ages,' confessed Julia.

'Don't worry – I'll mend it for you,' declared Ken nobly.

'Will you? Can you? Oh, Mr Pilbersek!'

Dee left them to it.

It was with a great deal of difficulty she got the door open. It took a bit of time to locate the kettle as it was buried under a cuddly teddy and what seemed to be a pile of clean washing.

A few minutes later, Ken bustled in and solicitously guided Blossom to a chair. In his bright-yellow suit, he reminded Dee of a cross between a mother hen and an overgrown canary. He clucked over Blossom, tutted and rolled his eyes as he found the cafetière hidden among the debris of an art project that involved a lot of pink glitter. The quest for the tin of freshly ground coffee was more challenging; it was eventually discovered in the fridge. Ken took the lid off the canister, inhaled and smiled.

The heady scent of pure caffeine wafted across the kitchen and hit Dee. Hastily, she dived into her bag for her emergency camomile. Tangling a pyramid bag of yellow-flowered calm on a string, she said, 'Tea for me please.'

Ken raised an eyebrow but obliged.

Dee watched, with concern, as Blossom took her first sip of the dark and dangerous brew that Ken had so lovingly prepared. She seemed to recall from her days as a Girl Guide that one was meant to give victims of crime tea with lots of sugar in it. Dee wasn't sure if it was because the psychological effect of tea was so soothing – after all, if one had a cup of PG tips or Tetley in one's hands, one felt that life couldn't be all bad – or if it was the sugar in the tea that helped to raise one's blood sugar levels. *But then, of course, so much has changed since I was a girl and perhaps now the advice is to knock victims out with caffeine.*

As she observed her, Blossom certainly seemed to revive. After only the first mouthful a slight smile played over her lips and by the third she felt strong enough to tell them what had happened.

'I was on my way to little Daisy Hubert's sixth birthday party when I found I had a puncture.' She broke off abruptly as an unpleasant thought struck her. 'Poor Daisy! Her birthday will have been ruined!'

Ken gently patted her hand. 'It's all right; she had a magical day. I went instead of you.'

'Did you? Did you really?' Their clown eyes looked lovingly at each other.

'So what happened next?' intervened Dee.

'Well, I looked for the puncture repair kit but I couldn't find it. It wasn't on the sideboard or dresser.' She gestured towards the chaos of papers, party hats and balloons on both these objects of furniture. 'Then I remembered I'd put it in the garden shed.'

'The garden shed? Why there?' enquired Dee.

Exasperated at Dee's dimness, Ken explained, 'The bicycle lives outside and the shed is outside!'

'Well I was just looking in the shed when little doggy started barking, didn't you Petal darling?' Petal, who was sitting at Blossom's feet, looking up at her adoringly, took this as her cue to start barking. After a bit of fussing Blossom continued, 'But before I could check what was upsetting her, I felt an enormous blow on the back of my head. I must have lost consciousness for a moment as the next thing I knew I was gagged and tied.'

As she started to cry again Ken gallantly leapt to his feet and held her once more. Dee rang for the ambulance as well as the police.

Not long afterwards, Dee was back at her own home with another cup of camomile in her hand, Cat on her knee and Zara for added company. 'Do you know, dear, I really am getting rather good at giving police statements – I suppose practice makes perfect.' A wistful look came into her eyes as she gazed out of the window. 'I can't tell you how romantic it was – Ken looked quite dashing with his red nose and the giant daisy in his lapel. It must have been something about the manly way he swept Blossom into his arms and held her so protectively.'

'Hmm,' was all Zara replied; her lips were a straight line and she tapped her fingers impatiently on the tabletop.

'Perhaps you had to have been there to have appreciated how touching it was,' commented Dee, a little deflated.

Zara was thoughtfully stirring her tea. 'No! It's not that! I was just thinking.'

'Thinking what, dear?'

'Well, isn't it a bit suspicious?'

'In what way?'

'Strange, that Julia – Blossom – whatever you want to call her, wasn't actually killed. She just received a bump on the head. And what's more, isn't it only in fiction that a bang on the head renders you suitably out of it for enough time for you to be tied up? Maybe Mrs May is right: perhaps Julia's 'Oh so sweetness' is just an act.'

Dee had been stroking Cat, but in her surprise, she stopped. Cat looked up reproachfully and Dee obediently resumed the caress. 'I think you're being a little harsh. Julia is a dear. Besides, how would she have been able to tie herself up, let alone lock herself in the shed?'

'She could have had an accomplice! Did you see how secure those knots were? Perhaps Ken and Julia are in it together! And the whole of today's drama was just to throw suspicion off them and you were a convenient witness. After all, they both admitted to having unpleasant dealings with Bernier and I'm sure if we dig a little deeper, we'll find that they knew Justin Harper too.'

Chapter 18

The following day Dee was slightly concerned about Cat. She was acting out of character; for the second day in a row, she was prepared to bestow on Dee the great honour of permitting her royal personage to be stroked by her.

She had opted for a Persian cat because she had been assured by a book about the breed that they were affectionate and adored human company. Unlike Dee, Cat had not read the glossy book, entitled, '*All You Need To Know About Your Persian Kitten*'. The book was packed full of advice and appealing feline photos. Not being *au fait* with this information, Cat persisted in being disdainful of most of the human race. She did, however, have a few chosen humans, on whom she lavished an extra dose of dislike – Zara for instance – but on the whole she preferred to ignore people; it was beneath her dignity to acknowledge them.

She submitted to a daily brush, comb and eye-clean from Dee as Cat did like to look her best. This slight personal vanity had its advantages; the book stated that washing one's Persian could be a challenge as cats tend to hate water but as you know, Cat had not read the book and consequently she positively skipped into her box whenever it was time for her to visit the professional groomers.

Now Cat had deigned to sit on Dee's knee and for this privilege, Dee knew she would have to pay the price. It would take at least fifteen minutes of using the sticky roller to remove the long silky hairs from her clothes before she could go out to the village. The effort would be worth it, though, as today Dee was looking especially debonair in shades of orange-gold saffron; a textured midi wrap skirt was topped by a low-slung, wide studded belt and her sandals were flat and stunning.

Cat purred contently. Soothing though stroking the feline was, Dee could not relax.

'You see, Cat, no matter how hard I think, I simply cannot make sense of it,' Dee confided to her uninterested feline friend. 'Who would want to kill both Andrew Bernier and that unpleasant Justin Harper? Even if we leave aside the whole clown angle, I just can't think who would have motive enough against both of them. One or other I could understand. After all, from what Zara has said, Bernier had troops of people that he had in effect blackmailed – or at least bullied – and it would appear that Justin Harper had a positive harem of wealthy middle-aged ladies whom he had misused. But what links the two?'

Cat flicked her long fluffy tail; she was beginning to find Dee's wittering annoying.

'One thing is for sure – it must be someone local. Could Zara be right? Could Ken and Blossom be in league together? They confessed that Bernier had been unpleasant to Blossom, and Ken had got into trouble when he went to warn the powers that be that Bernier was crooked. You never know, it's possible that Justin Harper made a play for Blossom and her savings. The way Ken feels about her, I have no doubt he'd defend her to the end!'

Cat, fed up with Dee's incessant droning on, dug her sharp nails into Dee's flesh before jumping nimbly off her knee. With great dignity, she strolled to the garden, where a sunny patch of catmint awaited her.

Dee stood up. 'Yes, you're right, Cat, I should be getting on. I've got a few bits I need to get from the village shop.' As she whisked the sticky roller up and down her front, her mind went in a new direction.

Perhaps it is Mrs May who is right. Is it possible that the motive for both murders is some local crazed vigilante? Both the victims were wrongdoers. If that is the case, then Mrs May is correct in putting retired Police Chief, Peter Wilson at the head of the suspect list.

She picked up her wicker basket, fortunately, unaware that Cat, from the comfort of her fragrant bed, was purring *'Gracious, the woman can't stop talking even when she's alone.'*

156

Across the village, in their stylish home; Robert and Paul were enjoying their Sunday brunch over the newspapers. Today it was scrambled eggs and smoked salmon with a toasted muffin. The salmon was from a local smokehouse and exceptionally good. As usual, they sat at their small table in the sunny bay window. Paul was picking out news headlines and commenting on them and Robert was thinking of other things. The only thing that was out of the ordinary was what they were drinking, or rather what Robert was having. Paul had struck to his normal cafetière of coffee, rich and aromatic, but Robert did not feel up to its brutish punch, so was sipping Earl Grey from one of his mother's delicate porcelain cups. Pale and subtle in scent and taste, it had a sliver of lemon floating in the amber liquid.

'The situation with China doesn't seem to be getting any better,' muttered Paul, not looking up from his iPad.

'Hmmm,' said Robert. He was contemplating Blossom, or Julia as he tended to think of her. He regretted what had happened to her; it was unfair after she'd been so kind to him when his mother died.

'Robert? Are you listening to me?' There was an edge of irritation in Paul's voice. Robert looked up sharply and yet again, even after all these years, was struck by how good-looking Paul was, with his blue eyes and classic features.

'Sorry, did you say something?'

'I just asked if you wanted me to put some toast on or have you had enough?'

Robert glanced down at his plate; he'd hardly touched his breakfast but Paul hadn't noticed.

'No thank you, I'm okay.'

This seemed to annoy Paul and Robert suspected it was he who wanted toast and that he was hoping to be able to carry on reading the news while Robert made him some.

'You seem rather on edge. Is there something bothering you?' Paul's tone was accusatory rather than solicitous.

Robert shrugged. 'Not really,' he said, while inside he felt that he was disappearing down a black hole of despair. There was an aching void of loss now that his mother had gone. He had no control over it; he felt like a man drowning in a vast ocean, never knowing when the fatal wave would swallow him up. Then there were so many other things beyond his control: Bernier, Harper and now this incident with Blossom. Paul was right, he was on edge; he expected at any moment there would be a knock on the door and the police would arrive.

He smiled and stood up. 'Let me make you some toast.'

'Okay, if you're making some I'd like a slice,' said Paul looking back at his iPad.

Robert was getting out the breadboard as Paul added, 'Can't think why the chancellor thinks that's a good idea; the man's a fool.'

Robert need not have worried about the police banging on his door; both Josh and Nicholas were fully occupied. It might be a Sunday morning but they were at the police station. There were the normal shouts and sirens to be heard. Nicholas, neat in freshly-pressed clothes sat at his tidy desk, surrounded by his bonsai trees. He was reading the report he had just received from the forensic accountant who was looking into Harper's and Bernier's finances. It was only an outline report; both the men's financial dealings were so crooked it was going to take the forensic accountant months to sort them out properly.

Nicholas decided to talk it through with Josh. He left his office and walked silently over to where Josh sat at a shared desk, his area defined by crumbs, crisp packets and a collection of expensive-looking coloured pens. He didn't hear his boss approaching and continued drawing.

Looking over his shoulder Nicholas was surprised; he hadn't realised Josh was so talented. With confident strokes, he was drawing an anime figure. The drawing had the same sweep of the eyes, fine nose and defined full lips that Josh had thanks to his Korean heritage, but this figure was a girl – a very attractive girl. She had a tiny wasp waist, accentuated by the corset she was wearing, her large feline eyes were green and the cascade of curls were picked out in scarlet, orange and gold. Her assertive stance was every inch familiar – here was Amelia FitzMorris in anime form; the only major difference from reality was the pointed pixie ears.

Nicholas decided he need to talk with Josh – the forensic accountant report could wait – but the boy really needed guidance on keeping his professional and private life separate. He batted away a vision of Zara, curvaceous and vivacious at the salsa club, and cleared his throat.

Josh looked up but at that moment, Nicholas' phone rang. Nicholas hoped it wasn't Peter Wilson yet again. The man's hectoring calls, full of assertions and demands were beginning to wear him down.

He glanced at the screen, it wasn't Peter Wilson, it was his mother.

He knew the call would be long, full of embarrassment and far from professional so he went back to his office to take it, leaving Josh to add an elegant sword to his figure.

Peter Wilson was too busy to phone Nicholas that morning although he did have plans to give him some helpful hints about the case that afternoon. For years Peter Wilson had indulged in brunch at the Golf Club on the first Sunday of the month. Originally this had been post a vigorous round of golf; these days, as his able girth testified, he skipped the golf and just went straight for the fried eggs and bacon.

The fine spell of weather was continuing so Peter thought about walking past the tennis courts, crossing the main road and navigating the edge of the rolling green golf course until he reached the wooden clubhouse. The thought was fleeting and he reached for his car keys. They weren't there. He always left them in the bowl on the sideboard as he came in the door. That was where keys had always been kept ever since he and his long-dead wife moved into the bungalow thirty years ago. He swallowed and felt a surge of panic – was he imagining it? Was he getting forgetful?

Pushing the thought away, he opened the drawer of the sideboard where spare keys were kept. There in the drawer was the car key he'd been looking for and the spare. He chortled in relief; he wasn't going senile, he had just misplaced them.

The five-minute drive to the Golf Club had his heart pounding. He swore under his breath. *Why does everyone drive so fast? Have none of these idiots ever read the Highway Code? If I wasn't retired I'd have the area swarming with speed traps!*

He parked the car in front of the clubhouse, next to the space marked *President*. A young couple walked past with their golf bags. He didn't know them; there was a time when he'd known every member of the club by name, but then they let anyone become a member these days, not like when he was Secretary.

He walked up the steps and in through the main door with its plaque reading, *Little Warthing Club House, Erected 1955.* He still felt riled by the other drivers on his journey there, but then he had an excellent idea. He'd call that young Corman chap, tell him to put up some speed traps and get some unmarked cars patrolling the area; that would soon sort out the lunatics using the roads. Back in control, he was able to relax.

He walked by the boards with the names of previous presidents, treasurers and secretaries written in gold. He noticed the trophy cabinet with its gleaming cups looked dusty; he'd complain to the club's president and explain that in his day they had higher standards.

Someone, he couldn't remember their name, said 'Hello' and he smiled as if delighted and shook them by the hand before proceeding to the restaurant.

The club's restaurant was excellent and always busy. He scanned the room with its mix of tables put together to accommodate different groups; from couples to quartets all the way up to groups of twelve.

He didn't know anyone apart from the ghastly, noisy woman who'd been a friend of Bernier; he had an idea she was his dance partner or was it bridge? Well, whichever it was she was a loud, obnoxious woman. As if on cue the woman let out a raucous peal of laughter. Peter directed a piercing glare at her but she was far too busy gossiping with her friends to notice. He sat down at a small table as far away as possible from those annoying females. He could remember the days when women weren't allowed to be members of the golf club – it was altogether a better time.

Forty minutes later he called to a young waitress as she passed his table. 'Where's my food? I've been waiting for over half an hour. It's just not good enough. Let me tell you I will be sending a stiff letter of complaint to the president,' he said angrily, his multiple chins quivering and his ponytail bobbing.

The skinny girl didn't look in the slightest abashed. She jutted out her chin and with her hand on her hip said loudly and with a hint of a sneer, 'Look mister, don't you go speaking to me like that – you haven't even ordered.'

The restaurant had gone quiet and everyone was looking at them. Peter Wilson's orange and yellow MCC tie felt too tight and he couldn't swallow.

'Of course I have, you stupid girl,' he muttered under his breath. Suddenly he didn't feel hungry, he just wanted to go home, away from all those painted harlots looking at him.

He stood up and his chair crashed to the floor. He put his shoulders back and marched out.

If only Justin Harper was still around, or better still, Bernier – he always loved listening to my stories.

At the back of his mind, in a region that was misty and uncomfortable, he had a sense that there had been something not quite law-abiding about those two men and what made his chest tighten was the question, *Did I do something to bring them to justice?* He couldn't remember, in the same way there were days that just vanished and he had no recollection of them at all.

Chapter 19

Dee locked her front door and turned to face the outside world. The sun was shining and she felt her choice of ethnic saffron was just right for the mood of the day, The lilac was in full bloom and its heavy scent sweetened the air. A cream clematis which climbed her fence had popped into flower. Smiling, she took a moment to enjoy it all before gazing up and down the road. She was surprised to see that someone had put up posters on every available surface.

Oh, dear! That will have lots of people up in arms. The local councillors will be inundated with complaining emails.

The residents of Little Warthing took a dim view of people sticking up bills. She adjusted her shopping basket in the crook of her arm and walked up to the nearest poster. She was curious to know what it was advertising.

Close by there was a poster which was plastered on a telegraph pole just in front of her house. The background was a garish clown – red and white paint on his face, with blue diamond eyes and a small straw boater. Inwardly, Dee shuddered but bravely she read on:

'The One And Only Clown Fair Coming To Your Area.'

It listed the attractions: a haunted house, bumper cars, and a bucking bronco.

Well, the bucking bronco and bumper cars might be fun, but I think I'll give the haunted house a miss – slightly too close to the reality of my life, thought Dee.

At the bottom in black was the name of her village, the playing field to be precise, and the date of the event: next weekend.

I'll give Zara and Amelia a ring later and we can go together.

'I suppose you will be going,' stated a booming voice flatly.

Dee spun around to see retired Chief Inspector Peter Wilson standing behind her. His height and bulk made him a menacing figure at the best of times, but just at the moment, she was rather sensitive to threatening situations. She took a step backwards and noticed Mrs May, grey and wizened, lurking behind him.

The latter spoke, or rather hissed, 'You and that daughter and granddaughter of yours …'

The actual words they used were neutral enough, but the tone and manner of both Peter Wilson and Mrs May were decidedly accusatory.

Dee smiled politely. 'Probably. What about the two of you?'

Mrs May sniffed. She was wearing a grey nylon sack of a dress. Dee seemed to recall seeing the very same outfit in a rather distressing drama she'd watched about asylums – or was it prisons?

Mrs May's wiry arms stuck out from the short sleeves. They were pale and wrinkly. She placed her hands on her hips and somehow made the gesture seem aggressive. 'Might as well. The noise will be appalling. There'll be whistles, jingles and raucous music. There'll be no peace to be had at home, so I might as well go down and take a look.'

'I'll be there.' Peter Wilson stood erect and attempted to pull in his large belly. 'I'll be keeping an eye on things. These fairground types can cause trouble.' His stern countenance took on a boyish bashfulness as he added, 'Besides, I've always loved fairs. The shooting galleries are my favourite. I remember when I was about thirteen, I won a huge teddy.' He smiled at the memory, and then his face darkened. 'My father clouted me when I got home, said I'd been wasting my money.' He looked sadly down at his polished shoes. 'I suppose he was right.'

'But you had fun! Surely that's a good thing to spend money on?' said Dee encouragingly.

Mrs May's pinched face relaxed a little. Dee noticed and wondered, *Is that a wistful look or has she just got indigestion?*

'I once won a toy clown at a fair; I got it on the hoopla stand.' A note of pride crept into Mrs May's voice. 'I got the hoop right over it. The woman on the stall had to let me have that clown. Just as well, as it was the only tuppence I had to spend. I've still got it – the clown, I mean. I keep it on my bed.'

'Have you? Do you really?' asked Peter Wilson incredulously. Mrs May looked self-conscious, but he was too busy blushing to notice. 'I've still got Mr Ted. Since my wife died, he sleeps on my bed too.'

Fascinating though these revelations were, Dee was lost in a sudden memory. She remembered a fair many decades before. Her parents had taken her and some of her giggling girlfriends to it. Her father had challenged them to eat as much candy floss as they could. Her mother had laughed as the girls devoured great pink sticky clouds of the stuff. It was one happy childhood memory, but what made her think of it was Mrs May.

That long-forgotten ghost of a child was returning to Dee's memory and she could see Mrs May as she'd been then. *What was her Christian name?* Dee couldn't remember. Even then she hadn't been someone to be remembered – grey and painfully thin. Her mother had never been waiting for her outside the school gates, unlike Dee's mum who was there rain or shine, smelling of fresh baking and her arms open wide for a hug.

Mrs May never had friends back for tea. Dee had an idea that her childhood house had looked as bleak and unwelcoming as her present home.

There had been something amiss there – was it alcohol? Her mother? Her father?

She recalled her own mum once shaking her head sadly and mumbling 'poor mite' as a nine-year-old Mrs May had scurried past.

Now she recollected seeing her as a child at the fair, clutching her clown and running past Dee and her friends and the candy floss. It had stuck in her mind because the girl had looked happy. Dee had never before – or since – seen her happy.

'Like I was saying, an apple doesn't fall far from the tree.' Mrs May was talking and Dee realised she'd probably been speaking throughout Dee's reminiscences.

'Sorry? What? I was miles away,' confessed Dee. 'What were you saying, Mrs May?'

The vicious tone was back in her neighbour's voice. Vindictively she continued, 'We were just commenting that your Zara was always very friendly with that Harper. Just how well did she know him? That's what we want to know!'

Peter Wilson took up the attack. 'Can't be a coincidence – you and Bernier, Zara and Justin!'

Dee wasn't to know that the retired policeman was puffed up by a resurgent sensation of his own power and that his bellowing was washing away the episode at the Golf Club.

'Sorry, I don't quite follow.'

Mrs May scoffed. 'It's obvious isn't it; both dead, both clowns. I was saying that the apple doesn't fall far from the tree.' She had a gleeful look in her eye.

Dee swallowed, and – every inch the lady of poise that her mother had raised her to be – she smiled graciously. 'Well, I must get on with my shopping. Perhaps I'll see you both at the fair.'

On the way to the village shop, she took out her mobile phone. Determined not to let the village sourpusses rain on her day, she dialled Zara. Amelia answered.

'Hi, Granny. Mum's driving; you're on speaker.'

She told them about the fair and was gratified by the whoops of joy that greeted the news.

When Nicholas Corman heard the news, the last thing he felt like doing was whooping for joy.

'Here, Gov, have you seen the posters? There's a clown fair coming to Little Warthing! Wicked!' Josh was elated.

Nicholas sighed. 'That's the last thing we need, more clowns in Little Warthing. This can only end in tragedy.'

Nicholas was not only person in the area who did not anticipate the upcoming event with delight. In the deli, for once there was little talk about how ripe the Brie was, and instead, all the chat revolved around the possible rides and attractions at the fair.

'Yes, I'll be there!' smiled Sophie as she wrapped a block of aged Parmesan in waxed paper and handed it to a customer.

Vivian Plover, who was waiting impatiently to be served, tutted loudly, her stiff hair and crisp linen frock crackling in disapproval.

As the previous customer departed, Sophie turned to smile at Vivian and her husband Christopher. 'I take it you won't be going.'

Vivian's thin lips quivered beneath their coating of red lipstick. 'Certainly not! All that noise. I can't think what the council was playing at giving permission for the fair to take place on the playing fields. It's simply asking for trouble. We all know what those sorts of people are like. I can tell you, Christopher will be locking up his garden shed that night.'

Sophie was about to pull Vivian up on exactly what she meant by 'those sorts of people' but Christopher spoke. His noble features creased with puzzlement. 'Always do.'

'You always do what?' snapped Vivian, eyeing her husband, who was obediently standing just behind her and holding her wicker basket.

'Lock my garden shed. I've got some valuable kit in there.' His eyes took on a gleam and he beamed at Sophie. 'Have I told you about my new sit-on mower? It has—'

'The last thing Sophie wants to hear about is your dreary mower!' Vivian stated emphatically.

Christopher looked down at his polished brown brogues and muttered, 'Not dreary at all, latest model with—'

Vivian threw him a glacial look and he fell silent.

She turned back to Sophie. 'As I was saying, the council should never have allowed the fair to come to Little Warthing – it's bound to end in tragedy.'

Christopher, still carefully standing a diffident pace behind his formidable wife, murmured, 'I rather like fairs.'

Vivian swung round to glower at her husband; he might tower above her but she was undoubtedly the imposing partner.

Fearing for Christopher's wellbeing Sophie quickly put in, 'David is going with Tristan.'

Her son and the Plovers' godson were friends.

'Yes, Tristan is down from London for the weekend – I think a group of them are going to the fair. I just hope he doesn't come home late and wake us all up. Now I'll have some of that Parmesan and do you have any Black Bomber?'

Over at the Flying Pheasant, Marcello spent the week feeling disgruntled that his parents needed him to work on the day of the fair. He would much rather go on the bumper cars with his mates, David and Tristan, than wait on tables. He was a few years younger than the others and the thrill of being allowed to play with the big boys was just as strong as it had been when he was eight. Mentally he sighed; the pub was bound to be full with all the visitors so there was no alternative for him than to contribute by acting as a waiter.

Knowing that it couldn't be helped only partly alleviated his melancholy, which by Saturday had mellowed to mild unhappiness. His parents' suggestion of a family brunch in the pub garden cheered him a little, especially when he smelt the bacon sizzling in the pan. His mum always got her bacon from Sophie's deli; it was local, organic and sublime. Without bothering to shower he padded barefoot down the stairs, with his hair dishevelled and his baggy PJ bottoms crumpled.

As he walked into the kitchen his mum looked up from the stove and smiled. 'At least put a T-shirt on, love.' Alex came into the room; her wheelchair made a low humming sound and she had an empty tray on her lap. She glanced at her brother's skinny chest. 'Yuck! That's the last thing I want to see first thing in the morning. For God's sake put something on and come and help – I've already laid the table outside.'

There was a knock at the door and Marcello recognised Dee's bright and cheerful voice. 'Morning!'

He swore under his breath and was about to ask who on earth calls at this time in the morning but when he glanced up at the kitchen clock, he realised it was nearly eleven, so not exactly the crack of dawn.

He scurried upstairs to get a T-shirt and when he came down he found that everyone was already sitting at one of the larger tables in the flower garden. His mum had made up his plate, two eggs, extra bacon and ketchup on the side.

His mum was explaining to Dee, 'With running the pub we hardly ever get to have lunch or supper as a family so I do like it when we can have breakfast together, but this morning we are running a bit late so we won't have long before we'll be opening for lunch.'

Gina was wearing a red summer dress; it had the hint of the 1950s fit-and-flare and showed off her curves, and the colour suited her Mediterranean colouring.

'I do hope I'm not intruding,' said Dee, looking at Gina with concern. 'It's just that I did want to drop off the Indian cookbook you lent me. You were right, it's brilliant, all those easy recipes and lots of helpful photos. I do so like to know what things are supposed to look like, even if mine rarely do turn out right.'

'Rubbish, you're an excellent cook,' laughed Gina, patting Francesco's black Labrador. The dog was never fed from the table but that didn't stop him from dreaming.

Francesco, sitting perched at the edge of his sit, ever ready to spring into action, was not a relaxing person to have breakfast with. He was looking dubiously at the empty table in front of Dee. It was in contrast to everyone else who all had plates heaving with fried eggs, bacon, sausages, mushroom and tomatoes. 'Surely I can get you something to eat?'

Dee smiled. 'No, honestly, my tea is just what I needed and I've already had breakfast. I must say this garden is looking wonderful. It's amazing how much it's come on in just a few weeks. All those poppies have popped since I was last here and your wisteria is positively laden with flowers.'

Francesco would not be deflected. 'Something light? It would only take me a second to whip you up some scrambled eggs and smoked salmon.'

'No, honestly, you just sit and enjoy your breakfast. You need your strength. I imagine you will be rushed off your feet with the clown fair today.'

Gina poured Francesco another coffee; privately Dee thought this was unwise as he was wired enough and definitely didn't need any more caffeine.

Gina looked around the table. 'More coffee anyone?' Both her children proffered their empty mugs, then she turned to Dee. 'Yes, you are right it will be manic here – all hands on deck. But we're lucky we have two willing assistants.'

She grinned at her offspring; Alex rolled her eyes and Marcello scowled.

Through a mouthful of bacon, Marcello grumbled, 'I just hope it's not like last Saturday afternoon when you two disappeared off – and you say *I'm* not responsible.'

Dee caught a glance between Gina and Francesco.

Alex nodded. 'Yeah, Mum, Dad, where were you? And neither of you were picking up your mobile phones when you're always telling us not to turn them off.'

Again that look between Gina and Francesco! But what does it mean? Were they having a romantic encounter somewhere? Gina certainly looks a little flushed at the memory. After all, it must be challenging to find any privacy with adult children in the house. But why is Francesco frowning? Goodness, I do hope ...

Her mind flashed back to the previous Saturday; the worry about Blossom, Petal's remarkable skill at being a rescue dog – if a rather small and fluffy one – and Ken being a knight in shining armour and liberating his damsel in distress, all the time wearing a clown nose and a brightly checked suit.

Surely not! Their absence just when Blossom was abducted must be purely coincidental!

Simultaneously, both parents replied but with very different tones.

In one of those cool, firm voices that brook no dispute, Gina said, 'We were back by opening time.'

Francesco thumped his fist on the table making the plates rattle and Dee's tea swish in its mug. 'I will not have disrespect in my home.'

There was an awkward silence.

Dee spoke with the brightest tone she could muster. 'Sounds like we all had busy days last Saturday! You've probably heard all about poor Blossom?'

She scanned Gina and Francesco's faces for their reaction. *Perhaps they will give something away – a guilty glance – whatever that might be.*

But she was disappointed; both of their features just puckered into suitable looks of concern.

'Yes, how is Blossom doing?' enquired Gina. 'She must have been so frightened.'

Dee decided she had better stop staring into her hosts' faces. *I can't have them thinking I suspect them of two murders and abduction.* 'She's doing remarkably well, I think. But Alex, you probably have a better idea of how both Ken and Blossom are; you work with them, don't you?'

Alex picked up her plate and turned her wheelchair towards the pub. Nonchalantly, over her shoulder, she replied, 'It's a big company; I see them around occasionally but it's not like we're bosom buddies. We should really be getting a move on – look at the time. Dad, you need to open the doors in five minutes.'

Taking the not-so-subtle hint, Dee rose. 'Yes, I mustn't keep you. Thanks for the tea.'

She left more puzzled than when she had arrived.

Chapter 20

'Mrs May was right,' commented Dee as she headed towards the playing field with Zara and Amelia.

They were walking among a throng of folk all surging in that direction. Most of the village appeared to be going to the fair and judging by the number of cars lining every side street, there were also a good number of people from the wider area.

'About what?' enquired Zara as she dodged around a young couple who was pushing a pram with an excited toddler in tow.

'The noise – she said it would be loud.'

'That's part of the fun!' Zara had to raise her voice to be heard.

They crested the hill and queued as the crowd were funnelled through a turnstile and kiosk to pay.

The playing field was transformed into a children's wonderland of attractions, merry-go-rounds with tame horses for the very young, and terrifying life-defying bungee jumps for the cocky teens. Every stand had its own megaphone spewing out music, and every attraction was manned by a clown.

Dee had a brief sensation of sensory overload. Her eyes darted from the swing pirate ship seesawing back and forth against the blue sky to the slow-moving aeroplane ride for younger kids. There were bumper cars with their long flickering mayfly tails, a teacup ride and carnival games like ring toss with giant stuffed animals hanging from the ceiling as prizes. Dee noticed that Amelia was looking towards the two-storey haunted house with its bright graffiti on the walls, a skeleton lolling out of a broken window and a curling slide at one side, while Zara was eyeing up the shooting gallery with its flashing lights and pop-up targets.

It wasn't just the attractions that assailed Dee's senses; there were so many people, all exuding a heightened emotional energy:

a child crying as his red balloon floated away high in the sky and a group of hyped-up teenagers walked past, triumphantly carrying an enormous panda. Then there were the smells, sickly sweet candy floss and doughnuts, pungent onions and hotdogs, all with a hint of engine oil.

For Dee, who liked things to be neat and tidy, the discarded wrappers and rubbish that littered the ground were distressing.

Amelia broke into Dee's ruminations by saying, 'I don't think I've ever seen so many clowns.'

In honour of the evening, she was sporting a tutu in pink and turquoise hues. It was liberally sprinkled with flashing lights and sequins, which twinkled in the sun. Her face makeup shimmered with added glitter as well. By comparison Dee and Zara were more modestly dressed. Dee was wearing dark denim jeans and a floaty Indian top she'd picked up in Goa, or was it Kerala? She felt Zara was quite entering into the spirit of things as she had opted for a green wrap dress. *Presumably, she has no intention of enjoying the more vigorous attractions – in that dress the bucking bronco is definitely out!*

'Where do we start?' smiled Zara as a stilt-walker tottered past.

'Candy floss!' declared Dee, deciding to throw herself one hundred per cent into the carnival spirit and hoping that a sugar rush would help. She led her family over towards a kiosk. The candy floss was being expertly spun by a small female clown, whose voluminous dress was cut short to show off her bloomers and stripy stockings. Dee inhaled the familiar scent and gazed at the translucent pink confection growing ever larger on its wooden stick.

'Bliss!' she declared after having a sweet feathery mouthful.

'That looks good,' commented Blossom Bim Bam.

Dee, along with Zara and Amelia had been so intent on their candy floss that they hadn't noticed Blossom and Ken approaching. They were in full clown makeup, Blossom frivolously bright and Ken more subdued.

'You're here in your professional capacity, I see! Can I get you some candy floss?' asked Dee.

'You're very kind,' beamed Blossom, the large daisy on her hat bobbing away, 'but not before a show. The fair organisers have asked us to do a bit of a party piece.'

Ken glanced at Blossom with indulgent disapproval and made a slight tutting sound before explaining with the utmost gravity, 'The fair organisers wanted us to raise the cultural level of the event and demonstrate what the art of clowning is all about.'

Dee nodded solemnly, trying not to smirk. *I just adore Ken's overly dignified demeanour all wrapped up in a checked suit and face paint.* She looked at Blossom, all in pink and with her air of childish joy, and at Ken, who somehow managed to exude a certain dignity regardless of his comic outfit.

I do wish Zara hadn't sown the seeds of doubt in my mind by her suggestion that perhaps my two favourite clowns might have staged the whole garden-shed rescue. She glanced from one to another again. *Surely not! Sweet Blossom and cuddlesome Ken clown killers? Never!*

But the whisper of suspicion lingered.

By way of distracting her wayward thoughts, Dee said, 'So you work together on accounts during the week, and then come the weekend you perform together as clowns – how romantic!'

Blossom blushed – at least Dee thought she did – it was hard to tell underneath all her makeup.

Ken took command. 'Um, yes well, we must get on! We must not be late.'

And they headed off; Ken marching purposefully and Blossom skipping in his wake. Dee watched them go, wishing she could just revel in the romance.

There's nothing like thinking one's neighbours may be murderers to put a dampener on enjoying their growing romance ... But talking of romance, could there be anything going on between this pair?

She had noticed Mrs May and Peter Wilson. They were talking to each other – or more probably, shouting – in order to be heard above the din. He was in his normal uniform; hair swept back in a ponytail and MCC tie while, not surprisingly, she was all in grey.

Well, I definitely don't want to have to speak to them!

She turned to find that Zara and Amelia had sated their need for candy floss and were debating what they wanted to do next. They were just pondering the merits of the bumper cars versus the shooting gallery when Josh lolloped up. He hadn't quite grown into his limbs and the way he moved reminded Dee of a young giraffe.

He looked at Amelia, apparently both Dee and Zara were invisible to him. Evidently Amelia in sparkling pastels appealed to his romantic, or was it adventurous, side.

'Wicked!' he said, not clarifying if he was referring to the fair or Amelia.

'Yay, wicked!' she replied.

Generally, Dee liked the younger generation and felt they were much maligned, but just sometimes she feared the age of eloquence was dying out.

Could it be all those one-word texts?

'Haunted House?'

'Wicked!'

Courtship over, they headed towards the aforementioned haunted house without a backward glance at their elders.

Dee was about to inquire if Zara's wrap dress was up to a ride on the bumper cars when she heard the familiar cultured voice of Nicholas Corman. 'Dee. Zara. Good evening!'

'Nicholas, how lovely to see you. Or are you on duty? Should I call you Inspector?' enquired Dee, all the while thinking how attractive it was to have a Cary Grant amidst the trainers and hoodies. His suit might stand out but it was in a good way; rather like Zara's wrap dress was unusual amidst the females in overly tight jeans with unsightly muffin tops.

'Nicholas, please. I'm off duty tonight.'

Dee looked at him and then gave Zara a significant glance. Zara was instantly alert; that smile of Dee's was often deployed when her mother was up to something.

'What perfect timing! Zara was just saying she wished she had someone to show her how to fire a rifle at the shooting gallery.'

Zara, who'd been a proficient shot since the age of nine, gave her mother a wry look. Gallantly, Nicholas proffered an arm to both Dee and Zara.

Dee shook her head. 'No! No! You two run along and have some fun! I fancy my chances at the hoopla stand. I wonder if I can win a goldfish or don't they have live animals anymore?'

With a wave she turned on her heels and started striding away. After a few steps a new thought struck her.

I know what! I'll go and watch Ken and Blossom.

Josh had been surprised by the tightness in his chest when he had seen Amelia through the throng of people. He had never realised before how darn sexy a pixie eating candy floss could be. He actually felt his heart beating from nerves as he approached her and then when he noticed the look of happy recognition in Amelia's feline green eyes, his body had been flooded with joy.

He'd hoped she'd be at the fair but with all these crowds he hadn't been sure he'd bump into her. Earlier in the week he'd toyed with the idea of texting her and arranging to meet but he'd chickened out; he worried that would be too formal, too much of a statement and worse still, it would have laid him open to a crushing rebuttal.

They threaded their way through the crowds, side by side but consciously not touching. There was a bit of a queue for the Haunted House.

Josh paid. 'My treat!' he insisted as he took the ticket from the bored young clown.

They negotiated the rickety stairs into the entrance. The second they stepped into the house they were plunged into total darkness. It was a thick, impenetrable blackness. Josh's hands brushed against the walls and it occurred to him that not only was he in the dark but that he was also in a very small space. He swallowed down a wave of claustrophobic panic. As he took a step forward a spider's web stroked his face. As it touched him he had a vision of an enormous spider lurking somewhere in the darkness. He swallowed again. Then he heard Amelia's soft tinkling giggle and his heart soared, all thoughts of menacing arachnids vanished. When they stepped into the next room and a frightening illuminated clown face lurched at them from out of the ceiling, accompanied by a nerve-jangling shriek, Amelia's chuckle blossomed into a full-throated laugh. *This girl is fearless,* thought Josh with growing admiration.

Tentatively, they sauntered into another passageway. For a second, nothing happened. The suspense built then the floor began to heave and move in unfamiliar directions. Their arms flailed as they struggled to maintain their balance. Amelia fell back against his firm chest; automatically his arms swooped around to embrace her and he had a brief sensation of her warmth and citrus scent. She regained her footing and they walked on laughing, but now it seemed quite natural that they were holding hands.

She pulled him towards an open window, and they stood side by side, fingers intertwined, gulping in the refreshing air. From this height they could watch the fair go by. Amelia tilted her head back and her fiery curls quivered. She smiled up at him. 'That's better, I was finding it difficult to breathe.'

'It was rather hot in there,' agreed Josh while thinking he'd never been happier.

This was definitely a mistake, thought Nicholas as he tried to scrape some disgusting pink bubble gum off the sole of his polished shoes. *Ridiculous having a fair and a clown one at that. I'd forgotten how much I hate all the noise. And why does no one use the bins? There is litter everywhere. And as for all those parents letting their offspring get their faces painted, have they no sense of responsibility? So unhygienic! As for them allowing them to eat candy floss! Words fail me! Pure additives and sugar – what's wrong with an apple?*

He denied, even to himself, that the reason he was there was that this fair was in Little Warthing, and that one Zara FitzMorris lived in Little Warthing. What was more, Zara had a mother, and Nicholas didn't need to be a detective to guess that Dee would insist that Zara accompany her to the fair. Earlier he had thought about calling in on Dee and arranging to meet at a given place. He would never have been bold enough to contact Zara directly but it was a fairly safe bet that she would be with her mother. He had dismissed the idea as it occurred to him that it would hardly be professional – after all Dee was a suspect in a murder case. He could not quite imagine himself standing in front of a disciplinary panel and justifying meeting a murder suspect by the bumper cars. Besides which it would be setting Josh a bad example.

This is ridiculous – I'm going home to work on my model train set and find some solvent to get this bubble gum off my shoe.

With determination he turned and began striding towards the a exit. It was then that he saw her – a vision of civilisation amid all the skin-tight jeans and bulging midriffs. Cool and calm, she stood there in her elegant wrap dress, her saffron hair glowing in the evening sunshine. She was playfully eating tufts of pink fluffy candy floss and in an instant, he forgot all about sugar and additives. *How enchanting!*

He could not believe the ease with which they greeted him and now here he was gallantly squiring Zara through the throngs of people towards the shooting gallery. He held a protective arm around her as he steered her safely around a spilled turquoise ice slushy and fended off a large helium balloon that was threatening to bump into her face. They stood to one side to admire a clown juggling flaming torches and the fire risk didn't even cross Nicholas' mind.

They reached the shooting gallery with its line of tin ducks tracking along the back of the reinforced tent. He briefly scanned the ceiling where all the stuffed toy prizes hung. *I wonder which one I'll win for her – perhaps the panda.*

As they waited for their turn he found himself being unusually talkative. 'I'd forgotten how much I love fairs. Don't those children with their faces painted to look like clowns look adorable?'

A deafening blast of Queen's iconic '*We Will Rock You*' came through a nearby speaker and Nicholas couldn't stop himself from smiling into Zara's eyes and joining her in singing along. He paid a wiry clown who had a cigarette laden with ash in the corner of his painted mouth.

Patiently, he showed Zara how to load the rifle. She watched him intently and when he saw the light in her jade eyes, he felt his chest swell. Stooping down he put his arms around her to demonstrate how to hold the firearm. He had to deliberately take a deep breath to calm his pounding heart.

'What's up with your breathing?' asked Zara.

'What?' stammered Nicholas.

'Your breathing – you seem to be breathing rather deeply.'

'Oh yes – well – making a good a shot has a lot to do with breathing correctly.'

'Ah! So that's what it was.'

He couldn't see her face as he was behind her but he sensed she was smiling.

I thought she'd be impressed, he mused, snuggling into her back.

'Nicholas?'

'Yes,' he murmured dreamily.

'I think you can let go of me now.'

He straightened with a jolt. 'Oh, yes, right. Okey dokey.' He started to perspire. *Did I really just say 'okay dokey'?* He coughed, cleared his throat and in a deep, authoritative voice said, 'Just remember to squeeze the trigger, don't jerk it. This is a repeat loader so you have six shots.'

'Thanks, I'll try to remember.'

He took a step back and observed her. *Her stance is really rather good. Arms relaxed, head nicely over the barrel. I must be a decent enough instructor, if I say so myself.*

Zara inhaled and squeezed the trigger, there was a satisfying *ting* as the first duck flipped down.

Beginner's luck – jolly good for her confidence.

Zara took another shot and again there was a *ting.*

Oh I am glad – even if she misses the rest she'll be happy.

But Zara had no intention of missing anything. After four bullseyes, the clown attendant was looking even more disgruntled and Nicholas was confused.

When the sixth *ting* rang out and the final duck fell Nicholas started to laugh.

Handing the rifle back to the clown with a gracious smile, Zara said, 'I'll take the giant panda, thank you. Oh, and you may want to get the sights looked at, they pull a bit to the right.'

With great aplomb, she presented Nicholas with a stuffed panda of enormous size. Its large black eyes twinkled at him.

'I guess you've done this before,' he said.

She laughed. 'Perhaps I should have mentioned I was junior commonwealth champion two years in a row.'

Dee watched as Zara and Nicholas sauntered into the mass of people. It was easy to pick them out in a crowd by their absence of trainers and hoodies. *They do make a distinguished couple – not exactly cutting edge, more retro, him in his ironed chinos, collared shirt and shiny shoes and her in a dress. But then all things retro and vintage are in vogue at the moment so perhaps they are on trend.* She smiled as she imagined Zara's expression if she heard her mother describe her as vintage. *I do hope Zara allows the inspector to show off his prowess at the shooting gallery. It might be asking a bit much to expect her to summon up a whimper of admiration but I hope that she at least has the sense to let him put his arms around her to demonstrate how she should hold the rifle.*

Now enough of Zara, what am I going to do?

She scanned the scene; there was some noisy contraption which people were paying to be strapped into before being hurled in all sorts of directions rather like astronauts training for a flight. *I don't think I fancy handing over good money just to vomit.* Her eyes wandered over to the haunted house. *No, I won't go there, I don't want to cramp Amelia and Josh's style. No, I still think the hoopla stall is my best bet – or better yet I can go and watch Ken and Blossom.*

Dee asked a skinny clown selling balloons where Blossom and Ken's show was. He directed her to a small side area where a mini big top was erected. She paid yet another clown and went in to find her seat. The big top was exactly how children's picture books depict circuses; right down to the sawdust ring and the smell of greasepaint.

Once seated on a rather hard bench, Dee politely declined the popcorn which was being sold by a young clown who was wearing a tutu even shorter than the ones favoured by Amelia. She settled down to enjoy all the sights and sounds. Looking around she noted that most of the audience was under six and wide-eyed in anticipation. Dee admired all their different outfits; most had their faces painted with red clown noses but there was a pirate and a good sprinkling of Disney princesses. *Adorable, and quite delightful in their frothy dresses.* She paused to consider. *But in this modern age aren't they all meant to be warrior princesses, empowered to go into battle and take over the world?*

She got no further in her musings as a dignified ringmaster, complete with a red tailcoat, top hat and moustache marched into the centre of the arena. He stood tall and erect, and a respectful hush fell.

Once he was sure he had everyone's attention he announced, 'Ladies and gentlemen, girls and boys, it is with great pleasure that I present the world-famous clowns, brought to you, with no expense spared ...' Over the speaker came a suspended-filled drumroll then, 'Joseph Popov and Blossom Bim Bam!' Upbeat show music erupted from crackling speakers and the audience gasped in anticipation.

They were not disappointed. To Dee's amazement, the show opened with Ken performing a series of cartwheels and flips onto the central arena. He was a blur of yellow-checked suit, oversized shoes and red nose. *How on earth does he keep his red wig and bowler hat on?* Blossom joined him, riding a unicycle. *Goodness – talented and beautiful.*

Blossom jumped off the unicycle to a storm of applause. She then set about preparing a meal which involved a lot of juggling of plates between her and Ken. A large plastic sausage was also thrown which elicited whoops of joy from the children. For the finale, Blossom smashed a rich oozing custard pie into Ken's face and the whole tent erupted. Dee's stomach ached from laughing so hard.

The talented duo took a bow and began to make balloon animals for their appreciative fans.

Dee quietly slipped away.

Who'd have thought that under Ken's gruff exterior was a tumbling, juggling genius? They work brilliantly together! I wonder if they could teach Petal, the pup, a trick or two? She would look adorable in a pink tutu.

Dee spent the next twenty minutes happily wandering around the fairground. It wasn't so much the attractions that she loved, it was watching the expressions on the people's faces: the apprehension of a teenage couple as they gripped each other's hands and waited to be mechanically hurtled into the sky, the excitement of an eight-year-old boy as he won a coconut. The crowds were now thickening. She was glad they'd decided to come early rather than later.

Amid the jostling multitude someone brushed against her just for an instant, but it was enough. Above the smell of sawdust and candy floss, Dee caught a whiff of something she had smelt before. A chemical smell. It was an odour with unpleasant connotations. Methanol, formaldehyde – embalming fluid.

She froze. *Someone who has just passed me has been in contact with a dead body!*

It was the same odour she had smelt emanating from Bernier and then Justin Harper. The hairs on the back of her neck rose as she deliberately calmed her breathing. She spun around and frantically trying to work out who it could have been amongst the sea of faces.

Not that couple with the child or the old lady with a Zimmer frame.

Then she spotted a figure in a grey hoody. There was nothing to confirm this was the culprit, only that in this sea of humanity it was the only figure not gawping at sideshows but rather furtively scurrying away between a booth selling hotdogs and a Try Your

Strength hammer and bell. It was such a fleeting impression that Dee had no real sense of the person's height, build or even gender. All that she knew was that she had to follow or risk losing this vital clue.

Somewhere in all this heaving mass of humanity is a murderer and I may be the only person who can stop them from killing again.

She was perspiring and with her heart beating fast, she worked her way through the crowd murmuring, 'Oh, I'm so sorry! Do excuse me!' as she collided with various bystanders.

She reached the opening where she'd last seen the figure. On her left, the queue for the hotdogs snaked around the corner and the smell of frying onions was enough to make her eyes sting. On her right, at the Try Your Strength booth, the bell dinged triumphantly as a middle-aged man in a vest and with many tattoos hit the hammer down. Dee stood and stared down the opening between the two stands. There was no sign of a figure; just generators, wires and cables, cars and the general background equipment needed for a fair.

I should go back and find that nice policeman, Nicholas, thought Dee as she plunged through the opening. Free from the crowds she started running, darting side to side, her eyes scanning for the figure. She looked behind a blue pickup, in the windows of a caravan, behind some stacked cans of fizzy drinks, but there was no one.

Dee stood and thought, *Oh well at least I tried, I'll have to go back to the fair and tell the others what I saw – or rather smelt. Not that there's anything they can do.*

She was turning around when simultaneously she caught a whiff of those cloying chemicals and felt a prick in her arm. Someone had stuck a needle in her and injected her with something that was taking immediate effect. As she sunk into helpless oblivion she thought, *So this is it! It's been a good life. I hope Zara and Amelia are not too upset and that they remember I want a willow coffin.*

And with that, she blacked out.

Chapter 21

Sometime later, after Zara and Nicholas had battled it out on the bumper cars and proved their bravery in the haunted house, they both agreed it was time to leave.

Nicholas tilted his head and looked into Zara's feline eyes, his eyebrows drawn together in concern. 'Should we try and find your mother?' He'd had a sudden wave of guilt that he had totally forgotten about Dee up until that moment.

Zara smiled. 'No, she's probably sitting in her cottage stroking Cat and having a cup of camomile tea.'

'In that case, shall I walk you back there?' he enquired. He was keen to prolong the evening.

'That would be delightful,' nodded Zara as she tucked her hand into the crook of his arm.

As the evening progressed the patrons of the fair were morphing from young families to rather rowdier young adults. The fair did not have an alcohol licence but, judging from the exuberance of some of the youngsters, that was not stopping them from drinking.

Nicholas escorted Zara through the crowd. 'I would be happier had I seen Dee home,' he commented with his forehead creased, after they passed two youths who were decidedly drunk. He gently guided Zara to the other side of him, so that his body could provide a shield between her and their unruly behaviour.

'Oh you don't need to worry about Mother, she is more than capable of looking after herself.' The smile playing around Zara's lips reached her eyes; she was amused at the notion of Dee, a martial arts expert, needing Nicholas' protection.

They left the playing field and began the walk down the hill to the village and Dee's home.

Nicholas was curious. 'Speaking of being able to take care of oneself, were you never tempted to take up Taekwondo like your mother?'

'It's not really my thing,' Zara replied easily.

'That's a pity,' he muttered, half to himself.

Zara pulled him up. 'Why?'

He looked at her seriously. 'Everyone should know some basic self-defence.' He paused, swallowed and with a certain degree of feigned casualness said, 'I could teach you.'

'Thank you,' was Zara's demure reply and he felt his heart leap.

They walked on in silence. When they got to Honeysuckle Cottage, the lights were out.

'Perhaps she fancied an early night?' suggested Nicholas.

Zara frowned, a faint line appearing between her eyebrows. 'I don't think that's likely, not with all the noise from the fair.'

She tried the door; it was locked. Nicholas noticed a tightness around her mouth and eyes as she used her own key to let them in.

The house had that dull sense of emptiness; there was no murmur of the radio or the gentle sounds of Dee making a final cup of camomile tea in the kitchen, nor was there the citrus scent that would suggest she was indulging in a relaxing bath by candlelight.

Zara looked hopefully at Nicholas. 'I'm sure there's nothing to worry about.' She smiled but her voice and body were tense and brittle.

Nicholas offered reassurance. 'Of course not – like you said, Dee knows how to look after herself.'

She ran upstairs to check Dee's room but soon returned shaking her head. 'I'll try her phone.' She did – no reply.

Nicholas could hear her breathing, fast and shallow. Calmly he suggested, 'Try Amelia, perhaps she's with your mother.'

She was just scrolling through her contacts when Amelia and Josh burst through the door. They were laughing at some joke and had evidently enjoyed the evening. Zara's nerves were so on edge that she jumped at the unexpected noise.

'Have you seen Granny?' she demanded, with more than an edge of concern in her voice.

Amelia raised her eyebrows, surprised by her mother's agitation. 'No, not since we left you.'

Zara paled. 'Where can she be?'

Nicholas regarded Zara; she was suddenly forlorn and vulnerable. Instantly he swung into professional mode. Calmly he stated, 'I'm sure there is a perfectly innocent explanation, but to be on the safe side I'll ring the local bobbies who were patrolling the fair. Perhaps they've seen her.'

As Zara waited anxiously, Amelia placed a comforting arm around her mother's shoulders. 'Chill, Mum! You know Granny, she's as tough as old boots.'

Zara gave a faint smile.

The call didn't take long.

'No joy! But they are going to keep alert and will ring if they find her.'

'Let's go and look for her,' Amelia suggested, glancing at Josh.

'We'll come too,' declared Zara then she wavered. 'Or should one of us wait at the house?' By way of a compromise she decided, 'I'll walk with you as far as the front gate.'

The night air was balmy. There was the subtle evening scent of stocks freshly flowering in Dee's front garden. The sounds of the fair music and the hum of people drowned out the normal noise of distant traffic.

They arrived at the gate at the same time that Ken and Blossom were passing by. They were both still in costume, complete with stage makeup. Blossom's cheeks were flushed and her eyes brimming while Ken's hands were clenched into fists and his knuckles were grazed.

Amelia looked at them and asked, 'Is anything wrong? You look as if you've been in some trouble.'

'Not at all!' snapped Ken, his jaw was tight and a vein on his neck throbbed visibly in the gap between his white makeup and his collar.

'In that case, have you seen my gran?'

Blossom looked into Amelia's eyes and opened her mouth to say something but Ken grabbed her arm.

'No!' he barked, and marched away, dragging Blossom in his wake.

'Well, really!' exclaimed Zara indignantly, thrusting her hands onto her hips.

She watched them depart to the left and as she turned around the sight of Peter Wilson caught her eye. He was returning to his home, which was on the right of Dee's, just past Mrs May's dismal abode.

'Oh look! There's Peter Wilson just coming home – perhaps he's seen her.'

Zara marched out onto the pavement and strode up to him. Nicholas followed; he was not at all sure that asking Peter Wilson anything was ever a good idea but he also knew he was powerless to stop her.

Before Peter Wilson could escape into his house Zara accosted him. 'Excuse me, Mr Wilson, you haven't seen my mother, have you?'

He was evidently feeling his bulk; he was puffing a bit and perspiration trickled down his jowls and onto his shirt. He paused, put a pudgy hand on Mrs May's front garden wall to steady himself and after taking a few moments to regain his breath, regarded her coolly.

'No, I haven't, but I've no doubt she is up to no good. I can always spot a bad 'un and that mother of yours is nothing but trouble. Why she wasn't arrested years ago is beyond me.' He transferred his malicious gaze from Zara to Nicholas. 'But then the police force is nothing like as effective as it was in my day.'

Nicholas bristled, more on Zara's behalf than his own. 'I say, Sir, there's no need to take that tone with Ms FitzMorris.'

His voice was calm and rang with authority but that didn't stop the retired police chief from squaring up to him. Peter Wilson had a good few inches and a great deal more weight behind him but Nicholas stood his ground.

It was Zara who defused the situation. 'This isn't going to help us find my mother! Amelia, you and Josh should go back to the fair … and for goodness sake, keep your phone on in case we have any news about Granny.'

Amelia nodded but her shoulders drooped as Zara's concern had managed to seep into her.

Josh nudged her. 'Buck up, we'll find her in next to no time.'

Josh's words turned out to be prophetic as the two of them hadn't got very far before Amelia gave out a whoop. 'Granny!'

And there indeed was Granny. She was leaning heavily against Mrs May. She looked extremely worse for wear but she was alive. She had lost a shoe, her clothes were torn and muddy, and she had a gash on her forehead that was bleeding. Bright red blood spattered down her face and onto her top. Her eyes were glazed and, though they were open, it was obvious she wasn't registering her surroundings. Mrs May's face was even more grey than normal and her lips were pulled in a tight line of determination. Dee might be petite and slim but Mrs May was also slight, and half-carrying her neighbour was obviously taking its toll on her.

'Mother, what happened?' shrieked Zara as she ran up to them, tears of relief coursing down her cheeks.

Dee just blinked vacantly.

Nicholas stepped forward. 'Here, Mrs May, let me take her.' He put his arm around Dee and began to gently lead her to the house.

Relieved of Dee's weight, Mrs May rolled her shoulder and stretched out her stiff arm. She glared at Zara and sourly stated, 'What your mother needs is a nice cup of camomile tea and a sit-down, before you start firing questions at the poor old dear.'

As Nicholas, half-carrying Dee, reached the door, he commanded, 'Josh, ring for an ambulance and—'

'No! Really I'm fine,' interrupted Dee, weak but alarmed.

Softly, Nicholas explained, 'Sorry, Dee, but I must insist. Not only do you need to be properly checked, but we might be able to get vital forensic evidence from your clothes. You'll need a blood test – you seem to have been drugged.'

Once inside the house Mrs May, of all people, got the kettle on, she even got some warm water in a bowl and very gently started to dab at the cut on Dee's forehead. Her movements were brisk and efficient but kind. Poor Zara and Amelia seemed to have been shocked into a kind of paralysis. Mrs May observed them with a pinched expression and narrowed eyes before setting to with a curt, 'Here! I'll do it.' Zara and Amelia watched her with wide eyes, their lips parted but speechless.

Dee, through her groggy haze, thought, *Who'd have thought that Mrs May had an inner Florence Nightingale just begging to get out and bring comfort?*

Zara pulled herself together enough to sit down on the chair next to Dee's at the kitchen table and to take her hand. 'Mother, now can you tell us what happened?'

Dee blinked, struggling to focus in a fog of confusion. She shook her head; it hurt. 'No, not really, dear.'

'Dee,' came the Inspector's firm but calm voice, 'just tell us what you do remember.'

'I'd been to see Ken and Blossom's show.' She smiled. 'Do you know they are surprisingly talented; they were really very good. They were juggling and there was a custard pie.'

'After that! What happened after that?' Zara's impatience came out in her tone and she gripped her mother's hand a little tighter.

'I was sort of wandering again, and then ...' She took a sip of tea.

'And then?' prompted Zara.

'I smelt something.'

'You smelt something?' Zara was baffled.

'Yes.'

'What?'

'Embalming fluid.'

Dee was feeling very drowsy and a bit dizzy. She started perspiring and went a definite shade of green. 'I think I'm going to be sick.'

Amelia grabbed the washing-up bowl and thrust it under her grandmother's nose. After a few moments, Dee smiled at Amelia and passed it back. 'False alarm.'

Nicholas had positioned himself on the chair across the table from Dee and he resumed the questioning. 'Dee, you were saying you smelt embalming fluid?'

She nodded.

'Where?' asked Nicholas, leaning forwards towards her.

'On someone passing by – in the crowd.'

'You saw them?' He sounded hopeful.

Dee shook her head and then wished she hadn't. 'No, but I sort of followed the scent.'

'Good on you, Gran! I always thought you were a bit of a bloodhound,' Amelia exclaimed and Zara glowered at her daughter.

'Then what?' asked the Inspector.

'Well, I saw a figure – darting between the hotdog van and the Try your Strength stand.'

Nicholas glanced at Josh, who was jotting it all down.

'And you could tell they smelt of embalming fluid?' Zara sounded incredulous.

'No, of course not, they were too far away.'

'Then why did you follow them?'

'I don't know,' replied Dee. 'They just looked sort of furtive.'

'Height?' enquired Nicholas, hoping to get some solid facts and take over control of the interrogation from Zara.

Dee shook her head.

'Man or woman?'

She shrugged.

'Build?'

'I'm so sorry – really it was just an impression. I think they had on a grey hoody.' She sounded doubtful. 'I looked around for a bit but couldn't see anyone. I was about to go back and find you and Zara when I felt a prick in my arm and I blacked out. The next thing I knew I was under a bush and Mrs May was beside me.'

Mrs May was sitting on the other side of Dee from Zara. Now everyone looked at her and she visibly puffed up with pleasure.

Nicholas gazed at her encouragingly. 'Mrs May, can you tell us exactly what happened?'

She swelled a little more, a faint rose pink infusing her sunken cheeks. 'Yes! Well, I wanted to go home. Such rowdy crowds of people.' She screwed up her face in disapproval. 'Anyway, I thought I'd take the back route. So I went to the edge of the playing field and over the style to the footpath. It's shockingly overgrown – the council really should do something about it, but what can you expect? Bunch of idiots, the lot of them! If I had my way—'

'Mrs May!' Nicholas cut her off in mid-flow.

She regarded him with distaste. 'Well it's like Dee said – there she was under a bush. I heard a sort of moan and thought it might be that Blossom girl's annoying little dog.' She sniffed. 'Ridiculous animal, but it sounded as if it might be hurt, so naturally I looked. You probably want me to show you where it was, so you can get forensics to check?'

Nicholas nodded and gestured for Josh to go with her.

As she left she patted Dee's shoulder. 'You'll be alright now, love.'

Close to tears, Dee smiled and murmured, 'I can't thank you enough.'

Chapter 22

The next day found Dee on her sofa with a rug over her lower half and pillows propping up her shoulders. Cat was lying in such a way that Dee could no longer feel her feet. She hoped it wasn't deliberate, but with Cat one never knew.

The room was overflowing with Dee's jungle of green pot plants which had been supplemented with an abundance of floral bouquets from well-wishers. Sophie had obviously visited the new florist's at the top of the hill and had bought a beautiful orchid, Robert had made up a posy from the pink roses and catmint in his garden and dear old Christopher had used binder twine to tie together a fragrant bunch of his sweet peas.

She could hear Zara clattering around the kitchen, her brisk but clumsy movements further evidence of how unnerved she had been by the events of last night. *She should be in here listening to these ghastly Zen bells and nature sounds – it might soothe her nerves.* It was the sort of background soundtrack one normally came across in spas or upmarket beauticians. Dee briefly wondered if anyone actually listened to it outside those settings.

'Here you go, Gran!' declared Amelia, as she deposited a stack of glossy magazines on the coffee table. Dee regarded the titles – *Yoga Today*, *Traveller*, *Gardening*, and *Nature*. 'Lovely, dear, but could you get my novel? It's by my bed.'

'Sorry, no can do! Mum's orders, She feels that a Lavinia Lovelace romance requires too much concentration and the steamy bits would raise your blood pressure. You must relax and recover. If I were you, Gran, I wouldn't make too much fuss – she's only just let you out of bed and onto the sofa. Knowing Mum, if you kick up any sort of bother she'll send you straight to your room.'

Amelia resembled a sympathetic pixie. She was wearing her trademark tutu, corset and heavy boots, but the hues today were all different shades of translucent green. Dee though it suited her complexion. *I rather think I'll miss this creativity in the way she dresses should she ever grow out of it.* She had a sudden vision of a fifty-year-old Amelia, a doctor of Criminal Psychology, being called to give evidence at the Old Bailey. The judge, in gown and wig, would listen attentively as Amelia, probably wearing a black tutu and corset to mark the seriousness of the occasion, gave her expert opinion. She smiled at the thought.

'In that case, dear, could I have some other music on?'

Amelia shook her head again. 'Sorry, Mum says it's either this or whale-song. They are meant to be best for healing.'

'But I've been listening to this album of Zen bells and nature sounds for hours,' sighed Dee. 'Couldn't I have something by that nice Ed Sheeran?'

'Certainly not!' came Zara's firm response as she strode into the room with a tray of camomile tea. 'All that *'I'm in love with the shape of you'* is far too exciting for an invalid. You have had a near-death experience, Mother, and you need to take time to recover.'

'But I'm not dead, am I, dear?'

'No! But you so easily could have been killed. The murderer had you at his mercy! Goodness knows what would have happened if Mrs May hadn't found you when she did!'

Dee nodded.

'What a surprise, Mrs May turning out not to be such a wicked witch,' said Amelia as she poured out a cup of tea for Dee.

'Well, yes, I must admit I was surprised by, er – well, by how kind she was. I didn't know she had it in her. I fear, I must have misjudged her. Given how long I've known her, I'm ashamed to say I've had the wrong opinion of her for half a century.'

Amelia laughed.

Zara was plumping Dee's cushions so she could sit upright and drink her tea without spilling it. Satisfied with her labours, she left her mother in peace and went to sit down in a nearby armchair.

Dee noted her daughter's expression. *This rather reminds me of when she was about five and went through that phase of wanting to be a doctor – or was it a nurse? Either way, I seem to remember hours of being confined to the sofa or bed while she ministered to me. She used to have that very same look on her face. It was quite a restful interlude – so much better than when she wanted to be a fireman.*

Dee took a sip of tea and turned her mind back to the present. 'I've been thinking about things.'

'Like what?' asked Amelia.

Hoping she sounded casual so as not to alarm Zara, Dee said, 'Oh you know this and that – what's been going on lately.'

Zara tensed and her eyebrows shot up.

'But what I've really been pondering is about the murderer.'

'I knew it!' declared Zara springing up from an armchair. She swooped down on her mother and felt her forehead. 'At least you're not running a temperature … but I really think you need to talk to a professional to help you process your trauma. That nice lady from Victim Support said she could organise everything.'

'No, dear, that's not what I was thinking about. Why don't you just sit down and listen to me?' She allowed Zara time to resume her chair before she explained. Try as she might, Dee just could not keep an edge of excitement out of her voice. 'I think I must be getting too close to the murderer. Why else would they go to all the trouble of sluicing themselves with embalming fluid like it's Chanel No 5 and then deliberately brushing against me in the crowd?' Dee looked gleeful.

Zara was horrified. 'Mother, did you just hear what you said? How can you be so happy about it? If the murderer smelt of embalming fluid it was probably because they hoped to use it on you. It makes me feel ill just thinking about it.'

'Darling, we know it's someone with local knowledge, so it shouldn't be too difficult for us to work out who it is.'

'Shame it was Mrs May who rescued you – I rather fancy her a mass murderer,' commented Amelia.

'Yes,' agreed Dee sadly, 'but it can't be helped.'

'Well, at least we've narrowed the suspect list down. How about Blossom and Ken? They were at the fair – they might have thought you were getting rather close to pinning the Bernier and Harper murders on them,' suggested Amelia.

Dee shook her head. 'No, they were too busy. I watched their performance … you know they really are jolly good. Ken's tumbling was brilliant and it was such a lovely touch that they made all the children balloon animals at the end.'

Zara's innate curiosity had obviously won over her caution and she leaned forward in her armchair. 'If Ken is so good at tumbling he is obviously extremely strong – quite strong enough to move a body to your veg patch or hoist one up a tree in Warthing Woods?'

'Well yes, I suppose so but like I said—'

Amelia butted in. 'And we know they had a history with Bernier bullying Blossom so there's a motive. I have my doubts about Blossom's character – can anyone really be that sweet?'

Zara sighed. 'So young and already a cynic.'

Amelia brushed the comment aside. 'I'm just a realist.'

Zara was becoming more animated as evidence for Blossom and Ken's guilt accumulated in her head. 'I always thought it was a bit fishy the way Blossom was just knocked on the head and not killed on that day Granny found her in her shed.'

Amelia bit her bottom lip. 'But the same can be said for Granny.'

Both Zara and Amelia looked speculatively at Dee. She flushed. 'I think we can take my innocence as read.'

Zara waved her hand in the air as if trying to extinguish the notion of her mother as the killer. 'That aside, there are plenty of other things that point to their guilt.'

'Such as?' enquired Dee, with a touch of truculence as she was still smarting that it even crossed her family's mind that she might be involved in wrongdoing. *After all, they should know I don't even drop litter, let alone commit murder.*

Amelia stated. 'Last night, there was definitely something off – Ken's got quite a temper behind that façade of face paint. And did either of you notice his knuckles were grazed?'

'I was drugged, not punched,' said Dee sourly.

Zara chipped in. 'Really, Mother, use your imagination. He could have got it in a scuffle – knowing you, I'm sure you struggled a bit. What I was most struck by was Blossom clearly wanted to say something to us when we were asking about you, Mother, but he was determined not to let her. Finally, and to my mind, the most compelling point is that they have, without a doubt, got a thing for clowns.'

Amelia was nodding in agreement and Dee was set on pricking their bubble of blame. 'That's all very well but like I told you, it couldn't have been them that abducted me. They were doing their show.'

Amelia widened her green feline eyes, and tilted her head so her cascade of red curls tumbled around her face. 'You thought it was rather dear them finishing their display by making balloon animals for the children?'

Dee nodded. 'Ken does a rather good giraffe.'

'So the show was actually finished?' queried Amelia.

Dee nodded.

'And how long was it afterwards before you were attacked?'

Dee thought for a moment before saying, 'At a guess twenty minutes, or half an hour, at most.'

'So plenty of time for them to change from friendly clowns to homicidal maniacs? Something had definitely happened when we saw them later that evening.'

Dee realised what Amelia said was quite true and nodded sadly. 'I do hope it isn't them. Imagine how sweet it would be if they got married and had a whole troupe of mini-clowns.'

She blinked away a tear as she envisaged Ken and Blossom juggling and tumbling along with a bevy of red-nosed, curly-haired tots with Petal, in a pink tutu, as their sidekick.

Zara noted her mother's distress and said, 'Peter Wilson.'

Dee looked up, confused. 'Sorry, dear?'

'I was just trying to cheer you up by suggesting other possible murderers than Blossom and Ken. Peter Wilson comes to mind. Mrs May is right, he is an obvious choice. He was so rude when he came home last night – anyone with such atrocious manners is surely questionable.'

Amelia nodded. 'Mrs May's comments about him being fitter than he looks since his knee op and perhaps seeing himself a righter of wrongs is all very plausible; after all, he is always saying, "Once a policeman, always a policeman."'

Dee could not agree. 'No dear, he thought Bernier was wonderful because the man was happy to listen to his dreary reminiscences.'

'Actually Granny, from a psychological viewpoint, I would say that his drive to right a perceived wrong, to punish a malefactor, would be all the greater if he realised he'd been deceived by someone he'd considered a friend.'

'I think you're clutching at straws, dear. Why would he kill Justin Harper?'

Amelia shrugged. 'We know Harper was into blackmail, so perhaps he had something on Peter Wilson. As a man with a good reputation, he couldn't allow his image to be tainted.'

Dee was still not convinced. 'I really can't see him messing around with clown makeup – it all seems a bit too theatrical.'

Amelia was adamant. 'Theatrical? What do you call a ponytail, an MCC tie and a heavy metal T-shirt?'

Zara sighed loudly. 'So our only options for alternative killers are a middle-aged clown and his sidekick or a retired policeman. It's a bit dispiriting. Poirot always has a library full of suspects.'

Dee paled a little as she regarded the beautiful posy of flowers that Robert had brought over. He had turned up with Paul, knocked on the door and popped in for a minute. It was a brief visit but long enough for Paul to mention he'd been in London the night before for a regimental supper. He'd said it casually, but it had struck Dee with force. *So Robert was alone last night? But surely not – not dear, kind Robert.* Then she had looked at his hollow cheeks, his furtive looks and his agitated movements and she had realised that the Robert she had been fond of for years was very different from the man plying her with flowers today.

'Mother?' asked Zara sharply.

Startled, Dee stammered, 'What? Sorry? I was miles away, were you saying something?'

'No, but you were unquestionably thinking something, and judging by the way you've screwed up your face and gone pale it's something you'd rather not contemplate. Come on, spill the beans.'

'No! Really, dear, it's nothing, just me being silly.'

Zara and Amelia exchanged a look, and then Zara said sternly, 'Mother!'

'I can't believe I'm even considering it. After all, he's one of my closest friends.'

Amelia was leaning so far out of her seat that she was in danger of toppling. 'Who?'

Slowly Dee raised her eyes from the flowers to her family and her face changed from pale to crimson. 'Robert.'

There was a shocked silence and both Zara and Amelia just stared at her open-mouthed.

Dee felt compelled to explain 'There are so many ties – Justin Harper was a beneficiary of Robert's mother's will and Bernier was all wrapped up in it – something to do with trusts and fees and even poor Blossom somehow got involved.'

Zara regained enough of her wits to murmur, 'But Robert? He can't possibly be involved! He's … gay.'

Amelia's face turned as red as her hair. '*Mum*! You can't say that – it's homophobic.'

Zara was now just as outraged as Amelia. 'Nonsense, darling! How can that possibly be homophobic?'

'You are making a generalisation based on his sexuality.'

Zara inhaled about to defend herself but Dee coughed and said, 'Normally I would think that the reason Robert couldn't be a murderer was because of his character. I like to think that my friends are nice people not murderers but since he lost his mother he does seem to have had a bit of a personality change. What's more, when they dropped the flowers off, Paul mentioned he'd been in London last night for a regimental dinner.'

'So?' asked Zara.

'Well it means, that loathed as I am to admit it – Robert could easily have popped up to the fair and …' She swallowed. 'I'd like to think he couldn't actually kill me as he has some affection for me.'

They sat in silence for a full two minutes before Amelia attempted to lighten the mood. 'Are there any other friends you think might be capable of multiple murders?' she joked.

She was surprised when her Granny said, 'Well, yes.'

'Who?'

'I hate to say it but I can't help being a bit suspicious of Francesco and Gina.'

Before either Amelia or Zara could remonstrate she explained, 'Just after Bernier was killed I was with the family and when Marcello mentioned his name and Alex working with him, she reacted very strongly. Obviously something unpleasant had gone on with Alex and Bernier and you know how protective Gina and Francesco are.'

Zara looked thoughtful. 'And what a temper Francesco has.'

Dee nodded. 'Speaking of which I witnessed quite a confrontation between him and Justin Harper.'

Amelia shook her head. 'It can't be them, they are always tied up with the pub.'

'Actually, about that – you know the afternoon that I found Blossom in her shed? Well, I heard from Alex and Marcello that both Francesco and Gina had mysteriously disappeared that very afternoon with no explanation.'

As if on cue there was a knock on the door, Amelia went to answer it and Francesco and Gina could clearly be heard asking if they could just pop in for a moment to see Dee.

When they came into the sitting room both looked pale and worried. 'We just had to come and check on you – we're so sorry.'

'Why?' asked Amelia a little sharply.

Gina turned to her in surprise.

Amelia persisted, 'Why are you sorry? It's not like you had anything to do with Granny being killed, is it?' She had her hands on her hips and was glaring at them rather like a fierce little pixie.

Hastily Dee intervened. 'What Amelia is trying to say is there is no need for apologies, it's just so very kind of you to call by when you must be exhausted after last night.'

'Last night?' queried Gina, looking from Amelia to Dee.

Zara explained, 'You must have been rushed off your feet with all the extra customers from the fair; it's so exhausting.'

Francesco shrugged. 'It's all good for business, but it didn't help Gina getting one of her migraines halfway through the evening.'

Dee looked at her. 'You poor thing – you do look a little pale.'

Gina smiled weakly. 'It's annoying but nothing like you've just been through.'

Amelia was still taking a combative stance. 'So you weren't in the pub, surrounded by witnesses all evening?'

'Er, no, I had to go to bed.'

Zara was on her feet, keen to stop her daughter from actually accusing the pair of murder and assault right there and then. 'And quite the right thing too. Now I must see you out as the doctor says Dee mustn't be overtired.' She bustled them out of the room and could be heard opening the front door and bidding them farewell.

She returned to the sitting room in time to hear Dee say, 'So Gina, like Robert, doesn't have an alibi for last night.'

'What do we do now, Granny?' asked Amelia.

'I have a plan,' smiled Dee.

Zara sighed. 'I was afraid you were going to say that. I don't suppose there is any point in saying *'Why don't you leave it to Nicholas'*?'

Both her mother and her daughter looked at her with total incredulity.

Chapter 23

Nicholas was taking a moment of meditative calm to bring tranquillity to his soul. By totally focussing on the bonsai acer tree on his desk, by absorbing its every line and leaf, he could almost block out the urgent sirens and frenzied atmosphere of the police station.

'You're not going to like this, Gov.'

Nicholas looked up at Josh. The boy's normally smooth forehead was creased and his aquiline eyes troubled. He'd given up trying to get Josh to not call him 'Gov' but he wondered if there was still hope for him ditching his trainers in favour of brogues. *Probably not.* In his mind, Nicholas ran through all the calamities that would fall into Josh's definition of '*you're not going to like this*' and settled on the most abhorrent.

'Don't tell me you've spilt Coca-Cola over the inside of my car again.'

'No, it's not that, Gov. It's worse.'

Nicholas wondered what could be worse than Coca-Cola on car upholstery.

'It's Dee FitzMorris.'

Nicholas leapt to his feet. His brows drawing together, he stared at Josh. 'Has she taken a turn for the worse? Has the murderer tried again? I knew I should have insisted on officers staying with her.'

'No, Gov. It's nothing like that.'

He gripped the back of his chair, wishing Josh would get the hang of giving clear, precise information rather than inflicting an emotional drumroll on Nicholas, presumably to build tension and add to the dramatic effect of any statement he might make. Trying to keep his agitation out of his voice and to role-model professional calm, he sighed. 'Well, what is it?'

Josh rolled his eyes and with a hint of glee – or admiration – said, 'She's been getting Amelia to go all around the village telling everyone that she's got her memory back. That she remembers everything ... including who attacked her! And, as soon as she is back on her feet, she's going to tell you.'

Nicholas swallowed and stroked his chin, much as Confucius might have done when confronted by a confusing conundrum. He glanced at his bonsai tree but serenity eluded him. 'She's been getting Amelia to go around the village saying she knows who attacked her?'

Josh nodded eagerly and helpfully repeated, 'And saying that as soon as she's back on her feet she's going to tell you who murdered her.'

Nicholas blinked at Josh, trying to process what he'd just been told. 'Good grief, why doesn't she just ring me and tell me who it is? Doesn't she realise how much danger she's putting herself in? The murderer could try and do away with her before she speaks to me.'

With Zen serenity, Josh exhaled. 'I think that's the general idea, Gov.'

Nicholas let go of the back of his chair and tried to ground himself by grasping the innocent stem of the acer tree between his finger and thumb. He gave up the attempt, threw up his arms and bellowed, '*What?*'

By way of comfort, Josh added, 'She hasn't got her memory back, but according to Amelia she's certain this is a sure-fire way of luring the killer out in the open.'

Nicholas and Josh were at Little Warthing in less than half an hour. Josh glanced over at his boss, he was leaning forward in his seat as if the gesture could get them there more quickly. *This is probably not the moment to point out to the Gov that he's just broken several speed limits.*

They screeched to a stop outside Honeysuckle Cottage. With a single movement, Nicholas had undone his seatbelt, leapt from the car and marched up to Dee's front door. As Nicholas hammered on it, Josh's thoughts wandered. *I wonder if Amelia will be visiting her Gran?* He spent a lot of time hoping he would see her.

It was Zara rather than Amelia who opened the door. She was wearing an attractive green wrap dress he'd admired before and a neat pair of espadrilles with ribbons that wrapped around her slim ankles. Her eyes widened with pleasure at seeing Nicholas and through slightly parted lips she murmured, 'Nicholas, I'm so glad you're here – perhaps you can talk some sense into my mother.'

'Leave everything to me,' he declared, as he swept past her into Dee's sitting room.

Dee was looking serene and happy. The bloom of health was back in her cheeks, her eyes sparkled and the smile she gave him was positively buoyant.

Evidently, near-death experiences suit her, he thought dryly.

'Ah! Inspector. Josh. How lovely of you both to call in. I would make you some tea but Zara has gone all matronly and is refusing to let me off the sofa.'

Dee was sitting propped among her cushions with the plaid rug. Nicholas noticed that beneath the rug, not only was she fully dressed but she had muddy shoes on. Dee saw him glancing at her footwear and winked.

'I'll get the tea,' sighed Zara and left for the kitchen.

Once Zara was safely out of earshot Dee gave Nicholas a broad wink and in a conspiratorial whisper said, 'Just between us, Inspector, I'm bored to tears. I took advantage of Zara having a bath to do a spot of gardening.'

With a pinched expression and narrowed eyes, he replied, 'I wish you would confine your activities to just a bit of gentle weeding and pruning.' He sat down in the armchair opposite her. 'Josh tells me you've had Amelia going around telling all and sundry that you've got your memory back and know who the killer is.'

Dee's smile widened. 'Yes, isn't it thrilling? Frightfully Agatha Christie!'

'It's reckless and irresponsible, that's what it is!' he said severely.

Dee, as cool as the proverbial cucumber, smiled. 'I thought you'd say that! That's why I didn't tell you in advance.'

By the time Zara appeared with the tea, Dee's power of persuasion had suitably nudged Nicholas' thoughts to her way of thinking.

Zara actually walked in just in time to hear her mother say, 'Look, Nicholas, it really is the most sensible thing to do; we can't have a killer quietly going around the village murdering people or knocking them out. At this rate by autumn, we'll have no one left to celebrate at the Harvest Supper.'

Nicholas, legs crossed and shoes shining, was nodding. 'Yes! You do have a point.'

Dee drew her eyebrows together in concern. 'Of course, if the murderer has seen you and Josh visiting, then the whole thing is off as they will assume I've already told you all. Let's just hope that they haven't noticed you. After all even murderers have to do other things sometimes … you know, like buy loo roll or get their hair cut. Josh, be a dear and go and hide your car. If you ring Amelia she'll pick you up and sneak you in the back way. Then you can join us all on the stake-out.'

Nicholas made a practical query. 'How are we going to get secretly into your house without being seen? Always supposing this visit hasn't been noted. We can't both just stay – one of us must move the car – the killer is bound to know what my car looks like.'

Dee's face was totally alight. 'Fortunately, there is a handy little gap in the back hedge – the killer must know it as they used it to get Bernier into my chard, but it isn't overlooked so you or Josh can move your car and come back discreetly through that way. I must say, I think this will all be rather jolly!'

'Yeah!' agreed Josh happily. He was leaning languidly against the wall with a boyish grin on his face. 'Like a slumber party, but with the added edge of another possible murder.'

Dee corrected him. 'Well, dear, hopefully, we'll just be apprehending a murderer rather than falling foul of his evil intentions.'

Zara had been standing in the doorway, too shocked by what she was hearing to speak or even move. She had conveniently forgotten that not long ago she had been spurring her mother on in her quest for suspects. Now she marched into the room and slammed the tray down forcefully on the coffee table. The cups clattered and tea slopped onto the table. Standing tall she confronted Nicholas. Hands on hips and eyes blazing, in a frighteningly calm voice she said, 'Inspector Corman, am I right in saying that you are proposing using my mother as bait to catch a killer?'

Nicholas looked a little sheepish, but an encouraging nod from Dee prompted him to answer, 'Yes!'

Chapter 24

Dee always enjoyed playing the role of the hostess; she adored the theatrical nature of setting the scene for a magical evening of relaxed entertainment. *Although, of course, it doesn't have to be at night – brunches can be fun and teas are always amusing. But what am I going to do for this affair?* She looked at Cat for inspiration. Lying majestically on the back of the sofa, with her squashed face and long whiskers, she gave Dee a withering green-eyed glance. There were times when Dee wished her companion was not quite so obvious in her disdain for her.

'A James Bond-themed cocktail party would be fitting.' She spoke out loud, theoretically for Cat's benefit but in reality, it was a habit she'd acquired since living alone.

She was startled when Nicholas spoke; she'd quite forgotten he was there. He had insisted on staying while Josh moved the car. 'Sorry Dee, what was that? I didn't quite catch what you said.'

He looked both apologetic and embarrassed. Dee was not to know that she'd caught him mid-scroll as he looked for possible new model railway purchases on his phone.

Dee suspected that if she admitted the truth Nicholas might give her a look that would rival Cat's. 'Oh, nothing, nothing at all. It's very kind of you Nicholas to play watchdog but I'm sure it's unnecessary.'

'Let me be the judge of that. You just carry on as if I'm not here.'

He went back to looking at his phone and Dee wandered into the kitchen, still not sure what she was going to do.

Nicholas would probably think that having the James Bond theme was rather frivolous and that I wasn't taking my crime-busting role seriously. Besides which it would fall a bit flat without real martinis, and he wouldn't pop on a dickie bow. Besides which, too, I don't feel like making all the fiddly 1950s canapés.

Her eyes alighted on a splendid basket of juicy red strawberries by the kettle; a gift from Sophie along with the orchid. The strawberry season was well underway. Dee always made the most of it, buying fresh-picked every day when her appetite exceeded her garden's produce.

Excellent – I'll wash them, take off the stalks and put them in my cut-glass bowl next to some paper napkins and everyone can take one as they want.

She took out her favourite heavy glass jug and matching glasses. What she really wanted to do was mix sugar syrup with orange-flavoured liqueur, add champagne and serve over ice with lots of lime wedges but this evening called for clear heads, so instead she sliced half an orange, a lemon and a lime and poured in filtered water. The orange, yellow and green looked refreshingly bright and she smiled as she popped it in the fridge to cool.

We need something savoury. I do love cucumber sandwiches, cut into dainty triangles but I think they'd be too twee for this evening.

She opted for French savoury cake cooked as muffins for easy eating. They took no time at all and Dee enjoyed the rich sounds of olive oil and eggs being beaten into the flour and the warm scent of rosemary and sun-dried tomatoes. The heavenly smells only intensified as they baked.

Dee did hope that this evening would be more John Le Carrie than Enid Blyton but nonetheless, she was aware that lashings of ginger beer would go rather well with the muffins and strawberries.

For the next couple of hours, the little gap in the hedge behind the potting shed was made much use of. First, Amelia and Josh squeezed through it and crept up the garden path and into the kitchen. Amelia had picked Josh up outside the village and then smuggled him back in. Judging by their suppressed giggles they were finding it all rather fun. Dee suddenly thought of the French Resistance and heroic young women secretly hiding armies, but a quick glance at Amelia in ripped tights and biker boots dispelled that idea.

As they burst through the French windows and into the kitchen, Amelia had Josh firmly by the hand. The young pair only acknowledged Dee and Nicholas with a nod. Josh, casual in his trainers, slacks and T-shirt, only had eyes for Amelia.

'We'll hide out in the spare room!' Amelia declared as they ran upstairs.

Dee watched with her head tilted to one side. *Should I intervene? I'm not at all sure leaving poor Josh alone with Amelia in the spare room is a good idea. Perhaps I could make some alternative suggestion, something like, 'Don't you fancy sharing a French savoury cake muffin in the sitting room?'* I wonder what *stake-out etiquette is.* She looked over at Nicholas but he had his back to her and was preoccupied, looking out of the French windows. *Surely he should say, 'Not whilst you're on duty, young fellow!'* She guessed he was watching for Zara.

Half an hour earlier Zara had left by the front door. On the step, she had loudly declared, 'Well, if you're sure you're okay being all alone, Mother, then I'll be getting home. See you tomorrow!' She had swished down the road and roared off in her car.

Dee had waved her away, thinking that acting had never been her daughter's strong point and recalling many hammed-up roles she had had in school plays. The most painful recollection had been Zara as Titania in *Midsummer's Night Dream.* Dee could only assume she'd been given the role because of her striking red hair; it certainly wasn't because of her acting talent.

Nicholas did not have to wait long. Zara soon appeared, a vision emerging from the veg patch. She had changed out of the dress she had been wearing earlier and was now in a well-cut bottle-green jumpsuit paired with a pair of tan plimsolls. She was dressed for action. Dee wondered if her daughter really thought she was going to push Nicholas and Josh to one side and personally manhandle any would-be murderer.

Nicholas was totally lost as he recalled the youthful crushes he'd had on all the dynamic female leads in *Charlie's Angels.*

Zara slipped back into the house. Despite her initial resistance, she was now totally entering into the spirit of things. Her eyes shone as she took Nicholas as firmly by the hand, just as Amelia had taken Josh.

'I know just where we should hide – it's going to be rather like playing sardines. It may be a bit squashed but I'm sure we can manage.'

Dee just heard him rather weakly say, 'In my professional opinion, this is quite unnecessary,' before Zara bundled him into the coat cupboard under the stairs with her.

Dee observed their departure and muttered to Cat, 'I didn't have to bother making the muffins.' She decided that her efforts wouldn't go to waste; she poured herself a glass of citrus water and popped a muffin on a side plate before wandering into the sitting room and settling herself on the sofa.

How on earth will both Zara and Nicholas squeeze into that tiny space? Dee imagined them in the dark, with Nicholas' left leg propped against the vacuum cleaner while murmuring an apologetic, 'Oh, I'm so sorry, did I just nudge you with the broom handle?'

Cat followed her into the sitting room and Dee confided in him, 'I suspect that Nicholas will make a bid for freedom before too long.'

He didn't get the chance, as at that moment the doorbell rang. Adrenaline shot through Dee's body, her breath became shallow and she pressed her palm against her chest where it had suddenly become tight. The night of the fair came back to her in vivid clarity; she recalled what it had felt like to be weak and helpless.

Perhaps this isn't such a good idea after all.

She heard the front door open. Her heart seemed to be beating out of her chest. Her hands felt sweaty and she was about to scream for help when Blossom's curly head appeared around the sitting room door.

'It's only me! I hope you don't mind me just coming in – the door was open.'

Dee wanted to scream, 'Yes! I do mind! Leave me alone!' But her mouth had gone dry so she couldn't make a sound.

Blossom regarded her with wide innocent-looking blue eyes. 'Oh, dear! I can see you're not doing so well – you're as white as a sheet. I've brought you some cupcakes.' She held out a plate of her signature pink cupcakes. They appeared delectable; all neat and perfectly baked with a generous swirl of pink icing and sprinkles on each one. Dee recalled Snow White and that irresistible poisonous apple and suddenly lost her appetite.

'Do have one!' said Blossom, her blue eyes twinkling as she took a step towards Dee and the sofa.

Dee pushed herself further into the cushion. 'Oh – er – they do look delicious!' she stammered.

'They taste even better than they look. *Do* have one! I made them especially for you.' By this time she had thrust them right under Dee's nose.

Dee's voice came out as a tight squeak. 'Perhaps later.'

Blossom stared her in the eyes and with a force Dee would previously have thought her incapable of and said, 'I insist!'

Tentatively, Dee took one and pretended to have a nibble. Blossom's shoulders relaxed and she lost that tight pinched look she'd had around her smile. The rational part of Dee's mind knew she had only feigned having even a crumb of the suspiciously beautiful cupcake, but her imagination could not stop suggesting that her lips were tingling; swelling with some noxious substance. And was her throat tightening? Was it getting difficult to breathe?

Blossom sat down. 'I think we need to talk about what happened the night of the fair.'

'Do we?' said Dee, feeling that this had all been a dreadful mistake.

'Yes! Zara and Amelia have probably tipped you off. You see, they saw us, and then I overheard Amelia in the village shop telling the assistant you'd regained your memory.'

Dee sat, or rather lay, on the sofa, a bit like a bunny caught in the headlights. Fear rendered her unable to respond.

'You probably think it was very wrong of us.'

Dee, picturing Bernier and Harper's lifeless clown bodies, did think it was very wrong – but looking at Blossom's intent gaze, she felt now was not the time to judge.

'But you see, Ken and I take the clown honour very seriously.'

'I'm not quite following,' stammered Dee.

There was a bang at the door and Ken rushed in. He was breathless and flustered. He glanced at Dee on the sofa. 'Thank goodness I'm not too late!' He then looked at Blossom. 'You shouldn't do this alone.'

Blossom replied serenely, 'It's all right. She's had some cupcake.'

Dee felt her lips begin to tingle again.

'I know you think your cupcakes can solve anything, but sometimes it takes more.' Ken looked as if he was struggling to stay patient. 'How much has Blossom confessed to?' he asked Dee in a more businesslike tone.

He flopped down on the other armchair and began to rub his – what Dee presumed were sweaty – palms on his trouser legs. His knees seemed to have taken on a life of their own and were jumping up and down. Either he had just developed a facial tic or he had decided that now was the moment to repeatedly wink at Dee.

Dee swallowed. She didn't like the odds. It was now two against one. She felt that between them, Blossom and Ken could do quite a bit of damage to her before Nicholas and Zara got out of the cupboard.

'Not a lot,' she stammered.

'I was just confessing—' said Blossom helpfully.

Ken flinched. He was too far from being the calm accountant, or even the tumbling clown.

'I came just in time! You see, it wasn't Blossom's fault. It was mine. I've always had a terrible temper.'

Unbeknown to Dee at this point, Zara tried to escape the cupboard and come to her rescue but Nicholas held her back. There was the sound of something clattering to the ground from under the stairs.

'What was that?' Ken asked sharply.

'Mice,' Dee said firmly. 'Now what were you saying about confessing and your temper?'

'Yes, my temper has always been a problem.'

Blossom gave him a little pat on his arm. 'But you are *getting so much* better at controlling it.'

'But just think of all that trouble it would have saved if only I had got to grips with it earlier. Take all that aggro with Andrew Bernier. Everything would have been so much better if I had just let it go.'

'Andrew Bernier? So you took decisive action to stop him?' asked Dee eagerly. Curiosity had overcome her fear.

The tic had ceased but all his features, from his eyes to the corners of his mouth, sagged downwards. 'I tried,' he admitted sadly, 'but like I told you when you came to interview me … when I attempted to tip off the accountancy powers that be, it backfired on me. He was always so matey with anyone important. Chums with the great and the good at the golf club and all that tosh.' His face was a tragic mix of anger and despair.

Blossom raised her eyebrows in concern and gave him another pat. He looked deeply into her big blue eyes and his features softened. She took up the story. 'You see, somehow Bernier found out there were some … er … um—'

'Irregularities,' Ken said helpfully.

Blossom smiled and nodded. 'Yes, irregularities in my taxes.'

'Irregularities?' enquired Dee politely while hoping the conversation was not about to get beyond her.

'Nothing major,' said Blossom swiftly. She held a cupcake up to Ken which he took and bit into. She smiled with satisfaction and turned back to Dee.

'You see, I have a car, from work – part of the job's perks – but I find driving a bit alarming. I prefer my bicycle but I do use it occasionally if I need to go to the supermarket, stuff like that.' She turned her wide eyes on Dee. 'Don't you find people are so horribly aggressive on the road and they drive so fast?'

'And Bernier?' prompted Dee.

'He found out that I hadn't declared it properly. And then there was the work trip.'

Ken chipped in, his eyes brightening. 'Have I ever told you, Blossom, how very fetching you looked on that trip in your pink polka-dot bikini?'

She blushed. 'Oh, Mr Pilbersek.'

They both giggled.

'And Bernier?' persisted Dee.

Reluctantly Blossom bought her attention back from bikinis to dead accountants. 'The company had paid for the flight to Florida and it seemed a waste not to add a few days on the trip and have a holiday.'

Dee nodded encouragingly.

'When that horrible man found out he started making all sorts of threats – nothing explicit – just hints. That's when Ken tried to help.'

'So you took steps to deal with him? Decisive action to make sure he couldn't hurt Blossom any more? Something more decisive than just having a word with a bigwig at the golf club?' Dee asked looking hopefully at Ken.

Ken looked blank. 'No!'

'So you didn't—'

'Didn't what?' asked Ken.

Had Dee's hearing been more acute she would have heard Nicholas hissing, 'For goodness sake, don't say it!'

But Dee failed to hear his warning, so she carried on, 'Kill him! Oh, I'm so relieved. And if you didn't murder him presumably you didn't do away with Justin Harper either. I can't tell you how glad I am. You and Blossom make such a lovely couple. It would be a shame if you both ended up in prison.'

Blossom and Ken stared at Dee, too shocked to speak. Blossom's blue eyes grew even larger and Ken's mouth fell open.

This gave Dee time to think of something. 'But if it wasn't you who tried to abduct me on the night of the fair, why were you both looking so dishevelled?' She glanced from one to the other in the hope of an answer to her confusion.

Ken blushed. 'That's what I'm so ashamed of!'

'What?' persisted Dee.

'Well, when we were on our way home, some louts started bothering Blossom … and there was a bit of a scuffle.' He stopped talking and looked at his shoes.

Blossom carried on, 'He's a bit embarrassed as he didn't manage to fight them off. But he did do brilliantly! I was so proud of him. He was so brave even though he was outnumbered.'

This praise was enough to give Ken the courage to raise his head. He glanced at his watch. 'We should be going. We need to practise our new tightrope-walking act.'

'Right-ho,' said Blossom happily. 'Enjoy the cupcakes!' were her final words as she disappeared out of the door.

Dee didn't have time to confer with Zara and Nicholas about these revelations as next Peter Wilson arrived. He knocked loudly and then barged in. She caught her breath and gripped a nearby cushion, holding it in front of her for protection.

He was big and cumbersome. He rather reminded Dee of a large bull, but one with an MCC tie and ponytail rather than a ring through his nose.

He marched in and straightaway she thought, *I see what Mrs May means by him being very agile since his knee op.*

He surveyed the sitting room and boomed, 'Oh good! I was hoping to catch you alone! I understand from that odd granddaughter of yours that you have got your memory back.'

His voice vibrated through the house.

Dee winced at the volume. *The poor man must be profoundly deaf – which isn't his fault – but is it pride that stops him from wearing a hearing aid? At least Nicholas and Zara will be able to hear every word he says. Actually at that volume, so will Amelia and Josh upstairs. So if he does strangle me at least I'll have the consolation of knowing he won't go unpunished, but who will look after Cat?*

Peter Wilson stood looming over Dee. He paused and then launched into what sounded like a prepared speech. 'I see it as my duty to maintain law and order. Standards today are slipping left, right and centre. People feel free to flout the law as they please. Even highly-respected and likeable chaps, like Andrew Bernier – or good-looking charismatic types, like that Justin Harper, seem to think they're above the law. Someone has to make a stand. And if I don't, who will?'

'The police?' suggested Dee.

He snorted in disgust. 'Don't be ridiculous! The force now is full of incompetent idiots like that Nicolas Corman.'

There was another loud crash from the cupboard under the stairs.

'What was that?' asked Peter Wilson.

'Mice!' said Dee. She leaned forward. 'So you decided to do something about it?'

'Yes!'

Dee smiled. Her curiosity was finally paying off. Peter took her smile as all the encouragement he needed. He looked pious. 'Some people might say it's wrong to take the law into one's own hands. But there are times a responsible citizen, especially a retired police officer, must not just sit on the sidelines!'

Dee sat up straighter and, looking directly into his eyes, said, 'Yes. Quite! So you ...?'

'Rang the police!'

Outrage clear in every syllable, Dee exclaimed, 'What? That's *all* you did? After being so rude about dear Nicholas?'

'Yes! Well, what else could I do?'

It was a despondent clan of sleuths that ate Blossom's cupcakes and drank tea together half an hour later.

'So that's that, then!' said Dee sadly.

'Wicked cupcakes!' said Josh.

Nicholas tried to sound positive. 'Don't be too despondent. I'm sure we'll get to the bottom of this.'

'Well, I'm spending the night with Mother, just to be on the safe side,' commented Zara.

At about eleven, Amelia, Nicholas and Josh said farewell to Zara and Dee. They left via the back garden and the gap in the hedge as it was closer to Amelia's car and she was giving the gallant boys in blue a lift back to their car.

Zara and Dee only had time to put the kitchen to rights when they were surprised by a knock at the front door.

Dee froze, tea towel in hand.

Zara stiffened, her brows raised above her wide green eyes. She mouthed to her mother, 'The killer?'

Dee shrugged.

There was another knock.

'Should I get it?' hissed Dee.

Zara grasped her mother's arm and shook her head. She whispered, 'We should ring Nicholas!'

'There's no time for that, dear,' said Dee, removing Zara's hand from her arm.

'Then pretend you're out.'

'That's hardly likely with all the lights on. Besides if that is the killer we can hardly just let them go.'

Zara glared at her mother. 'Why not?'

Dee sighed. 'We just can't – you go back to the cupboard under the stairs and I'll answer the door.'

'Let me get my mobile; I can ring Nicholas from the cupboard.'

There was a rattle of the door handle. Dee supposed the potential murderer was seeing if it was locked.

Dee knew it wasn't and hastily propelled Zara to the cupboard. She was only just in time as the front door opened.

She turned to see Gina, in a vivid blue dress, and Francesco in jeans and what looked to be a silk shirt. He'd left undone the top three buttons which gave Dee an unnecessary glimpse of his hairy chest.

Gina spoke. 'We needed to see you, so we came round as soon as we'd shut the pub up.'

Francesco took a step forward, his dark sharp features taut. 'It was very foolish of you to have Amelia go all around the village telling everyone that you've got your memory back and know who the killer is.'

Dee swallowed and for the umpteenth time that evening agreed with those sentiments. As her mouth was dry it was difficult to speak so she nodded in agreement.

Francesco looked at her with steely black eyes and vehemently declared, 'Harper and Bernier, they both deserved to die; the world's a better place now they're not in it. I am glad they are dead.'

Dee glanced over at Gina who had an unaccustomed grimness about her mouth and her eyes were hard. 'Bernier made our Alex's life a misery.' Gina's fist was clenched and Dee took a step backwards. 'She'd done so well then she made a simple auditing mistake and he found out and kept hinting he was going to make trouble for her.'

Francesco was puce with rage beneath his tanned skin. He spat the words out. 'Then that damned Harper got in on the act and kept saying how God would see to it that Alex's life would be so much easier if we would just donate to his mission.'

Gina put a restraining hand on his shoulder. 'But that's not why we're here.'

'It's not?' choked out Dee.

'We want to let you in on a secret.'

About you killing them both? But why the clown makeup? Could it be an Italian thing?

'You do?'

Gina smile. 'Although I think you already have some suspicions – I saw you looking at Alex and Marcello when they let slip we'd both been away from the pub on the afternoon Blossom was locked in her shed.'

Dee stammered, 'No, not really, not at all. Would you like a French savoury cake muffin? I made them with sun-dried tomatoes.'

Gina blinked. 'Not now, perhaps later. As I was saying you probably want to know where we disappeared off to.'

'No, not at all, none of my business. Cupcake? I think there's one left.'

Gina shook her head. 'Are you … alright? You seem a bit confused after your ordeal. When we were here earlier it was difficult to talk with – er – Amelia there. She's very – er – protective.'

'I'm fine, absolutely fine.'

'Well, as I was saying we want to let you in on a secret.'

Dee shut her eyes. *Why didn't I listen to Zara and pretend to be out? We both could have hidden in the cupboard.*

Gina looked at her anxiously. 'We trust you can keep a secret?'

Dee nodded vigorously.

Gina and Francesco exchanged a significant look, and then Gina said, 'Shall I?'

Francesco nodded.

Gina, slightly flushed, swallowed and turned to Dee. 'This may surprise you.'

Dee felt she was way beyond surprise.

Gina smiled and in a rush announced, 'We're getting a puppy! She's the sweetest little border terrier.'

There was a moment of silence while Dee gaped at them as she tried to process this information. In return, they looked expectantly at her.

Zara had evidently been able to absorb the news more rapidly than her mother. Loudly, she exclaimed, 'Well! Really!'

Francesco and Gina jerked their gaze to the cupboard door under the stairs.

'What was that?' whispered Gina.

'Zara,' said Dee lightheaded with relief and beaming.

'In the cupboard under the stairs?' queried Gina, confused and incredulous.

Dee's head was swimming and she was rapidly moving from elation to a cortisol crash. 'Yes! She's checking for woodworm. Now I mustn't keep you; you must be longing for your beds. I know I am.'

Dee started making gestures towards the exit but Gina stopped her. 'We still haven't told you why we wanted to speak to you.'

Dee paused. As they hadn't called in to confess to being homicidal maniacs she didn't really care what their reasoning for the visit was. All she knew was that suddenly her lavender-scented sheets were calling her. 'I thought it was to tell me about the puppy,' she said while throwing open the front door.

Gina laughed. 'Well, sort of. You see, we want a favour. We would like to surprise the children. She's adorable, they'll love her. The breeder has offered to drop her off early afternoon on Saturday. The pub will still be open so it will be hardly ideal.

Could we have her dropped off here and we'll pick her up as soon as we possibly can?'

'I'd be delighted. I can't think of a more enjoyable way to spend an afternoon,' Dee replied honestly before firmly pushing them out of the door and carefully locking it.

Chapter 25

When Dee finally flopped into bed she felt totally exhausted but sleep eluded her. She'd had her final cup of camomile tea with Zara and had added a teaspoon of honey for the shock. *And this evening has been made up of one shock after another.*

She'd bathed in a cool lavender-scented bath and even sprayed her pillow with more soporific lavender, but it seemed that all the camomile and lavender in the world couldn't lull her into slumber. Her mind was whirling.

Of course, it's a relief that dear Blossom isn't a murderer – it really would have destroyed my faith in human nature if it had turned out that she could be so cute and pink one minute and a crazed killer the next. Even with Ken egging her on, she is far too gentle to go around killing people. And her cupcakes are divine – if she was a murderer it would be a bit like discovering that Mary Berry had a dark side. Dee shuddered. *And it seems that Peter Wilson is an objectionable individual but quite harmless.* She recalled the inconsiderate way he habitually played his radio at full blast and amended her judgement. *He's only marginally harmful.* Finally, she thought of Gina and Francesco. *What fun – a puppy. I shall look forward to Saturday afternoon.*

She decided to try her breathing and relaxation exercises – breathing in deeply for a count of three then exhaling for a count of five while tensing and relaxing her muscles, starting with her face and finishing with her toes. But as she completed the exercise her mind was flooded with a new thought. She drew her eyebrows together and pursed her lips. *Of course, they might be lying. Anyone who is happy to kill and is disagreeable enough to desecrate my veg patch isn't going to be shy about lying.*

She rolled onto her side, her cool cotton sheets caressing her. She took a deep breath and closed her eyes. *If only I could wind the clock back and return to those halcyon days when it never occurred to me that my friends and neighbours weren't exactly who they appeared to be.*

There is a glimmer of hope that Ken, Blossom, Peter Wilson, Gina and Francesco are all telling the truth, otherwise, they would have taken advantage of me being supposedly alone to bump me off in order to stop me from telling Nicholas who the killer was.

The thought gave her little comfort and she smiled to herself but her relief was short-lived.

Robert! It can't be Robert – of all the people in the village it would be most heartbreaking for me if he was guilty. I'm very fond of him, besides which, his mother would be so disappointed.

Her mind ranged for alternative suggestions. *Sophie and David? But what would the motive be? Christopher and Vivian Plover? But again why? And there are all those people at the golf club who knew both Bernier and Justin Harper who might well have good reason to do away with them but if they are not personally known to me, why choose my chard to dump the body?*

Feeling like a defeated failure, Dee fell into an uneasy sleep.

It must have been about two in the morning when she woke up from an uncomfortable dream. She could not remember the details, but it had left her with a feeling of foreboding. She lay in her comfy bed listening to the gentle rustles of a summer night. The moon was full and cast a mythical glow over Little Warthing and the surrounding countryside. She tried to think of happy things in an attempt to get back to sleep. After half an hour of focusing on flowers and fruit, she gave up, pulled on her dressing gown and slippers and went downstairs.

She made herself a camomile tea and took it into the garden. Cat came with her. Her feline companion languidly wove her way through the flowerbeds. The night-flower scents and the cool dew-laden air soothed her. Then, suddenly she realised what the nagging worry was. She was able to see clearly the fear that was keeping her awake.

Mrs May. She gripped her cup so hard that her knuckles showed white. *She hasn't popped in to check on me all day – there hasn't even been a phone call. Ever since she rescued me she has been so solicitous – rather too solicitous – inquiring multiple times a day how I am getting on, then today, nothing.*

'Oh Cat, I think I've made a terrible mistake. Let's hope it's not too late.' Cat gave Dee a withering look. 'Of course, the murderer would be certain I hadn't seen them. They were so careful to keep out of sight and to inject me from behind. Mrs May, on the other hand, could so easily have walked past them or noticed them from the corner of her eye.'

Leaving Cat to her night foraging, Dee dashed back inside.

I should wake Zara but the poor thing is quite exhausted and needs a good night's sleep... Besides which, she wouldn't let me go.

Still in her dressing gown and slippers, with her heart beating fast and a tingling of fear running up and down her spine, she carefully opened the front door. *If I make any sound at all Zara is bound to wake up and make a fuss.*

Zara was sleeping in the spare room that overlooked the road, so Dee continued to creep in silent stealth across her small front garden. Even in her agitated state, the gardener in her noted, *those hollyhocks are coming on a treat. They're taller than I am and it won't be long before they flower, but I must make the time to get in here and do a bit of deadheading the other plants.*

She reached the pavement but suddenly thought, *there's someone there! But who would be out and about and this time of night?*

She felt her shoulders tighten and started to sweat. Instinctively she drew back and crouched behind a bush. Well-hidden, she peered around the foliage and examined the figure. *He's right by Mrs May's gateway, but is that because he was walking past or has he just come out from there?* She felt slightly sick. *Am I too late?*

She screwed up her eyes. *It's definitely a man and that slim build looks familiar.* As if sensing he was being watched, the figure swung around. Dee bit her lip to stop a gasp from escaping and froze in the bush. Blinking rapidly she found herself repeating over and over again in her mind, *No, no it can't be, it simply can't.* But it was – there was Robert.

For what seemed like an age, he stared in Dee's direction but finally satisfied he turned and walked away. Dee closed her eyes and shook her head, feeling betrayed. Then, *Mrs May!*

She dashed up to her neighbour's door. One or two lights were on. This was not unusual. Mrs May, like many people who live alone, tended to keep an upstairs landing light on and one downstairs. What was unusual was that the front door was open.

Perhaps I should call the police, or at least Zara, thought Dee, as she hurried into the front hall.

She had never been inside Mrs May's home but she was not surprised to find it much like Mrs May herself: grey and sterile. There was a pervading smell of bleach. Dee glanced in at the kitchen, and the living room and even peered through the window at the back garden. All was immaculately boring. It was all eerily devoid of life. Dee took a deep calming breath which did little to quell her beating heart.

With stealth that Cat would have been proud of, Dee mounted the stairs. On the landing, she paused to listen again. Still no sound. She had rather hoped to hear the reassuring grunt and whistle of Mrs May, deep in slumber and snoring loudly.

Her eyes had grown quite accustomed to the half-light, but there was not a lot to see. The landing was uncarpeted. There were no pot plants or paintings to gladden Mrs May's heart as she climbed the stairs to bed. All the time Dee's heart felt as if it was bounding outside her chest and try as she might, she couldn't calm herself. *So much for practising my deep breathing most mornings while doing my Taekwondo forms.*

Dee paused, and her nose twitched. *What's that faint smell?*

It was somehow familiar. It was a fragrance that fought for Dee's attention over the odour of the bleach. Then it came to her

– embalming fluid!

I'm too late! thought Dee desperately, as she opened the nearest door.

It was the bathroom – bleak but mercifully free of dead bodies. She tried the next door. This time it was a bedroom, the master room judging by the size. The open curtains allowed the full moon to shine in. Bleak was too optimistic a word to use to describe the desolate room. It was grey and barren. The only furniture was a prison-style metal bed. On it, positioned with surgical precision was a sheet and a thin pillow. On that emaciated pillow was the most surprising thing of all; a stuffed clown doll. Its broad smile shone out valiantly against all the grey, its red wool hair splayed out against the cushion. The blue-button eyes gazed directly at Dee. While she was trying to come to terms with what she was looking at, Dee heard someone behind her.

'So, you're here at last. I have been waiting for you.'

And there was Mrs May herself. She was still in grey from head to foot, but instead of a shapeless dress she wore protective goggles, a thin plastic apron and gloves. On her feet was a pair of Wellington boots.

'Mrs May. I … er … I was worried about you,' stammered Dee staring with wide eyes. 'I thought you might be in danger.' She inhaled and rather weakly finished by adding, 'I came to save you.'

Mrs May's laugh echoed out through the silence. 'Well it looks like you got that wrong, doesn't it?' She cackled again. 'But you never were that bright, were you? I know you always came top of the class and on prize day you were so sickening – with your shiny hair and your arms full of cups – but that was just because you were little Miss Popular. I always knew I was cleverer than you and now I've proved it!'

The moon glinted on her protective goggles. There was no hiding the gleam of satisfaction on her face.

Dee struggled to make sense of what she was saying but everything was so jumbled in her mind. Mrs May in this foolish outfit, the gruesome corpse in her chard, the grotesque figure of

Justin Harper tied to a tree with his habitual grin painted in garish red, Blossom tie and bound, herself assaulted in a noisy fairground and her memory of an unhappy, unloved schoolgirl.

'So was all this – Bernier, Harper – just some way to get back at me?' asked Dee. She was incredulous.

'It didn't start off like that,' admitted Mrs May philosophically.

Dee swallowed. 'Then why?'

'Well, I think I got the initial idea after I retired.' Her tone was chatty only her protective clothing and the maniacal look in her grey eyes suggested that this was rather more sinister than a normal neighbourly catch-up.

'When you retired?' Dee was in total confusion.

What can retiring as a librarian have to do with becoming a multiple killer with an obsession for clowns?

'Yes! You see, when I was head librarian, I was somebody. People looked up to me. They had to do as I said or take the consequences. Then suddenly no one listened to me!' Her pale complexion began to suffuse with purple. 'Do you know how often I told that Andrew Bernier to clean up after his dog? He never listened; just laughed in my face. I must have said to myself a hundred times "I am going to strangle that man!"' Her expression lost its anger and was replaced by smug satisfaction. 'Then one day I did.'

'But how? He was small, but surely you weren't strong enough?'

'It did take a bit of thought. I must admit, originally I'd planned on using my sleeping pills but Zolpidem isn't fast-acting enough. Handy thing about being a librarian is you pick up all sorts of useful information. Insulin was easy enough to get hold of – a little squirt of the stuff and as you know you're out of it. So I made him suitably subdued and strangled him.'

Dee bit her lip but she just had to ask the obvious question. 'And the clown makeup?'

A note of asperity came into Mrs May's voice. 'Like I keep telling you, he was a fool.'

It was only now that Dee noticed that in her right hand, Mrs May held a syringe.

Dee swallowed again. *I need to play for time. If only I'd done the sensible thing and woken Zara but too late for that ...*

'But why my vegetable patch?'

'You asked for it! You deserved it! Have you any idea what it was like to move in here, then to find that you of all people were my neighbour? This place was meant to be my dream home! It was going to be a fresh start for a happy retirement – and what do I find but you! Here in Little Warthing! It was just like being back at school, with you as Queen Bee and everyone loving you. I had to make them all see who you really are!' She spat out the last sentence.

There was a pause before Dee quietly asked, 'And Justin Harper?'

'I thought he loved me!'

She sounded so pathetic Dee almost walked over to her and put her arms around her bony shoulders, but somehow the mortuary attire deterred her.

Mrs May sniffed. 'I haven't felt like that about anyone since you stole away my first love and married him. Then that Zara of yours took up with my Justin Harper and he never gave me a second glance. He'd only been after my savings. He never cared for me at all!' She sniffed again, then brightened. 'It was most convenient in the end, what with him living so close to the wood where you go bird recording. I must say, my wheelbarrow has been very useful this summer.'

'Insulin again?'

Mrs May nodded. 'And with Blossom, but I didn't get the dose right.'

'And me?'

Mrs May smiled broadly. 'With you, I wanted to have a little fun, so I deliberately gave you half a dose.' She laughed. 'It's been hysterical! You were so pathetic! So grateful! It's been like watching a comedy. What with you sending Amelia off to spread the word, that you knew who the killer was. Like I said, you're not that clever, are you? It was so obvious. You always have read far too many Agatha Christies.' She waved the syringe in the air and, through her guffaws, spluttered, 'Then yesterday when you were smuggling policemen in and out of your house. I could see everything out of this bedroom window.' She gestured with the syringe to the plain plate window behind Dee with its thin curtains. 'It was like Piccadilly Circus, with all the comings and goings.'

Her shoulders heaved with laughter and tears rolled down her cheeks. She pushed her goggles up and dabbed away at her eyes with a handy tissue.

'But enough of this. It really is time to deal with you.'

Mrs May took a threatening step towards Dee.

If ever there was a time when all my martial arts training should come in handy, now is the moment.

Dee inhaled deeply, drew herself to attention and solemnly bowed to her opponent. *Mrs May might be a deranged multiple-murderer with no dress sense but one should always show respect.*

Mrs May stopped and stared, then she began to laugh once more, a barking, derisive laugh which stopped only when she sneered, 'Who are you kidding? As if you could ever bring yourself to hit, let alone kick, an old lady!'

Dee paused as the truth of Mrs May's words sunk in.

Mrs May was finding the whole situation highly amusing and it occurred to Dee that she had never heard her laugh as much. 'That's probably your worst character flaw – you have principles. Fortunately, I don't.'

She took another step towards Dee. The plastic suit crackled and the rubber boots squelched.

Desperately Dee glanced around the barren room for inspiration. There was only the bed. She leapt onto it, totally destroying its impeccable neatness. For a second she looked down on Mrs May and contemplated surprising her with an aerial attack, but just in time thought, *There's a high chance I'll just end up impaled on that needle and injected with whatever's in the syringe.*

She leapt off the bed on the other side. *At least the bed is a sort of barrier between us.*

'This is all quite futile you know.' Mrs May's voice was icily calm and she took relentless step after relentless step, coming ever closer, despite the bed.

'Why don't we talk about this, over a cup of camomile tea?' Dee was beyond fear; she was now in survival mode.

'You and your bloody cups of camomile tea. This has all been most entertaining but now it's time to finish it.'

'You won't get away with this! Zara has already called for the police.'

Mrs May laughed and took another step.

It's a bit like playing grandmother's footsteps with the risk of death at the end.

Dee picked up a pillow and hurled it at Mrs May's head. Annoyed the other woman punched it away and it fell with a thud on the floor.

Mrs May cursed. 'Do you really think this is some schoolgirls' pillow fight in the dorm?'

Dee grabbed the toy clown.

Mrs May gasped. 'Put Mr Clown down!'

Dee raised an eyebrow. *There is someone Mrs May cares about!* She catapulted the clown over Mrs May's head.

Mrs May let out a howl of anger as it fell to the floor by the door. She turned to retrieve the much-loved toy.

Dee took advantage of both her adversary's distraction and the fact she'd turned her back. She bounded onto the bed and then sprung onto Mrs May's back, tightly wrapping her legs around the women's waist while at the same time grabbing her right arm. She held it so that the woman couldn't stab at her.

Mrs May staggered under the assault but she didn't fall. Instead with her left arm clutching Mr Clown protectively to her bony chest and her right arm extended out, she pivoted round and round in little circles while Dee clung on. Mrs May's cries were animal-like in their rage. Dee could feel her, all bones and fury, beneath her.

For Dee, terror had been overtaken by a laser-like clarity and determination; the more Mrs May screamed and flayed the tighter Dee gripped.

Eventually the inevitable happened and Mrs May over-balanced and sprawled onto the floor, dislodging Dee and sending the syringe flying across the room.

Side by side they lay panting on the linoleum floor. It was at exactly the same instant that they both registered what had happened and lifted their heads to locate the deadly syringe. It had rolled under the bed and lay there innocently.

In a fraction of a second the two women exchanged a glance then both lunged towards it. Dee, unencumbered by wellies, protective goggles and rubber gloves, was swifter. She threw herself under the bed, her fingers reaching for the syringe. But just as her fingers touched it, she felt Mrs May's claw-like fist grab her ankle in a painful grip. The jolt sent the syringe rolling further away, beyond her reach to the other side of the bed.

It was in that moment that Dee made a dramatic discovery. Mrs May had been wrong – if her life depended on it, Dee could kick an old woman and kick hard.

With all her force she raised her free leg and smashed it into Mrs May's face. Her slipper came off on impact. Mrs May grunted, obviously surprised and winded but most important of all she let go of Dee's other leg.

Free, Dee sprang to her feet. She glanced at where the syringe was – by the window – and back at Mrs May, who was rapidly recovering. Then she looked at the door.

She had a split second to make a decision: fight or flight?

She bit her lip, thought of Zara and Amelia, and ran towards the shut door. She fumbled with the handle – surely Mrs May hadn't had time to lock it. Her sweaty hands couldn't get a grip and all the time she could hear the woman staggering to her feet and going for the syringe.

In her desperation she rattled the door, she twisted the handle but all to no avail.

Mrs May was behind her now and let out a low chuckle.

Should I turn and fight or do I try the door one more time? Dee knew her life depended on her making the right choice.

She could hear Mrs May's lumbering breath as she took a step closer and could imagine her raising her arm with the syringe in her fist and the moon glinting off the silver tip of the needle.

'Please God! Please!' Dee whispered out loud.

Mrs May gave another chuckle; she was closer than Dee had thought. 'God can't help you now!' she sneered and at that instant, the door opened.

Dee dashed through and slammed it behind her, hearing Mrs May shriek as it hit her in the face.

Dee lost her other slipper on the top step. She kicked it away and half-jumped, half-ran down the stairs. Behind her, she heard the bedroom door open and footsteps pursuing her down the stairs.

Near the bottom Dee tripped. She grasped at the bannisters but it was too late to save herself. With a painful thud, she hit the ground, rolling so she was face up and looking into Mrs May's cold grey eyes. The woman with a smirk of satisfaction grunted and raised the syringe.

Dee blinked and at that very moment, the road outside was flooded with sirens and flashing lights. Mrs May looked up for a fraction of a second and that tiny fragment of time was all Dee needed to grab Mrs May's foot with both hands and jerk with all her strength, pulling her feet from under her and successfully sending her sprawling onto her back.

Dee rolled back onto her feet and ran out of the front door, into the road and Zara's arms. Policemen leapt from cars in every direction and there was Nicholas Corman, with Josh close behind.

Dee began to cry, sobbing heaving tears of relief and Zara cradled her in her arms as if she were a frightened child awakening from a nightmare.

'It's all alright now, you're safe,' murmured Zara.

Dee buried her head in her daughter's shoulder and allowed all the tension to seep away. There was a lot of shouting over the noise of the sirens and she just wanted to block it all out.

She heard footsteps approaching and recognised Robert's voice, 'What on earth's going on? Is Dee alright?'

She could feel Zara nodding. 'Yes, just a bit shaken – she's had a rather trying experience.'

Dee lifted her head to assure him all was fine but she was taken off-guard by the sight of Mrs May, still in her Wellington boots and goggles, handcuffed and being led away by two burly uniformed police officers.

She looked so tiny and frail that Dee's heart went out to her – that was until she heard the string of profanities coming from that woman's not-so-frail mouth.

Robert stared. 'Where are they taking Mrs May? And why is she dressed like that?'

'She's the killer and she's just tried to murder my mother. Thank goodness I woke up and found that Dee was gone and rang the police,' announced Zara and then with a crisp tone added, 'but of course, if my mother had done the sensible thing and woken me or even rung the police herself none of this would have happened.'

Dee pulled herself out of Zara's arms, feeling the need to defend herself. 'That's very unfair. It wasn't as if I knew Mrs May was the murderer when I went over there.'

She glanced at Robert, but managed to refrain from mentioning that when she'd seen him on the road she'd assumed he was the killer.

'But why go over there in the first place?' Zara's relief at finding her mother safe was rapidly giving way to anger at Dee's foolhardy behaviour.

Dee took a step back and crossed her arms in front of her. 'I was worried about her. She didn't call yesterday and I thought she might have been attacked by the killer; so I went to save her.'

Mrs May let out a finally screaming oath, that rang out over the sounds of sirens, as she was helped into the police car.

Zara didn't say anything but she raised an eyebrow, a gesture which spoke volumes and infuriated Dee as she knew that all Zara was clearly thinking was true.

Robert let out a sigh and shook his head. 'I can't believe it. Mrs May? I was just here a bit ago. Since Mum died I've had the most terrible insomnia and I often walk around the village at odd hours. If only I'd seen you, Dee, I could have helped.'

Again Dee managed to stop herself from explaining, *Of*

course you didn't see me, I was hiding in a bush.

Ken hurried up, an anxious expression on his face and wearing sensible striped pyjamas with an old-fashioned wool dressing gown. By his side was Blossom; her pyjamas were suitably pink and frilly, she evidently hadn't been able to find her slippers as on her feet she wore her short wellies covered with daisies.

Robert was answering their stream of questions when Peter Wilson lumbered over. Dee was impressed by Peter Wilson's flamboyant silk dressing gown, despite it straining at the waist where he'd tied it over his large girth.

He looks just like a boxer. She looked again and amended that thought. *A heavyweight boxer.*

'I knew it! I always had my suspicions about her – eyes too close together. I can always tell. Once a policeman, always a policeman,' he boomed.

He gazed over at Mrs May's bungalow. 'Excuse me, I'll just go and see if young Corman needs my help.'

He strode over toward the door but was stopped by a young woman officer who barred his way.

While they argued it out Francesco and Gina came running up. This time it was Blossom who explained everything and Gina hugged Dee tightly to her amble bosom while Francesco exhaled oaths of horror.

Dee looked around at all her wonderful neighbours and felt a surge of love and happiness. 'Why don't you all come back to mine for a cup of camomile tea and some French savoury cake?'

'Oh lovely. I'll just pop home and get some more cupcakes,' exclaimed Blossom.

When Josh and Nicholas had wrapped up what they needed to do at Mrs May's, they walked over to Honeysuckle Cottage and were greeted by a convivial scene. Crammed around the kitchen table were Dee in her cream silk PJs and dressing gown, and Zara in a flowing emerald green nightie with a matching wrap, surrounded by Dee's neighbours who – all bar Robert – were also still in their nightclothes.

The sun had risen and the French windows were open to allow in all the fresh summer scents and sounds. Someone had lit several generously-sized candles which twinkled amongst Dee's pot plants and herbs. Blossom had indeed gone to fetch more cupcakes, Ken had got some of his and Blossom's favourite coffee while Gina and Francesco between them had come back from The Flying Pheasant armed with bottles of smooth red wine, a generous platter of different cheeses, crackers and quince jelly.

Even curmudgeonly Peter Wilson had generously supplied a bottle of fine brandy. 'For medicinal purposes,' he quipped while pouring everyone large measures.

'So how did you know Mrs May was the killer?' asked Ken, while offering Peter Wilson a pink cupcake in return for the brandy.

Dee, happily ladling quince jelly onto a cracker, said, 'I didn't.'

Ken would have asked more but Francesco spoke up. 'More wine, Dee?' She nodded and he topped up her glass before inquiring, 'But why did she do it?'

'Dog poo!' answered Dee succinctly before crunching into her cracker.

Francesco blinked and the rest of the table assumed they'd misheard what Dee had said.

Zara's brows were drawn together in puzzlement. 'But Justin Harper didn't have a dog.'

Dee nodded in agreement, 'No, the dog poo was Bernier's boxer dog. And I'm afraid it was also why she went for you, Blossom.'

Blossom blushed and protested, 'But it was only the once and it's my aunt's dog.'

'So, why kill Justin?' persisted Zara.

'Tragically she thought he loved her and I don't think Mrs May has had much love in her life.'

'But he didn't love her?' enquired Peter Wilson, leaning his bulk forward so his tummy rested on the table.

Dee shook her head. 'He was only after her money and when she realised it – well, it was too much for her.'

'So all of this was about dog poo and a bruised heart?' Robert was incredulous.

Dee swallowed a bit of Brie and expanded, 'That and losing her sense of purpose when she retired.'

Peter Wilson, who seemed to have most of the cheese platter on his plate, not to mention two pink cupcakes and a French savoury cake muffin, tut-tutted loudly. 'Woman should have taken up a hobby – I've found listening to the cricket a great solace since I retired.'

'We've noticed,' smiled Blossom innocently, her blue eyes wide and her pink lips smiling.

Gina looked earnestly at Dee. 'But why did she target you? I mean the first body ended up in your vegetable patch, the second where you were bound to find it and then tonight …'

Dee gazed wistfully out of the French windows and at the beauty and serenity of her garden and barely above a whisper replied, 'Because I had done something unforgivable to her.'

A shocked silence descended around the table and a few baffled looks were exchanged.

Eventually, Blossom queried, 'What?'

Dee paused and then, scanning the faces of so many friends seated at her table, gave a sad half-smile. 'I let her see my happy childhood and my daily joy now.'

Ken brushed over this and demanded, 'But why put clown makeup on her victims?'

Dee grimaced. 'You'll have to ask Amelia for a proper psychological analysis but I think it was a complex mix of factors. She had a bit of a thing about clowns probably stemming from the one happy memory of her childhood – winning a toy clown at a fair.'

Peter Wilson nodded. 'She mentioned that to me.'

'Then she was very taken with the notion of the clown representing the 'rustic fool'. With her self-esteem having taken a battering, she was desperate to publicly belittle others.'

Francesco didn't care for the sombre note that was threatening to overtake the celebration. He rose to his feet, smiled around the table and raised his glass. 'Here's to Dee – the hero of the hour.'

There were general jeers and whoops and Dee felt very content. *The village is finally back to normal.*

By eleven o'clock the next morning news had spread around the village. First to arrive on Dee's doorstep was Mrs Jenkins. She arrived between jobs, with her apron on and her mop and bucket in hand.

Leaning forward and eyes bright with the hope of first-hand gossip to spread, she said, 'Oh, Dee, it's just awful, all the goings-on. You must be exhausted. Why don't you let me spruce your place up and you can tell me all about it?'

Dee wavered; she didn't want to offend. 'That's very kind of you but ... er ...'

Fortunately, Zara arrived to rescue her. Striding up the path she announced, 'What my mother is trying to say is thank you, but she doesn't need any cleaning done and that we really mustn't keep you.' She swept into the house and firmly shut the door behind her.

The next visitor was far more welcome. Christopher Plover, accompanied by his spaniel, came with an enormous marrow. 'Thought you might like this, fresh from my greenhouse.' His distinguished features were wreathed with concern beneath his grey beetling eyebrows.

Dee patted his arm reassuringly. 'How lovely, I love stuffed marrow. Now don't worry, Christopher, I'm quite alright.'

He looked relieved. 'Good, good – so all's well that ends well, as they say.'

Christopher and his spaniel walked home, with him whistling the 'British Grenadiers' and the dog happily wagging its tail to the beat.

When Sophie popped in she brought a homemade coffee cake. 'I can't stop long; the world and his wife seem to be in the deli this morning but I did so want to give you this and say I'm thinking of you.'

'That's so kind. Zara, Amelia and I all love coffee cake. Please don't be concerned – I'm really fine.'

Sophie smiled before hurrying back to the deli.

Later, as Dee sat in her garden with Zara and Amelia and the rather fine cake Sophie had made for her, Dee made an announcement. 'Lovely though this is,' she gestured at all the flowers and foliage in their early summer abundance, 'I think what we all need is a holiday.'

'Oh, I do agree, Mother! A holiday would be just the thing after all this upset,' nodded Zara before taking a forkful of delectable cake.

'Where do you suggest? It might be difficult for me to make it,' asked Amelia innocently.

Zara and Dee exchanged knowing looks and both guessed that Amelia was silently rejoicing at the idea of both her mother and grandmother being away for a bit, thus allowing her unfettered freedom.

'Somewhere quiet, with no dead bodies,' suggested Zara.

'I know just the place. I went there once as a teenager,' said Dee.

'With Dad?' asked Zara.

Dee blushed. 'Er, no, actually your father and I had had, er, a little tiff.'

Zara sat up straighter and Dee hastily continued before her daughter could ask any questions, 'It's a little island in the Irish Sea.'

'The Isle of Man?' enquired Amelia.

'No, the Isle of Blom. It's near the Isle of Man and very similar but totally independent. From what I remember there's a stunning coastline for walking and even a steam train.'

'Sounds just the thing – let's look at dates.'

A few miles away, in his train room, Nicholas was talking on his mobile to his mother. 'Where do you want us to go to? The Isle of Blom? Why?'

'It's your father – apparently, it's very good for birdwatching. Now I insist you come, you've been looking rather pale. I think those clown murders really took it out of you. Some sea air is just what you need.'

'But, I—'

'I have already booked your ticket and our rooms.'

Nicholas knew his mother and that there was no point in arguing with her, besides which she was right – he did need a break, away from dead bodies. *And there won't be any of those on The Isle of Blom, especially with the FitzMorris ladies safely in Little Warthing. The Isle of Blom? I believe they have a steam train.*

Nicholas was correct about the steam train but he couldn't have been more wrong about the FitzMorris ladies and the dead bodies, as he was about to find out.

Books in the FitzMorris Family Mystery Series

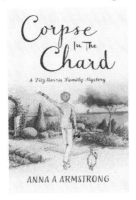

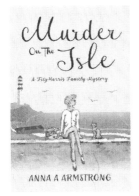

Printed in Great Britain
by Amazon